T0023845

PRAISE FOR CHRISTI CALDWELL'S ALL THE DUKE'S SINS SERIES

"Ribboned with subtleties about gender roles and class expectations that make this novel both thoughtful and delightful all at once."
—#1 *New York Times* bestselling author Jodi Picoult

"Christi Caldwell's crisp, sparkling writing is infused with emotion, passion, and a belief in the healing power of love. This is terrific Regency romance!"
—*New York Times* bestselling author Amanda Quick

"Emotional, funny, and filled with passion—everything I want in a romance."
—*New York Times* bestselling author Lorraine Heath

"What historical romance is meant to be. I devoured every word. Christi Caldwell has become one of my favorite authors." —*New York Times* bestselling author Laura Lee Guhrke

"A charming, romantic love story that shows Regency romance isn't just about dukes and duchesses and love isn't just for the upper classes."
—*USA Today* bestselling author Maya Rodale

"Packed with familial warmth and peppered with humor. . . . An endearing romance." —*Kirkus Reviews*

MORE PRAISE FOR CHRISTI CALDWELL

"Christi Caldwell writes a gorgeous book!"
—*New York Times* bestselling author Sarah MacLean

"A Christi Caldwell book never fails to touch the heart!"
—*New York Times* bestselling author Tessa Dare

"Sizzling, witty, passionate . . . perfect!"
—*New York Times* bestselling author Eloisa James

"Christi Caldwell is a must read!"
—*New York Times* bestselling author Mary Balogh

"Romance worth swooning over!"
—*New York Times* bestselling author Grace Burrowes

The Diamond and the Duke

CHRISTI CALDWELL

BERKLEY ROMANCE
New York

BERKLEY ROMANCE
Published by Berkley
An imprint of Penguin Random House LLC
penguinrandomhouse.com

Copyright © 2024 by Christi Caldwell
Excerpt from *Along Came a Lady* copyright © 2021 by Christi Caldwell
Penguin Random House supports copyright. Copyright fuels creativity, encourages
diverse voices, promotes free speech, and creates a vibrant culture. Thank you for buying
an authorized edition of this book and for complying with copyright laws by not
reproducing, scanning, or distributing any part of it in any form without permission.
You are supporting writers and allowing Penguin Random House to continue to
publish books for every reader.

BERKLEY and the BERKLEY & B colophon are registered trademarks of
Penguin Random House LLC.

ISBN: 9780593334959

First Edition: February 2024

Printed in the United States of America
1   3   5   7   9   10   8   6   4   2

Book design by George Towne

This is a work of fiction. Names, characters, places, and incidents either are the product
of the author's imagination or are used fictitiously, and any resemblance to actual persons,
living or dead, business establishments, events, or locales is entirely coincidental.

If you purchased this book without a cover, you should be aware that this book is stolen
property. It was reported as "unsold and destroyed" to the publisher, and neither the author
nor the publisher has received any payment for this "stripped book."

To Mom and Dad,
who when I couldn't read as a child,
found me a tutor who, despite my frustration and
struggles, would not only teach me how to read, but
who'd also instill in me a love for books and storytelling.
To Larry DiPalma for teaching me how to read.
To my husband, Doug,
for encouraging me to pursue my dream of writing,
and supporting me even though
I'd never earned a penny doing so.
And to my children, Rory, Reagan, and Riley
who taught me about struggle, perseverance,
deep-abiding love, and the truest meaning
of the words: happily ever after.
Every word I've ever written,
every book I've ever published is because of you.

Part One

I know not how it came, nor when it begun; but creep, creep it has, like a Thief
upon me; and before I knew what the Matter was, it look'd like Love.

—*Virtue Rewarded,*
Samuel Richardson

Prologue

My dearest Wesley,

*You insist on knowing my favorite flower, so that you can
return and shower me with those blooms, and yet, how
can you not realize, I do not need gifts or sonnets or the
jewels you talk of gifting me. I wish only for your return.
But as you persist, and I do not want you to believe me
coy, I shall share. It is . . .*

Lovingly Yours,

Over the years, Lady Ellie Balfour had become very adept at certain skills, none of them ladylike: Swordplay.
Pretend dying. Running. Hiding.

Usually, she'd been running *and* hiding from her thank-
fully now-dead father, the heartless Duke of St. James.

At this precise moment, however, she found herself on
the fringe of the Leeds property for altogether *different*
reasons—to avoid the very many reminders of how much
everyone hated her.

Strangers she could have dealt with. Her late sire's cruelty, she'd even come 'round to accept. But now this vast list included everyone she loved. From her brother, Courtland Balfour, the Duke of St. James, to his new wife, Cailin.

Oh, no one said as much.

But she knew they did.

After all, having grown up with the disdain and loathing of her late father, she'd become rather adept at recognizing when people directed that sentiment her way.

As a small girl, she'd been hard-pressed to identify anything to merit her father's disgust.

As a girl of fourteen, she couldn't say the same. This time, Ellie knew *precisely* the reason for everyone's loathing. Their disdain stemmed from what she'd done—Ellie had single-handedly coordinated Cailin's ruin and brought society rushing in on an intimate moment between the Duke of Bentley's daughter and Ellie's brother.

Granted, Ellie had only done so to help the couple hurry along with their affections, while at the same time helping save herself and her family from the uncertainty of their circumstances.

Ellie didn't blame them for their resentment. For how could they forgive Ellie's greatest sin when she couldn't even forgive herself?

It didn't matter that debtor's prison had been bearing down on Courtland and as a result their family faced financial ruin. Or that Courtland so very desperately loved Cailin.

What *did* matter was the reason for Courtland and Cailin's hasty union—*Ellie*.

Oh, everyone had been polite enough through the wedding festivities.

But she hadn't dedicated years of her life to battlefield prowess and sharpening her strategic capabilities to fail and miss something so very obvious as the evasive maneuvers of those people avoiding her.

They wouldn't even look her in the eyes.

Her right hand clasped behind her back, with her left

palm, Ellie circled the tip of the rapier she brandished at the enormous oak tree.

She took graceful lunges and engaged in that pretend battle.

Because battles were fun.

Because since she'd been a small girl playing at military general, she'd welcomed the distraction. Then it had been a distraction from the fact her father despised her and called her a "freak of nature," always reminding Ellie of how ugly she, in fact, was.

She lunged again, this time striking the tip of her weapon against the tree.

Sweating from her exertions, Ellie drew back.

Many people hated her.

She thrust a second time, making another mark upon that gnarled oak.

But she was *used* to being hated.

Breathless, her chest rising and falling fast and hard from her efforts, she stood, staring blankly ahead at that pretend foe she'd fashioned in her mind.

This time, however, it felt different.

Her brothers and sisters, they'd always loved her—even when the man who'd sired them had not.

Ellie brought her sword back up into position. *Guard.*

Courtland, Keir, Hattie, Lottie.

Lunge. Panting, Ellie propelled herself forward on the balls of her feet.

Her new sister-in-law, Cailin. No doubt, Cailin's bro—

"And recover."

Ellie gasped and spun; losing her grip upon her saber, the gleaming sword went sailing through the air, and she watched on in horror as the tall, broadly muscled gentleman, clad in crimson uniform, neatly stepped out of its path.

Her sword landed with a noiseless clatter upon old leaves blanketing the forest floor.

Horror rippling through her, Ellie stared briefly at the article, and then looked back once again to Cailin's brother, the Duke of Bentley's illegitimate son, Lieutenant Wesley Audley.

He smiled bemusedly at her weapon.

Now she'd almost gone and killed Courtland's new brother-in-law.

"Splendid," she muttered.

"Ah, you *were* attempting to run me through, then, little general?"

"No!" she exclaimed. "My apologies. I was most certainly *not* trying to kill you. I—"

She caught the glitter in his emerald-green eyes and instantly stopped. "You were teasing."

"I assure you I'm usually far better at jests."

"Yes, well *I'm* usually quite skilled with a sword."

Suddenly, it seemed very important he know *that*. Ellie might never have possessed the social graces and elegance of her elder sisters, but when it came to handling weapons, there wasn't a more skilled woman in the kingdom.

"I can see that," he commented, and, dropping to his haunches, he retrieved her saber. He studied it for a moment. "I observed you a bit while you practiced."

She eyed him warily. "I didn't know you were there."

"No, you were very engrossed in your battle."

"A master never allows themselves to be caught unawares."

That tactic she'd learned long before the military books she'd often read, back when she'd been avoiding whatever punishment her father sought to mete out.

Her shoulders sagged. "Great, I failed at this, too."

"What was that?" the lieutenant asked, cupping a hand around his ear.

"I asked how long you were watching me."

"No, you didn't."

Ellie scrunched her nose up. "If you knew what I'd said, then why ask?"

He shrugged. "Fair enough."

"How long were you there?" Ellie persisted, *needing* to know.

He held her sword out. "Long enough to know you are, in fact, as skilled as you say."

In an instant, she forgot all about the fact he'd come upon her while she practiced her swordplay, and she fell more than a little in love with Lieutenant Wesley Audley.

For his words weren't the clear platitudes Courtland gave her. Courtland who—God love him for being a wonderful brother and joining in her battlefield games—didn't know a thing about weaponry or military combat.

Lieutenant Audley smiled. *He truly had a lovely smile.*

"Your sword, little general?"

Her sword?

Ellie blinked wildly. Her sword!

She quickly took back her weapon. "You know something of fighting, lieutenant," she said. "Do you believe I'm skilled enough to face Boney's men?" It was a question she'd never have the answer to herself.

All of her siblings combined would have collectively groaned at that query and pointed out a lady's place in the world. Lieutenant Audley, however, considered her words a moment.

"Some of them," he allowed.

How easily it would have been for him to say: undoubtedly, yes. After all, she'd have never known the difference. Instead, he spoke truthfully to her and she appreciated him all the more for it.

"Are there suggestions you might give me?" She pulled a face. "My *sisters* are forever insisting women should only worry about things like flowers and sonnets and anything not related to fighting."

"Why can't it be both?"

She snorted with laughter, before catching the solemnity of his gaze. "You're serious."

"Deadly so. Flowers have any number of benefits."

"Even for soldiers?"

"Especially for soldiers."

"Now I know you're funning with me."

"I wouldn't dream of it."

He looked just beyond her shoulder, and as he approached an ugly plant near her, Ellie followed the lieutenant with her gaze.

"Like that one."

She stared skeptically at the hideous bloom. "*That* one?"

"*This* one. It's called the Stinking Iris."

Ellie laughed again.

"It has all manner of benefits," he said. "You can apply it to a wound or bruise."

Her amusement faded, and she widened her eyes. "Truly?"

He nodded. "When I worked in the mines, there were any number of men who had poultices made from the flower, and the same can be said for battle."

The lieutenant beckoned her closer.

"And," he whispered, when she was nearer, "the iris *also* decorated Joan of Arc's battle standard."

"It did?" she whispered in return.

He nodded again.

Ellie clasped her hands to her chest. "The iris shall be the one and only flower I favor."

"A very wise choice, little general."

Her face fell, as she recalled: "The iris may help a soldier heal, but they don't prepare a person to fight."

He bowed his head. "You're right on that score."

Lieutenant Audley collected her sword and brandished the weapon. "A lesson, then?"

Ellie stilled. "Truly?"

"Would a soldier ever jest about any form of fighting?"

"Never!"

He launched into a lesson. "First, you hold your weapon in your hand that is dominant," he said, pressing the saber back into her hands, and as he guided Ellie through the proper way to hold the thing, her mouth . . . it went all weird, her tongue going heavy, and her fingers warm at his touch.

The lieutenant had big hands.

She hated big hands.

Her late father had big ones.

But the dead duke's unsullied, lily-white ones had been

nothing like this man's: callused and powerful enough to swallow her entire palm, tanned by the sun, scarred by . . . what, she knew not, but was so very curious to.

"Did you get all that?" Lieutenant Audley asked, and she had to tell her brain to tell her head to nod. Folding his arms across a powerful chest, the gentleman nodded to her. "Well?" he urged gently.

Well?

Ellie puzzled her brow and touched the fingers not holding her saber to her chest. "You . . . want me to *show* you."

He tendered a gentle smile, an encouraging one. "That is the point of a lesson, is it not, Ellie?"

Ellie.

Never had she minded the shortened moniker all her elder siblings had conferred. Until now.

In hearing this man speak it, Ellie found herself wishing she went by something more elegant—a *sophisticated* name belonging to a beautiful woman.

A question entered his eyes and chased away his slight grin. "What is it?"

"My siblings think it is child's play, and that women don't really have a place at being proficient with a sword."

"And what of you?" he ventured, strolling closer.

"I think it is essential all people, *especially women*, have the means with which to defend themselves."

Her stomach lurched. She'd said too much. He'd realize the hideous tales of her childhood and the rage she'd induced that had led her father to regularly attempt to thump the bad out of her. While her family had long suspected she was a child playing at adult games, she'd been motivated by the need to survive.

"I think that is a wise thought to have, Ellie," Lieutenant Audley finally said, and she slowly picked her eyes back up to meet his again.

"You . . . do?"

He nodded. "Why should you not know how to protect and defend yourself? Because you're a woman?" He answered his question that wasn't a question. "How many times have we seen in history that women are, in fact, as capable? Joan of Arc. Kit Cavanagh—" Eager excitement brought her back up.

"You've heard of her." That legendary woman who'd disguised herself as a man and joined the British dragoons to fight the French, all while she'd searched for her husband.

He nodded. "Indeed, and there are even more women who've gone to battle."

They spoke in unison.

"Deborah Sampson."

She and Lieutenant Audley shared a smile.

Her heart shifted in her breast.

Courtland had indulged her.

But never had he truly believed Ellie should hold a sword, or that it was something any woman, for that matter, should do. Not as this man before her.

Just then, someone came stomping through the grounds.

"Ellie?"

Her heart sank. "Oh, hell," she whispered, looking away from Lieutenant Wesley Audley.

Splendid. Just splendid.

"Bad?" the lieutenant asked.

"*Very.*"

Her *second*-eldest sibling—Keir. The eminently less fun of the twins. Less patient. Less understanding. Less *everything.*

Keir entered the clearing. "What are you doing?" he demanded, by way of greeting.

Ellie stuck her foot out. "As you can *see*, Keir, I'm otherwise bus—"

"Your skirts are a mess, Ellie," he interrupted, chiding her in that matter-of-fact tone of his.

Despite herself, despite the fact that she had certainly never cared about stains on her skirts, Ellie now, for the first time in the whole of her existence, wished she were someone else. She wished she looked a different way—that she wasn't lanky and painfully thin like a colt, but soft and rounded and feminine like her sisters.

"St. James is looking for you," Keir said.

She perked up. "He is?"

Normally, she'd rib Keir for referring to their brother, his twin, by his title. This time, she could only focus on the hope Courtland didn't hate her so very badly after—

"He wants to be sure you are staying out of trouble."

At that blunt pronouncement from her always-brusque brother, her heart dropped.

Of course.

"She's been no trouble," Lieutenant Audley assured Keir.

This time, that organ in her chest lifted and then soared. She swung her gaze back to the soldier.

Keir switched his attention to the slightly taller, absolutely broader gentleman.

"Lieutenant Audley," Keir, as awkward with social exchanges as his twin, Courtland, was affable and charming, offered a belated greeting.

Ellie gave her brother a triumphant look. "See, I'm no trouble."

"The lieutenant is just being polite," Keir said flatly, setting her teeth on edge.

"I assure you, I'm not," the gentleman insisted.

And in that moment, Ellie, lover of all things military, and detester of all things romantic, fell head over toes in love with Lieutenant Audley.

She went all soft inside. Her heart melted and her tummy fluttered and fireworks exploded, and as she stared at Wesley, Ellie couldn't stop the smile that felt silly. She loved h—

"What's the matter with your eye, Ellie?" her brother demanded, stomping across brush and sticks, and bringing her crashing right back to the present.

"Noth—" Her muttering merged with a grunt as Keir took her chin firmly in hand.

He angled her face up.

"You're blinking oddly," he muttered, peering intently at her face, and blast if her cheeks didn't fire ten shades hotter. "Or you were."

Batting her lashes *and* blushing? Egads, those were *both* surefire signs of "being in love."

"I'm fine," she said tightly, between clenched teeth.

Alas, her brother proved unrelenting.

"You're sure? Because you have mud on your face."

Keir whipped out a kerchief, and before she could open her mouth to advise him against it, he was already rubbing at her cheek with the white linen. "You've been playing pirates again."

Mortification brought her toes curling painfully in the soles of her boots again, and God help her, if she'd had a real sword, she'd have likely committed fratricide.

Her brother wasn't done.

"We can't have you running about the duke's estates with mud on your face and skirts, Ellie."

Around her brother's shoulder, she caught the lieutenant's smile.

Gritting her teeth all the harder, she yanked her gaze back to Keir, who continued to wipe away dirt from her face. She attempted to draw back, but he tightened his hold gently.

"Will you stop?" he muttered. "I'm cleaning you off."

"I was not *playing* at pirates, Keir," she said, ignoring his brusque request; praying to the Lord above that her brother would just let this go and spare her from further humiliation. She trilled a laugh. "I haven't played pirates in forever."

Why, it'd been at least a year now. It didn't need to be pointed out this time or ever that she'd shifted her focus to—

"That's right," he said. "Since Napoleon's havoc, you and St. James have moved on to playing war."

Frustration roiling in her breast, she wrenched away from Keir's grooming.

"Will you stop?" she snapped.

His jaw slackened, and surprise filled his dark eyes.

"I'm . . . not a babe who needs cleaning, Keir." She shot a surreptitious look at the lieutenant. "I'm a grown woman."

Keir snapped his blond eyebrows together. "If that's the

case, might I suggest you stop bothering the duke's son and return to the household so that you can resume your deportment lessons with Edwina."

Mortified heat touched every part of her person from the top of her head, all the way on to the tips of her toes. When she'd never even known toes *could* blush. Apparently, they could . . . if the humiliation was powerful enough.

Lieutenant Audley's quiet baritone cut across the awkward silence. "Lady Ellie really is no bother." And spoken in that firm, confident way, there could be no doubting the veracity of that assurance.

Ellie's heart danced wildly once more.

Keir inclined his head. "That is kind of you to say. However, I know with her antics, El—"

Ellie kicked her brother hard in the shins.

"Oomph." Her elder brother glared in return. "Ellie is something of a hellion."

"You have my assurance, it really is no bother. In fact, the lady"—*the lady*. As in *her*—"will be sparing me from tedium." Courtland's new brother-in-law inclined his head; a smile teased at the corner of his firm lips, his the first mouth she'd ever noted of a man, and she went all soft inside.

She couldn't help it. A sigh slipped out.

"That is gracious." Keir bowed his head. "I will, however, send on Ellie's nursemaid so she can collect her when you tire of—"

"She is a governess, Keir," she said through clenched teeth. "Miss Meads is a governess."

A lovely, oft-smiling woman who often had her head in a book, and was therefore easy to evade whenever they went outside.

"Nursemaids are for babies," Ellie added for good measure.

"Well, a baby is what you are, and will always be to me," Keir said, ruffling the top of her head, his succinct tones at odds with that bothersome pat.

Glaring sharply up at him, Ellie swatted him away.

In vain.

At last, he dropped his hand, and she opened her mouth to disabuse him of the idea that she was in fact a baby in need of watching over.

But then stopped.

Perhaps she should be grateful he still saw her as his baby sister. For if he didn't, there was no doubt he'd never, ever leave her alone with Lieutenant Audley.

Keir looked to the lieutenant once more. "You are certain it is not too much of a bother—"

"No bother at all." Wesley's assurance smacked of sincerity, and her heart continued to pitter-patter erratically within her chest.

Both men exchanged bows, and as Keir headed off to fetch Miss Meads, Ellie found herself precisely as she wished to be—alone with the lieutenant.

"Thank you for not making me go back with him," she said softly. "I . . . it is hard being there."

As soon as she said it, she regretted it. The last thing she wished to remind anyone of—especially this man—was the fact that she'd coordinated the fall of two people. Even if said couple were very much in love.

Why, the lieutenant was likely only being nice, too. He no doubt hated her as much as her own family did. The same way her late father always had. He'd known her soul was corrupt, evil like his.

Ellie looked down at the ground and the brittle-looking brown and gray leaves aged by the winter and left as a forlorn reminder of the seasons past.

A large, powerful hand settled on her shoulder, stealing her breath and bringing her eyes flying up.

"Your intentions were good," he said gently. "And my sister is very much in love with your brother, and I see your brother feels the same for her. So . . . it was not all bad."

Her eyes stung. "Thank you, Lieutenant," she whispered.

Stung? What in the holy mixed-up world *was* this? Dirt. It was nothing more. Nothing at all. Because she certainly did not cry. She'd not managed to do so since her father had thumped her back with a cane hard enough to send her flying, onto a metal soldier whose tiny bayonet had speared her knee, forever scarring it.

"Now," Wesley said, his tone more cheerful as he lightly squeezed her shoulder before releasing her, "would you like to continue our lesson?"

Ellie smiled. "I would like nothing more."

That was, aside from one day marrying Lieutenant Wesley Audley.

Chapter 1

LONDON, ENGLAND
ONE YEAR LATER

My dearest Wesley,

I know I once said there was nothing more beautiful than a blue, cloud-filled sky. I was wrong. There is something far more magnificent . . . knowing I share that sky with you. Whenever I wish to feel closer to you, I just look up.

Lovingly Yours

Perched on the window seat, her knees drawn up to her chest, Ellie shifted her focus from the rain slanting in sideways sheets upon the pavement, a deluge that left her stuck indoors, to the couple curled up beside one another on the green button-back velvet-upholstered Chesterfield sofa.

Cailin lay with her head on Courtland's lap and her legs flung over the rolled arm, reading from a letter, while Courtland remained with one hand stroking the top of his wife's head, and the other holding whatever title it was on fossils that so fascinated him and Cailin.

Ellie forced her gaze away from the bucolic tableau they

presented: a happily married couple, with the young wife's belly gently rounded from where their first babe rested.

Courtland and Cailin had been gracious. Certainly more gracious than she deserved, or than her machinations had merited.

But Ellie had been obliged to acknowledge one sad truth—her relationship with the pair had been forever altered. Following his marriage, and the pained lecture he'd doled out after he'd learned the truth about Ellie's involvement in his ruination, he'd stopped joining her in her gameplay, and instructed her to cease looking at the world as a battlefield plan there for Ellie to arrange.

And that proved the greatest regret of her life.

It shouldn't matter. Ultimately, in the end, all children were forced to hang up their scabbards and put away their wood pistols and swords and swap those pretend games for all that came with real life.

Absently, Ellie traced a fingertip over the window.

". . . what is it, love? You've those frown lines you get here," Courtland was saying as he touched the place between Cailin's eyebrows. "When you are upset." With those quiet murmurings, his words revealed an intimate knowing of the woman he'd wed, and Ellie found herself more than half longing for that.

Alas, she lifted the book from her lap and raised it to her face, giving the couple the privacy she ought, feeling like the worst sort of interloper.

A streak of lightning lit up a dark sky which would have better suited the night.

". . . my brother . . ." Cailin was saying. ". . . Wesley . . ."

A sharp crack of thunder rumbled the foundations of the house, shaking the windowpanes.

Ellie lost her grip on the book.

Thump.

It landed on the floor with a less-than-subtle *thwack* that briefly interrupted her brother and his wife's conversation as two sets of eyes swung her way.

"Dropped my book," she explained, unnecessarily. "Lost

my hold on the pages. The storm, of course. That sounded as if the lightning strike was close."

Her brother and Cailin stared at her.

"Not that I'm afraid of storms," she blurted. "I'm not." Except that was a lie. "That scared. I—" *You are rambling. Stop rambling. You are not a rambler.* Anything but. Ellie cleared her throat noisily and, leaning down, rescued her book. "I *haave* it!" she exclaimed needlessly, and then promptly cringed inside. Snapping the pages open, she quickly brought the volume back into place before her face.

"I see that," Courtland called over. "You . . . uh . . . may wish to turn it ar—" Ellie promptly flipped it right side up. "—ound," her brother completed that word and droll response.

Dedicating all her attentions and energies on her book, Ellie made a show at reading; all the while, her ears remained keenly focused on the parts and pieces of the discussion her brother and Cailin had resumed.

". . . heartbreaking . . . not so much as a word from her . . ." Cailin said, her voice catching with tears, and Ellie flipped the unread page noisily. ". . . she will not write him. She will not answer his notes. What am I to say when he asks?" Ellie's sister-in-law was saying. "That according to our brother Hunter, the woman you are in love with is the darling of Staffordshire?"

Ellie went completely motionless.

The woman he . . . loved? Her organ in her chest forgot its job was to beat. As in, Wesley Audley was in love with—

". . . that she's enjoying herself at all the local soirees while you are risking life and limb to keep England safe from that French frog?"

As in Wesley Audley was in love with a woman wholly undeserving of him and his love.

Hatred and jealousy mingled, and together, soured her tongue like the vinegar rag her father had advised her nursemaid to stuff in Ellie's mouth for using words he'd deemed inappropriate for a lady to utter.

He was . . . in love.

In all this time since they'd met lakeside, she'd thought of him. And more, she'd thought of him—and her—together.

Granted, he was more than a dozen years her senior, but she was no longer a child, and with every passing day where he was gone, she'd become a young lady, and he was to return and notice that she was no longer a gangly child.

Just . . . a gangly woman.

But neither would that matter, because he'd said that day at the lake she'd spirit and strength, and a skill with a sword that he'd admired, and—

Ellie gripped her book hard, her fingernails digging sharply into the soft leather and leaving crescent marks upon the cover and back.

The housekeeper appeared and dipped a curtsy to Cailin. "If I might speak to you, Your Grace, about the latest changes to the menu."

The latest changes, because with Cailin increasing in pregnancy and queasy from it, every meal was constantly changing.

As Cailin came to her feet, she offered a wave and smile to Ellie, which she quickly returned.

"I'll return shortly, love," the duchess said to her husband. She tipped her head up to receive Courtland's kiss.

Ellie hurriedly averted her attention from that intimate exchange.

The moment Cailin had followed Mrs. Dumfrees, Courtland returned to his book.

"Who was Cailin speaking about?" Ellie asked after her sister-in-law had gone, and she and Courtland remained alone.

Her eldest brother glanced over the top of his pages and looked confusedly her way.

Be breezy. You are breezy. "The woman who is not writing the lieutenant."

Courtland scrubbed a hand over his mouth.

For an instant, she thought he would not answer. For an instant, she thought he'd rightly point out her past actions barred her from possession of intimate details that did not explicitly involve her.

Though, in this case . . . they did. Her brother just did not know it.

"She also happens to be the young woman who urged him to go to his father, the Duke of Bentley, so he could make a better life for himself." Her brother's jaw hardened. "A better life, which in her mind included wealth and land, and attaining everything she could through *his* commission in the army."

The reason he'd joined the military, and risked his life even now, was a *woman*?

Ellie's chest tightened in an odd way, in a way she'd never believed it would or could because of a man, and yet now it did at the thought of the dashing Lieutenant Audley courting another woman who was decidedly not Ellie.

Courtland started to rise.

Ellie quickly stayed him with another question. "Do you know her?"

He stared confusedly at her.

"The young woman," she clarified.

Her brother shook his head. "Only that her name is Claire Sparrow. Her father is a part owner of the Cheadle mines with Hunter."

The second-eldest Audley sibling, following Rafe. Wesley and Cailin were the youngest.

"She has not bothered to write Wesley in all the time he's been off fighting."

Pain knifed away at Ellie's heart this time for unselfish reasons: because of the hurt he knew, and all for a woman who couldn't appreciate Wesley for the man he was.

There came a flurry of footfalls, and they both looked up. Cailin's lady's maid, Sara, rushed into the room, breathless.

Ashen, Courtland jumped up. "The duchess—?"

"Is fine," the young woman hurried to reassure him. "Her Grace was accompanying Mrs. Dumfrees, who was discussing the menu, and the duchess . . ."—Sara's cheeks pinkened—"fell ill in the hallway."

Ellie grimaced. Tossed her biscuits, Cailin had done. As

the poor expecting mother was always doing, everywhere, these days.

"She told me I should not send for you, Your Grace, but I thought you should—"

"I am glad you did," Courtland interrupted, hastening to the door, leaving Ellie alone with only the silence of the room . . . and—her gaze inched over to the hastily abandoned area her brother and his wife had occupied—Wesley's letters.

She dampened her mouth.

It is none of your affair . . .

It is absolutely none of your affair.

Not even a bit.

That was, aside from the fact that Ellie was head over heels in love with the lieutenant.

Her book forgotten, Ellie absently set it down beside her, and came slowly to her feet.

Keeping her eyes on the doorway, she inched over and stopped beside the note.

None of your affair. None of your affair. None . . .

Of its own volition, her gaze slid down, landing on that folded note.

Good, a person could not read a folded note. The only way to do so would be to pick it up, and open it, and well, Ellie certainly had more than enough restraint.

Or . . . she thought she did.

Just not where matters of Wesley Audley were concerned.

With a silent curse, her fingers dove for the page, and she quickly snapped it open and proceeded to read.

My dear sister,

I write this missive hoping to find you and Courtland and your unborn babe are each faring well. I am eager for the day I return, and hope it is one day soon where I am able to see your expanded family.

Ellie finished and turned the note over.

There was no mention of Ellie.

He did not so much as ask after her.

Not that she expected he should or would. Ellie was, after all, just another one of Courtland's many siblings.

She snapped the note shut and returned the letter to where Cailin had left it.

That, however, didn't mean Ellie didn't . . . hope that he thought of her in some way.

Though, knowing his heart was otherwise engaged—and by a woman so completely unworthy of him—it made sense why he should not.

And she was stunned to discover, she wasn't so very selfish as to want him at any cost. She wanted him alive and happy. Even if it meant, when he returned from war, he would belong to another woman.

Balling her hands into tight fists, Ellie squeezed and unsqueezed them; all the while she waged a silent war with herself. "Bloody hell," she exclaimed into the quiet of the parlor, and then, sitting down at Cailin's writing station, Ellie availed herself of a sheet of parchment and a pen.

Dipping it into an inkwell pot, she proceeded to write.

My dearest Wesley,

You must forgive me for the delay in my writing. My father discovered your notes. My only course, our only course, is to send our correspondences through a location where they're sure to not be discovered.

Lovingly Yours

Chapter 2

*I do not want you to worry after me or about me, or my
undying love or regard for you. My only want, my only
wish, is for you to focus on the battles you are fighting,
so that one day, you may come back to me.*

Captain Wesley Audley hadn't died on the mud-soaked
battlefields of Belgium.

He was one of the lucky ones.

Or that was what they said, anyway. That was what they
thought.

The docked ship that had carried Wesley back to England rocked gently on the channel.

He clenched his eyes tightly.

Nobody knew a goddamned thing about anything. Especially people who'd never set foot upon a battlefield.

But Wesley knew.

Just like every other man who'd ever been lanced with
the blade of a bayonet, or taken a bullet through his flesh,
Wesley knew death was easy.

It was *living* after sustaining those injuries that truly challenged a man.

One might as well be dead. For people didn't speak to you. They spoke about you and over you. It mattered not that Wesley had risen from mere lieutenant to captain, commander of his own forces. Or that he'd placed himself between Wellington, saving the great commander in chief's life.

When a man fell in battle, and lost the use of his limbs, he became useless to society. Those downed warriors became broken objects people either ignored, or worse, sought to fix. Never once did those people bother to seek the soldier's input.

Nay, men marched to war as powerful warriors and returned—in the eyes of all—nothing more than a feeble child.

Perhaps that was because they knew if they asked every man wounded in battle, they'd order you to let them die, instead of facing . . . *this*.

Lying flat on his back on a litter, his eyes closed, Wesley waited for the men he now relied upon to get him . . . anywhere. Waiting for them to carry him. Waiting for them to speak about him, and this time clinging to those voices to distract himself from the fiery pain that racked his body.

". . . I have been sent by His Grace," someone was saying.

It was an unfamiliar voice.

A somber, commanding one.

His father had sent someone to retrieve him.

What did you expect? You are a duke's by-blow and now a broken by-blow at that. Did you think he would have rushed to collect you?

No, but he had expected at the very least, Rafe would come to collect him. In his mind, Wesley had braced himself for the reunion with his eldest brother.

And he'd dreaded it.

Because he didn't want to be presented with the evidence of his brother's virility and intactness when he himself was so broken and battered—his leg mangled.

But his brother had a life of his own now. One that didn't even involve the Cheadle mining village where they'd grown up and worked. Rather, Rafe had since married and had a family of his own and a life . . . in London. Why should he abandon all that to come and gather up his crippled brother?

"Captain Audley, can you hear me?" the man serving as his nursemaid asked.

Wesley ignored him, a task that wasn't altogether difficult, given the pain ravaging his body and threatening to pull him back into that blessed haze of unconsciousness.

"The captain doesn't talk," someone replied for him. "Too weak from his injuries."

Too weak from his injuries.

That much was true.

There came a low groan as the floorboards creaked, and a slight shadow fell over Wesley's eyes. "Captain Audley, are you able to talk?"

Wesley wasn't altogether certain on that score. He'd been unconscious, and when he'd awakened had been too riddled with pain to do anything more than groan or moan. What he *was* certain of was he didn't want to take questions from the damned emissary his coward of a father had sent.

"Your father, the Duke of Bentley, sent me," the man said once more. "My name is Dr. Monroe. You were injured on the fields of Brussels. Do you remember as much?"

If laughing was something he'd been capable of and doing so wouldn't have run his weak body ragged, he'd have roared his hilarity.

Did he remember . . .

As if on cue, the staccato of muskets firing blared in his ears as the acrid sting of remembered smoke burned his nostrils.

". . . help. Put me out. I'm on fire . . . heeeeelp . . ."

A memory popped in of the young boy on drums who'd caught fire, the pungent odor of burning flesh so sharp Wesley could taste it still.

"You were at—"

"I remember," he rasped, those two words wrenched

from him the first he'd spoken, and even with his eyes closed he felt the looks pass between the men who'd been stuck caring for him the length of his journey home.

Home.

How goddamned hilarious that was.

"Good," the doctor said, a pleased-sounding quality to that avowal. "You are conscious and able to speak."

So he'd merely been testing Wesley? Gauging whether his patient's mind was intact?

Well, the damned joke would be on him.

There was nothing intact about Wesley's mind. Or, for that matter, his body or soul.

"We are going to make the journey to His Grace's London townhouse. I expect given the extent of your injuries, the carriage ride will bring you great pain." The doctor spoke matter-of-factly, doling out his words about the plans for Wesley and his condition the way he might deliver a scientific lecture on some tedious topic. "Therefore, we will take the journey slowly."

There was something underlined within that particular statement, something that suggested a greater journey than the ride to the duke's townhouse.

Drained of energy, Wesley squeezed his eyes shut more tightly and curled up into himself, taking himself out of the discussion with the doctor. There came the smallest of mercies as the doctor ceased peppering words and questions Wesley's way and turned them back on the men who'd overseen Wesley's care.

When Wesley came to . . . minutes . . . moments . . . hours? . . . later, it was to a blinding pain.

His eyes shot open, and he instantly groaned as the raging sun burned his irises, blinding.

How long had it been since he'd seen sun?

The world had gone dark for him, and he'd known nothing beyond murky shades of grays and blacks.

A tortured gasp climbed from deep within him, and Wesley arched his back in a bid to escape, but there was no escaping. Whimpering, he tossed his head back and forth.

"Halt . . ." the doctor commanded with the ease better suited to the commanding officers who remained behind on the fields of Brussels. "You're moving too quickly. You risk doing further damage to his leg. He'll need short breaks as we go, and then when we move, you must carry him with greater care."

Greater care.

As if that would make a difference.

"Captain Audley? Are you well enough to continue?"

What was the alternative? To tip the litter and dump his broken body on the hard cobblestones? If he'd been capable of stringing together a semblance of words to make that query aloud, he would have.

As it was, he managed only silence.

Several moments passed before the doctor spoke, calling for the men to resume their walk.

Wesley forced his eyes open a fraction, and then ducked his head sideways, arching into his pallet, both riveted by the orb hanging in the sky and pained by the length for which he stared. The hulking, crimson-clad soldier carrying Wesley periodically shifted, adjusting his hold upon Wesley's litter, as he did, pulling Wesley's face in and out of the sun.

Unblinking, Wesley stared sightlessly up.

God, how he'd loved the sun. How he'd missed the brightness of an uncomplicated sky.

He'd become so accustomed to skies black and gray and cloudy from cannon fire.

When he'd been away fighting, he'd sustained himself with the idea of living so that he might again feel those warm rays bathe his face and tan his skin. He'd imagined doing so with Claire's head upon his lap, as he read to her from those books she'd quoted in her letters to him, each note a lifeline to a future he longed to know. Until the line had, for a second time, been ripped asunder, and he'd had nothing more than a final note, and only silence from her—this time, that silence had been permanent.

Slipping between past memories and new hells, he felt

darkness clawing at the edge of his consciousness, and he welcomed that abyss, an endless hole he so desperately longed to drown himself in. Wesley surrendered to the blackness.

Along the trek from the wharf and during the journey in the duke's carriage, Wesley moved in and out of consciousness.

Slumped along the side of the conveyance they'd come and collected him in, Wesley pressed his forehead against the window, the fabric of the curtain scratchy against his cheek and brow, a vicious juxtaposition of the agony that raced along the line of his jaw from where a knife had cut him.

Under the bandage wound about his head, his skin throbbed.

Wesley squeezed his eyes shut as the conveyance bumped and swayed along the uneven country road. Every jolt to his twisted leg sent his stomach revolting.

"Nausea is normal." That quiet statement came from the opposite bench.

Wesley ignored the other man.

The carriage hit another rut, and this time, Wesley couldn't stifle the moan that filtered from his lips.

He promptly regretted it.

That sound caused his aching head to pound all the harder, and his stomach flipped over again.

"Do you need a bucket?" Dr. Monroe offered.

A bucket. To throw up into. The bitter irony was not lost upon Wesley.

He'd left for glory. He'd sought to build a name and future for himself so that he could be more, so that he could have more. He'd gone seeking honor and prestige, and a reputation as a man who'd risen up. Only to come back *this*.

As the carriage swayed once more, the curtains parted a fraction, and his visage reflected back.

His face covered with a heavy beard; a white bandage wrapped about his head; his eyes bloodshot and deadened. He was, in short, a caricature of the living, breathing man who'd marched naïvely off to battle.

"I trust the pain is significant. I understand from the attending doctors you refused all laudanum."

Yes, because during his time at the Cheadle, he'd witnessed men who'd been badly injured in mining accidents doused with laudanum. He'd seen firsthand the hell wrought on those who'd relied upon that mind-numbing elixir.

"There is no harm in—"

"Will you shut up?" Wesley's voice emerged as a harsh growl, lack of use making it raspy and raw.

That effort cost him dearly, and a blinding pain brought his eyes sliding shut, as flecks of light danced behind them.

Death. Death would be preferable to this.

And Wesley remembered no more.

That afternoon, the Balfours gathered in a parlor as they'd done so many times before at the Duke and Duchess of Bentley's expansive Mayfair townhouse, Chiswick Hall. The families were, as usual, also joined by the Duke of Bentley's eldest son, Rafe, and Rafe's wife, Edwina.

The general festiveness that usually accompanied such gatherings between them had been replaced by a dark pall, as the Balfours, this time, joined the Audleys in a show of support. After all, Ellie's brother Courtland had married the Duke of Bentley's daughter, joining their families as one.

This time, no one wished to be here. At least not for the reasons that saw them assembled—Ellie included.

Sandwiched between her elder sisters, unmarried Hattie and just recently married Lottie, on a pretty sofa, Ellie glanced around the solemn room.

It was the first time since her brother had married Cailin that Ellie had ever felt that way about a visit to this particular household.

The kindly, gracious duke had opened his home to her, allowing her to visit his libraries and gardens as often as she'd liked, and many of those times he joined her.

As such, for the duke's paternal warmth toward her, this

residence had felt far more like a home than the household she'd grown up in.

This time, however, being here did not bring Ellie the usual calm it normally did.

This time, she wanted to leave.

Because she was a coward inside. And yet, she had to be here. She had to be there when Cailin's brother, Wesley, at last returned home.

Despite the years he'd spent away, fighting Boney's forces, and falling in battle, he'd lived, and at long last, come home.

Her stomach churned violently.

Wesley had survived. She told herself that. She reminded herself of that beautiful reality over and over again.

It did not help.

For he'd almost not made it back.

From the whispered conversations she'd shamefully listened in on several weeks ago, Ellie had gathered that Wesley's injuries had been substantial . . . and had also come around the time Ellie had stopped writing him letters. More specifically, writing him letters as another woman.

It is my fault . . . it is my fault . . .

This is what her wickedness had wrought this time. After Miss Sparrow stopped writing, Ellie picked up doing so in the other woman's stead. With every note, she'd let Wesley believe his true sweetheart was the one still penning him notes.

She'd sought to assuage the guilt at her deception by reminding herself Wesley found hope and a reason to live from her letters—he'd about said as much in his return missives.

Ellie had reveled in every written word he'd sent in return . . . until, one day, Wesley had shared his dream of their being *reunited*.

From then on, Ellie's guilt became too great and she'd stopped.

That decision nearly cost him his life.

What would her family think if they knew what she'd

done? The duke and duchess who'd been like a mother and father to her these past few years?

Worse . . . what would Wesley say? What would he think?

A log shifted in the hearth and sent off a little *pop-pop-pop* among the embers, drawing Ellie's gaze over, and then she wished she hadn't looked.

His arms clasped behind him, the duke paced back and forth before the hearth.

Never before had she seen him in such a state . . . which was saying a good deal, as she'd seen him many ways these past years: Stunned when his daughter had been caught in a compromising position with Ellie's brother Courtland. Terrified and pacing in a similar way when Cailin had been giving birth to her first babe.

Even that day, with the lines at the corners of his mouth tense, and his skin pale, he'd not looked as he did now.

Just then, the Duchess of Bentley slid into her husband's path, cutting off his stride. The devoted couple exchanged quiet words.

Periodically, they nodded. His throat muscles moved, and his eyes gleamed, and the sight of that suffering . . . a portend of what was to come any moment when Wesley Audley finally entered the household, was too much.

Ellie wrenched her gaze away, stealing a peek at the clock atop the mantel.

"How are you reading right now?" Lottie said in hushed tones to their eldest sister.

"I need a distraction," Hattie said defensively, drawing her book close against her chest.

"A distraction?" Lottie whispered furiously. "A distraction? How can you think of being distracted? They said he is scarred beyond measure. Terribly injured, and you are somehow not worried about seeing him?"

Terribly injured. Scarred beyond measure . . .

Ellie's mind balked and recoiled as she forced herself to retreat from that quarrel, which painted an image she didn't want of Wesley Audley.

Because she preferred to remember him as he'd been years ago: powerful and laughing and wholly intact. She didn't want to think of him changed and broken and hurting—

Ellie sucked in a deep, shaky breath and looked over to where Courtland stood at the window, with Cailin beside him. The devoted, loving couple stared outside.

". . . what harm is there in me reading a book while we wait . . ." Hattie was arguing.

"I swear sometimes I wonder that I'm not the older sister," Lottie muttered, with a toss of her curls.

Hattie and Ellie exchanged a look. They might be different in many ways, but they were united in their opinion that since Lottie had a successful Season, and a quick marriage to one of London's most sought-after noblemen, she'd become somewhat unbearable.

"Now, do put that away," Lottie advised Hattie.

"I won't, and I certain as Sunday won't take orders from my little sister."

Lottie gasped.

"Please," the Duchess of Bentley interjected. "There is no harm in Hattie reading."

As her sisters stopped their bickering and silence fell once more, Ellie climbed to her feet and joined Courtland.

An anxious Courtland, whose gaze remained fixed on his wife, Cailin. Of course, devoted and loving husband that he was, the center of Courtland's focus wasn't his brother-in-law, Captain Audley's, impending return, but rather, Courtland's wife, the captain's *sister*.

As if he finally felt Ellie's presence, Courtland glanced over.

Worry remained etched in every line of his troubled face.

"Ellie," he greeted absently. "You didn't have to come today."

He'd say she hadn't had to come because he still thought her a child. They all did.

Courtland continued. "It's not too late if you'd rather—"

She cut him off. "I know I don't *have* to be here, Courtland. I *want* to."

Because to every member of her family, Ellie was still a small child, no different from her young nephew of two years, who had to be protected. Ellie hadn't made her Come Out yet, and she suspected even when she did make her entrance before Polite Society that treatment of her would not change.

"What have you heard?" she asked in hushed tones.

She felt her brother hesitate.

Courtland stole a glance in his wife's direction, and when he returned his attention to Ellie, he spoke in hushed tones Ellie struggled to hear. "They say he was speared with a saber in his right shoulder, and his left leg, it was mangled quite badly."

A pang struck. His rapier fighting arm, as he'd called it those handful of summers ago. That same arm he'd waved about so adroitly as he'd instructed Ellie on the proper way to really handle a sabre and—

Her heart cracked open.

"I . . . fear the duke is being optimistic in the welcoming he's planned," Courtland murmured.

As in, the duke hadn't allowed himself to think about the possibility that his son had been severely hurt. In his mind, he saw Wesley returning the same way Ellie had painted that return in her own mind.

Courtland tensed. "He is here," he called out.

Ellie stiffened.

Tension whipped around the parlor as everyone went motionless.

She managed to slide her gaze over to the window and her heart thumped.

Sure enough, a carriage had come to a stop at the front of the duke's household. Crimson-clad servants had already begun streaming from inside, rushing to meet Wesley.

Almost simultaneously, everyone found their feet. The duke led the charge, with the duchess flying fast beside him, impressively keeping up with her taller husband.

Courtland hurried to catch Cailin, and the two of them set off after the welcoming party streaming from the room.

Gathering her white skirts, Ellie lifted her hem a fraction and rushed to join the family in the foyer.

She took a position at the last place in the line, alongside Lottie.

Lottie clutched her flowers for Wesley Audley close to her stomach and stretched on tiptoes to catch a glimpse of him through the door.

Ellie's chest tightened, and she reminded herself to breathe even and easily.

And then . . . he was there.

Only, he was there as she'd not expected.

For in all her imaginings of his return, she'd never imagined him being carried on a litter by several servants.

Thwack . . .

Dumbly, Ellie glanced away from Wesley's prone form to the flowers her sister had dropped.

Lottie swayed.

Or was that Ellie?

Courtland rushed to catch Lottie by the arm, to keep her on her feet, so it must be Ellie's elder sister.

Ellie's legs knocked together.

The duchess sobbed softly, and then caught that errant sound of grief and despair in her fist.

All the while, Ellie stood motionless. Her breath came harsh and fast in her ears as she stared at Wesley.

Wesley remained motionless, his eyes shut, and his cheeks covered in a thick growth. But for the lowest, faintest groan to filter from his lips, he remained utterly silent.

What did you think? That he would walk through the doorway?

And yet, oddly, she realized that was precisely what she'd thought. For in her mind, Wesley was indomitable, possessed of a strength and power of the legendary gods, and as such, when she'd played out his return, he'd always been walking. He'd have moved with a swagger. In that romanticized dream of his return, he'd even sported a dashing scar down his cheek which would have only leant to his masculine beauty.

The servants carrying Wesley's litter paused near Ellie and adjusted their hold on the handles.

Suddenly, Wesley's eyes opened.

Ellie froze, her gaze locked with his.

Hunted.

Haunted.

He was a man who was both. As a young girl who'd been both of those herself, she recognized those emotions even within his pain-filled eyes.

"Hullo," she said, her voice so faint she wasn't sure if she'd actually spoken that greeting.

He glared at her; the coldness in that agonized gaze knocked her back on her heels, and she automatically took a step backward to escape it.

Suddenly, he spoke, his voice a harsh, angry rasp. "Leave me alone."

And a vicious pain racked her heart.

The servants carrying Wesley froze and looked desperately at the Duke of Bentley for direction.

"I said, leave me alone!" Wesley thundered. "All of you, just let me be." He thrashed his head back and forth, shouting, cursing, and Ellie proved a coward, because she retreated several steps.

What did you think? That upon seeing you, he would have hopped to his feet and recognized you as the woman who'd written him, and be miraculously cured?

But then Wesley closed his eyes once more and ceased his shouting and cursing. There was a flurry of motion as servants rushed forward, and an officious-looking man with wire-rimmed spectacles hurried along behind, and Wesley, once strong, powerful, indomitable, and smiling Wesley, was carried abovestairs.

When he'd gone, she and their families remained locked in silence broken only by the weeping of the duchess and Wesley's sister.

Ellie hugged her arms tight.

What if you'd continued writing . . . What if you were the one to pull back home, and in so doing, distract his attentions from where they truly belonged—on fighting?

Bile climbed her throat, and her breathing grew ragged.

In both writing those letters, and then not writing them, Ellie had wronged him.

And there could be no undoing what she'd done.

Ever.

Chapter 3

My dearest Wesley,

You will think me silly, but I abhor fishing. Something about seeing that hook stuck in their mouths makes me hurt for the pain they endure for nothing more than our own pleasures.

Lovingly Yours

With the hood of her cloak drawn up protectively about her face, and a small scrap of paper clenched in her hands, Ellie moved with purposeful steps through the streets of the Rookeries.

She kept her gaze forward as she strode the darkened pavement lined with decrepit buildings sporting broken windows and thatched rooves.

Though in truth, she didn't need the scrap of paper with the address written upon it. The memory of this place had been long seared on her mind and memories.

Even so, she held the bit of parchment. She plucked at the edges and held on tight because it grounded her.

And at last, she arrived.

Ellie pushed the hood of her cloak back a smidge, just enough so that she might better view the establishment.

There was nothing remarkable about the building. In fact, had she walked these streets ten times before it, she might not have even noted it.

A stucco-faced structure with a handful of wide steps that ran the length of the unit, its only odd piece of note was the plank-like wood slab several paces down that connected the pavement with the top of the main landing.

Besieged with equal parts fear and equal parts uncertainty, Ellie hovered there. The moment Ellie had left Mrs. Porter's some eight years ago, she'd vowed never to return. Between the remnants of the agony known at the woman's capable hands, coupled with the memories of the old horrors that had brought Ellie there, she'd wanted to keep that day and this place buried in the furthest recesses of her mind.

It wasn't her place to be here.

She knew it.

She knew it because after interfering in her brother's courtship of Cailin, and seeing the way he'd looked at her after he'd discovered her treachery, Ellie vowed to never again interfere in *anyone's* life.

This time, she had to break that promise.

A bolt of lightning streaked across the gray morning sky and a light rumble shook the ground.

Ellie shivered and burrowed deeper into the garment.

It is the Lord. It is the God you ceased to believe in reminding you he is, in fact, very real, and that he is also very, very displeased with you for proving wicked once more.

Stop it.

Her being here—*this* was different. For surely it didn't count as an interference if she were here to undo a previous interference?

Wind whipped up around her. That sharp, sudden gust sent the skirts of her cloak and day dress slapping angrily against her legs, and she tightened her hold upon the parchment in her hands. Too late.

The little scrap slipped from her hold and took flight, rolling swiftly along a barren white pavement, traversed by none.

With her gaze, Ellie followed its path, onward, back toward her family's waiting carriage at the end of the street. And it was likely the Lord's hand at work once more, urging her to get herself back to that conveyance and away from the steps of the building she'd no place being near.

Another bolt of lightning illuminated the sky so dark it might as well have been night, followed close by a crack as something nearby was struck, and struck loudly.

Ellie found her feet. Collecting her hems, she raced up the small, crude ramp, and knocked just as another great rumble of thunder shook the ground.

And yet, the panel was drawn open almost immediately, by a kindly, but nondescript-looking woman in a serviceable uniform and white cap upon her brown hair.

"Hullo," the familiar woman said as she let Ellie inside.

"Hello," Ellie returned that greeting from deep within the folds of her hood.

It was funny how much older people seemed to children. When Ellie had first met the woman before her, she'd taken her for her mother's age. Now she saw she wasn't many years older than Hattie.

"How may I help you?" she asked Ellie.

Ellie hesitated a moment more, and then pushed back her hood. "My name is Ellie."

Recognition dawned in the lady's pretty brown eyes. She gave her a gentle smile. "I know you, my lady."

Ellie's entire body tensed. She remembered her.

"I remember everyone who's ever come through those doors," Mrs. Porter said, accurately reading Ellie's unvoiced thoughts. "You have my assurance that I'll not speak of your visit or the reasons behind it."

The older woman spoke with the same soothing gentleness she had all those years ago.

Mrs. Porter motioned for Ellie to enter.

Ellie followed the bonesetter over to a pair of pretty carved wood side chairs. They were positioned the way they might have been in any formal parlor for entertaining. Only this wasn't a place for simple meetings.

Ellie skittered her gaze about a room she'd only been in once before. Just like that, it all came rushing back to her: The agony. The screams.

Sweat popped up on her skin.

". . . Please, do not kill me . . ." Ellie begged through her tears.

"I am not killing you. I am saving you. I know it hurts. Bite down on this. You may also scream around it."

"Beautiful, are they not?"

That question ripped across Ellie's remembrances.

Gasping, she whipped her gaze in Mrs. Porter's direction.

The smiling woman before her stared patiently back behind her wire-rimmed spectacles. Even as a small girl, Ellie had recognized in her the manner of a person capable of putting another soul at ease by her own self-possession and calmness.

"Mrs. Porter?" Ellie asked, searching for some hint of what the bonesetter had been talking about.

"The flowers," the other woman clarified. "They are a symbol of friendship, joy, and new beginnings."

Ellie's gaze went to the white vase filled with a dozen or so yellow roses.

She shook her head dumbly. "I . . . did not know that," she murmured, because she was expected to say something.

Joy. It was not joy that brought her here.

And yet . . .

Friendship. That was why she was here, and new beginnings. A fresh start, which she desperately longed for. Not for herself, per se. But for another.

"Many attribute to them the warmth of a sunny day."
Behind the wire rims of Mrs. Porter's spectacles, her eyes
glimmered. "Perfectly needed on a day like this."

As if on cue, another rumble of thunder shook the foundation of the establishment. "Indeed, it is."

I am speaking to her about the weather. Aside from rain
and fog, it was the most typical English thing in the entire
kingdom.

They didn't speak for several moments.

A cozy fire burned in that metal grate, radiating a soft
warmth; it did little to ease the chill. Over the years, there'd
been more tender touches given to this room. A fresh coat
of paint. Newer furnishings.

Tick-tock. Tick. Tock. Tick. Tock.

Ellie looked to the timepiece atop the mantel. Even a
pretty new clock.

"It was a gift," Mrs. Porter shared.

For a second time, Ellie blinked in confusion, and it
took a moment to deduce she now spoke of the golden sunflower clock across the room.

The lovely timepiece was etched with leaves, and an
intricately curved stalk was an extraordinarily cheerful
article . . . but for a bronzed serpent that snaked its way
down the stem. Age had lent a perfectly apropos green patina to his scaled skin.

Another shiver glided along her spine, and unbidden memories slipped in, dragging her back, her late father's harsh
admonitions beating against her brain like a well-played
drum.

*"My God, you defiant, vile chit . . . if you weren't cast in
Eve's image, I don't know a rotted female soul more wicked
than you . . ."*

Riveted still by the sight of that bronzed snake, Ellie
drew more tightly into herself.

For mayhap the late duke had been right after all.

Lies.

Temptation.

Evil.

The serpent represented all those worst parts of a person, the worst parts of *Ellie*.

"Not in all cultures," Mrs. Porter remarked, snapping Ellie back to the moment.

Ellie pulled her gaze from the timepiece. "Ma'am?"

"I was referring to what you'd said about the snake." She nodded her chocolate-brown head toward that clock. "We tend to equate the serpent with Eve's transgressions: lies, temptation, evil."

Ellie recoiled. Good Lord, she'd spoken aloud.

"In Greece and Egypt and even indigenous parts of North America," Mrs. Porter continued, "the snake represents rebirth and renewal."

"Rebirth and renewal," Ellie murmured. "I prefer that."

"Yes, I find it sometimes helps a good deal to . . . reframe the way we tend to think about things."

Hers was a positive way of looking at life. Only an eternal optimist could see a serpent and see salvation and not Satan in its reptilian form. And yet, she'd seen many who'd suffered as Ellie had. How had she retained light through that darkness?

Mrs. Porter steepled her fingers. "You wished to see me," she said, in the gentlest tones, ones reserved for wounded souls and battered animals.

Even so, Ellie faltered.

Her gaze slid to the entryway, and she troubled at her lower lip with her teeth, more than half expecting to see her brother or sister-in-law or the Duke of Bentley charge forward with an accusatory finger jabbed her way and harsh words on their lips, calling her out as the interferer that she was.

"You may speak freely, my lady," Mrs. Porter said in that temperate, soothing way.

Ellie hesitated.

Suddenly, the woman opposite her stiffened. For the first time since Ellie arrived, Mrs. Porter's eyes went dark.

"They hurt you again."

"No," Ellie said hastily.

They being "he," as in her late father. "He died."

"Gone on to hell he did, at last to join all the other wife-and daughter-beaters."

The bonesetter spoke with the vitriol of one who'd known firsthand such suffering.

Ellie glanced about at the modest, surprisingly cheerful-looking room. Memories again tugged at the corner of her mind, dark thoughts that threatened to drag Ellie back to a different time, but this same place.

"... it's going to hurt, lass ... I will not lie to you ..."

Then had come the screams. Ellie's screams, which pealed around her mind and this office.

She drew in another steadying breath. "It is not me." This time.

It would never be her again.

"He is a soldier. He is ... changed since his return. Both in body and in mind."

"War has that effect upon a man."

"Yes, I expect it would."

Mrs. Porter gave her a knowing look. "But then, life in general has that effect upon all people, does it not?"

"It does."

As a girl she'd loved to play with swords and imagine herself a soldier, and imagined going away to fight, and resented all the men who'd been afforded a dream that she, and no woman, was ultimately allowed. As a woman who'd read in the papers the names of second and third sons of lords who'd lost their lives in battle, she'd come to appreciate that war was no game, and the men who returned likely did so changed.

The image of Wesley being carried on a litter slipped in, angry and pale and weak and in pain.

"Is he your husband?" Mrs. Porter asked, pulling her to the moment.

"No, I'm not married." Nor would Ellie ever enter into that miserable state.

"Ah, a sweetheart, then."

Heat filled her cheeks. "No!"

The bonesetter gave her an amused look.

Ellie modulated her tone and spoke with a greater calm. "No," she repeated. "He is my brother's brother-in-law."

"The fellow can be both of those things."

"But he's not," Ellie said calmly. Though, how long had she secretly wished that it'd been Ellie whom Wesley penned those lovely lines to? He'd written words seductive and beautiful enough to make even her, a lady who'd vowed to die a spinster, contemplate marriage—to him, and only him.

Mrs. Porter looked at Ellie a moment more. "Break or injury?"

Ellie breathed a silent sigh of relief at this safer, less personal questioning.

She shook her head. "I don't know. He returned several weeks ago. From what I've heard spoken amongst the servants and family, the doctors who've come in are unable to form a consensus on the nature of his injury, but he's not improved."

"Of course they're unable," the bonesetter muttered. "I'd expect each one is more pompous than the next."

Mrs. Porter proceeded to pepper Ellie with questions. "Where's the gentleman's injury?"

"His leg."

"Upper, lower, or knee?"

"His knee is bent at a gruesome angle, leaving his entire lower leg deformed," she said, her heart aching as she recalled that day long ago in the duke's forest when Wesley had schooled her on how to handle a sword. How effortlessly he'd once moved.

Ellie continued. "He is in a great deal of pain," she said as her mind recalled the first glimpse she'd had of Wesley—his scarred features ravaged with misery and pain.

Suddenly, without a word, the bonesetter headed over to the cluttered desk in the corner. "Where is it? What did I do with it?"

Muttering to herself, Mrs. Porter searched among the piles and piles of papers, clippings, and books, and in her search, she dispelled a little cloud of dust.

The eccentric woman batted at the air with one hand, while with her other, she continued her search.

Ellie hastened over and joined the bonesetter at the foot of her desk.

Mrs. Porter muttered under her breath. "Ah, here it is."

Then, uncorking a pewter hip flask, she downed a long swallow.

Ellie watched her as she drank from that container.

Given the manner of atrocities and horrors witnessed by the bonesetter, Ellie rather suspected she'd require spirits to get her through the memories she carried. Ellie herself had been here but once, and that one morning was indelibly stamped upon her memory.

Ellie's gaze locked on that familiar small container the bonesetter pressed against her mouth, and once more, the past knocked away at Ellie's mind, sucking her back, re-calling that cold metal touching her own lips right before Mrs. Porter had set to work on—

"Can you help him?" she asked, more sharply than she intended.

With the flask halfway to her lips for another sip, Mrs. Porter paused and looked over at Ellie.

Drawing in a slow, even breath through her nose, when Ellie spoke, she did so more calmly. "Can you help the gentleman?"

"My lady, didn't you, yourself learn, I can help anyone?" The bonesetter smiled with all the confidence only a woman so very capable where most men were not, could, toasted Ellie, and then drank deeply.

When she'd finished her swallow, Mrs. Porter wiped the back of her spare hand over her mouth and put her libations down.

"But the people who come here have to want my help. It isn't their friends, family, or sweethearts who need fixing."

"He's quite stubborn and angry," Ellie confided. "Thus far, he's rejected all efforts to help him."

"When he's ready, you bring him to me."

This wasn't just any person. This was Wesley Audley.

The duke's beloved son who'd once smiled and laughed and been charming and kind, and now he was dark, angry, brooding, and roared everyone away. There'd be the matter of convincing that man to visit Mrs. Porter.

Only . . . .

"I . . . don't know how to explain my knowledge of this place," she finally managed to say, directing that admission to the dusty wood floor. "If I do share it with him or his father, there will be questions."

Her siblings had never gleaned the extent of the horrors visited upon her. They hadn't known her horrific *fall* that day hadn't *really* been a fall. Rather, it had been a beloved governess who'd whisked her off to Mrs. Porter . . . only to be sacked by the duke for having done so, against his wishes, and replaced with a cruel woman with a streak of mean to rival Ellie's father.

She felt the bonesetter's eyes on her.

"I'll tell you what no one ever told me," the bonesetter said, and Ellie lifted her gaze to the other woman's. "It isn't our fault that men are brutes."

She stiffened.

"My lady, a woman can spot a kindred soul a mile away. You may come from royalty, but men are men. They're nasty, cruel, and bent on their own pleasures. That is one thing we can all rely on in life, regardless of how or where we were born. But neither does that mean we women wish to relive our pains and share them freely with others."

She caught Ellie by the same arm she'd healed all those years ago. "Am I right?" she asked quietly.

Ellie nodded.

They weren't all bad. Ellie had only ever known kindness and love from her brother Courtland, and Keir—in the way that he was best able to show emotion. She'd also discovered for the first time, in the Duke of Bentley, that not all fathers were bastards. But not all bad didn't mean all men were good, and she'd been given enough reason to never entrust herself and her future to anyone.

Mrs. Porter grunted and gave Ellie's arm a firm pat. "As

for how to convince this fellow and keep your secrets your own? That's for you to sort out. A clever girl like you has spirit and wits enough to convince a wounded soldier to pay me a visit."

"If I bring him, you will help him?"

Mrs. Porter nodded. "*When* you bring him, I will fix him."

If Ellie brought him, Mrs. Porter would help him.

All it required was for Ellie to convince a reclusive gentleman to leave his home and make the journey to Mrs. Porter's establishment in East London.

As of now, there was a greater chance she could convince the duke's cattle to fly the London sky.

Chapter 4

My dearest Wesley,

*When I was a girl, I'd hold my arms out as wide as I
could, and run as fast as I could, and try to fly like a
bird. I wish we could do that, somehow. Fly away,
together, to a world where there is only you and I in it.*

Lovingly Yours

Will he live . . . ?" There it was.
       Not for the first time. Not even for the second,
third, or fourth time.

That question about whether the great Captain Wesley
Audley would survive.

It was a question that had drifted in like a murky specter
floating past when he'd been in a battlefield tent, with men
screaming and surgeons scurrying around.

And it was the same question when they'd strapped him
to a litter and carried him from the fighting fields of Brussels, with Wesley preferring the peace represented by an

eternal sleep to the fiery pain that had held him in its grips the moment a bullet had pierced his thigh, and another through his shoulder.

That question had been whispered in hushed, desperate words spoken by his father, the Duke of Bentley, and Wesley's eldest brother, Rafe, as servants had carried Wesley, feeble and unable to open his eyes from the pain of being jostled around a carriage, and then abovestairs, and blessedly to his chambers.

And this time, with Wesley seated in some kind of roll chair, being pushed by a servant, his father trailed behind him, putting that very question to the doctor.

Powerless.

Pathetic.

Pitiable.

Every last unfavorable *p* word and then some rolled around his brain, and he gritted his teeth.

He'd reverted back to being a babe, one who was at the mercy and whim of those tasked with caring for him, and this reversion from the strong, capable man that Wesley had become filled him with a restive frustration, and he wanted to toss his head back and roar at the unfairness of it all. He'd gone from a captain, in command of men in battle to . . . to . . . this.

The servant shoving the damned chair guided Wesley down another corridor, and Wesley snapped.

"Stop," he gritted out that lone syllable.

To no avail.

His father and doctor continued speaking in hushed tones behind him, and the servant continued shoving Wesley along, until they reached the entryway to the Duke of Bentley's massive library.

Rage tightened his gut.

He slammed his hands down on the arms of the chair. "I said, stop this goddamned contraption."

The servant abruptly complied, bringing Wesley to such a quick stop, his body lurched forward, and the parts of him that had been bullet fodder on the battlefield screamed in agony and protest, and as pain held him in its throes, a black curtain fell briefly over his vision, momentarily blinding him.

"Wesley," his father began, in those same concerned, pained tones he'd used since Wesley's return. "You—"

"I do not want to sit in a damned library," he barked, his voice raspy and hoarse from lack of use.

Not with company, anyway.

The duke wrung his hands. "Dr. Monroe believes it will do you good to have a distraction," he entreated, and looked over the top of Wesley's head to the doctor there.

"You've been home a number of weeks now, and Dr. Monroe is confident you've made significant progress."

"Significant progress?" Wesley echoed. Is that what this was? "I'm in a goddamned chair, unable to walk."

"The pain will continue to recede," Dr. Monroe interjected. "However, I cannot verify you'll ever be fully free of it. Certain weather might affect the muscles and ligaments more. I also believe—"

"The doctor believes it is equally important that you tend to your mind's healing, too," the duke finished for the tall, bespectacled doctor.

As if on cue, the footman collected a handful of books from a nearby table that had until now gone unseen by Wesley.

Wesley stared at the small pile of leather volumes held his way.

"*Tend my mind's healing, too,*" he silently mouthed, and then Wesley tossed his head back and roared with laughter.

That cynical mirth brought pain shooting through his body, and yet, he only laughed all the harder, welcoming the pain. His mind.

They actually thought a good book would erase the memories of those darkest moments, when the world had caught fire, and screams and gunshots and cannon fire had filled the smokey air?

This was why they'd forced him out of his damned rooms and tried to roll him in a wheelchair beside a hearth like he were some old doddering man, content to read a story because there was nothing else for him to do at this juncture in his life.

Which . . . there wasn't.

Not really.

Crippled by the war, he could not even walk the length of his chambers without the support of a cane.

"I don't need a damned story," Wesley hissed. "I need to be left the hell alone."

"And you will." The duke spoke soothingly, like Wesley was a child. With that, Wesley's father glanced to the silent, dutiful servant at the helm of Wesley's infirm chair; the decision ultimately made by a duke accustomed to having his every wish met.

The same liveried footman who'd helped lift Wesley from his bed and into his chair complied with that ducal nod, and pushed Wesley forward, into the room.

A warm, welcoming fire threw off heat, and as they guided Wesley closer to the hearth, he stared blankly at the flames dancing within.

At last, they stopped.

"Captain Audley." Dr. Monroe spoke in lofty tones Wesley expected inspired confidence *in some*. "As I was saying to His Grace, your arm is showing marked improvement since you returned."

"No thanks to anything you've done," Wesley snarled.

The stiff, arrogant fellow pursed his thin lips. "I do believe it will soon be time for me to make a determination about your leg."

As in, cut it off.

Wesley growled. "Go bugger yourself."

Dr. Monroe's bushy white eyebrows went flying up.

The duke pressed a hand over his eyes.

"Well, I never."

"You know what you can never do?" Wesley snapped. "Come back and bother me."

Wheeling on a heel with a speed and ease Wesley resented him for, the doctor grabbed his bag and stalked off.

"Dr. Monroe," the duke begged, running after him.

"Both of you can stay the hell out," Wesley roared. *So that I might enjoy reading a good book . . .* and he continued laughing, even though it hurt him from his teeth on down to his toes.

And Lord help him, Wesley knew it was wrong. He knew the duke was undeserving of his rage, that he'd sought to dissuade Wesley from going to war from the beginning, but Wesley was hopeless to contain the tidal wave of frustration and fury at his own circumstances.

And then mercy of small mercies—there was a God after all—the occupants emptied from the room.

"And shut the door," he said tiredly, closing his eyes.

The panel was immediately closed, with a soft click.

And then peace.

Peace.

Wesley's shoulders sagged, and he slumped in his chair.

It was a funny word, that.

Peace.

Peace existed . . . until it didn't. Until tyrannical men took it upon themselves to amass power, collecting it the way a child might toy marbles.

Wesley forced his eyes open, and he stared emptily into the flames.

Only, there could be no turning back.

There could be no undoing the rivers that ran from clear to sanguine, filled with the blood of too many innocent men, men who were pawns upon the chessboards of more powerful men.

A spasm racked his chest.

Or, in some poor fools' cases, those men made soldiers of themselves, all in a quest for glory, in a hope of being more, and making more of himself . . . for another.

Cynicism brought his lips quirking up painfully at the corners.

How ironic. In his hope and quest to be more for Claire Sparrow, he'd lost . . . all.

Ultimately, losing her.

If you ever even had her to begin with . . .

Delicate and lovely with plump cheeks, given to blushing, and with blond ringlets, she'd been captivating to him. He'd courted her in secret. The times they'd managed to steal away—he from the mines and she from her father, the owner of Cheadle's mines—had been few. But those moments, and thoughts of more, had sustained him.

During his darkest days fighting, her letters had fueled him, filled him with a need to survive so he might have a new future.

With her.

Until, for a second—and final—time, her letters had stopped. At some point, between feverish dreams, as his flesh had burned and the field doctors had dug the bullets from his skin, he'd acknowledged her defection was for the best.

That the dreams he'd carried of a life and future with sweet Claire Sparrow of Cheadle were best shut away and buried, forgotten forever.

A log slipped in the metal grate of the hearth, and the fire hissed and popped; the flames forked into two, putting Wesley in mind of Satan's horns, and he stared enrapt. Lost.

And his mind slipped back, drifting to a recent time . . . back to the Mont-Saint-Jean Ridge.

Wesley's fingers tightened reflexively upon the arms of his chair, his fingernails making marks in the soft wood.

Images flashed in his mind, brief snapshot moments that peppered in and out.

"*. . . Jaysus, 'e's on fire . . . someone put him out . . .*"

Wesley's breathing grew ragged and shallow in his ears as he fought in vain to ward the memory off.

"*. . . heeeeeeelp me. For God's sake, pleeeeeease . . .*"

The screams continued—in Wesley's mind?

Or from his mouth?

The frantic cries of that soldier burning alive had pierced across the field. Other men had been furiously fighting their own battles, and there'd been no opportunity to put out the flames licking at a lad, no more than seventeen.

But Wesley had intervened. The moment he'd felled the

soldier intent on killing him, Wesley turned to helping the boy.

What'd happened was all jumbled. The past mixed up with the present, both intricately twined and unable to extricate from the other.

Wesley's hands fluttered, his palms coming up as the scene continued to replay in his mind, feeling the sting of fire as he'd shoved the man down, rolled him over, and patted him until the flames had gone. The soldier's entire right arm had been charred black.

His breathing came shallow and ragged as it had in the midst of that battle and fight to keep the young man from burning alive; his chest moved up and down in violent heaves.

Click . . .

He dimly registered it.

A bayonet being cocked. Wesley tensed and braced himself for the explosion of gunfire to follow.

It did not come.

Because there were no guns. At least not here.

There was no fire, except for the safe, comfortable, contained one within the metal grate.

He was not in Brussels, but in the Duke of Bentley's household.

And that click was no hammer of a gun, but that of the door, signifying someone had entered.

Wesley gritted his teeth.

His father.

Rafe.

The duchess.

Cailin.

Between the four of them, they were unrelenting, determined to drive Wesley mad. His shoulders shook with empty mirth. That was, a different kind of mad.

Who was it this time . . . ?

Narrowing his eyes, Wesley glared at that still-shut panel, the hesitant person on the other side having sense enough to contemplate a path in. And for a moment, he thought his

damned tenacious family had second thoughts, and intended
to leave Wesley to that which he craved most—his own
company.

The person on the other side pushed the door open a
crack, and then widened it enough to slip inside.

Alas . . . there was to be no reprieve this day.

Only . . .

Wesley stared on as a slender figure slipped inside.

It was none of the four. Nor, for that matter, was it Dr.
Monroe or any of the many servants assigned the unenvi-
able task of serving Wesley.

The young woman drew the door shut behind her and
hesitated there at the entryway.

Attired in flawless white and ruffled satin skirts, she was
no servant.

A handful of inches past five feet, she was taller than
most women, but of a height ideal for most men. Her waist
was trim, and her breasts small.

She wasn't a figure a person would take note of . . . but
for her curls.

More curls than he'd ever seen upon a single person;
those unruly strands had been wound like a golden coronet
about her head. Some four sapphire-studded hair combs
attempted—and failed—to hold those heavy-looking corkscrew tresses in place, and yet, even with that, a handful
had escaped their restraints and hung about the slender lady's narrow shoulders.

There was . . . something vaguely familiar about her.

Nay, those curls.

Wesley tried to recall them. He tried to recall *her*.

He'd a vague recollection of arriving back in London,
carried on that litter, and opening his eyes to find this woman's heart-shaped face staring back at him, with stricken
eyes.

But her identity, it eluded him. It didn't make sense he
would know her. His time among the peerage had been limited. There'd only been the short time when he'd first come,
years ago, asking Bentley for a commission, and then a brief

return when Cailin had been married, and her husband arranged for Wesley to be present.

The young lady did a glance about the room. Her gaze skipped over where he sat shrouded in the dark.

Wesley opened his mouth to tell the woman to get the hell out. To go back to whoever had sent her to keep him company—but then stopped.

The latest thief of Wesley's solitude ventured not toward him, but rather, off in the opposite direction.

She trailed slowly along the floor-to-ceiling-length shelving units brimming with leather volumes. More books were contained upon their mahogany shelves than Wesley had ever known there could be.

The mystery woman paused periodically, leaning up on her tiptoes to better peruse a title, before sinking back onto her heels and resuming her casual search.

It was an incongruously innocent exploration, at odds with the tumult that had gripped him moments before her arrival.

Wesley didn't know who the slender slip of a lady was, but he wanted her gone.

He wanted to rid himself of the reminder that he was forever broken and damaged, his mind and body equally and permanently destroyed while the world around him was composed of the unscarred, untouched.

Sitting there, tension thrumming within him, Wesley gritted his teeth and waited for the young woman to make her selection, and then get the hell out.

Chapter 5

My dearest Wesley,

You mourn our being apart, as I do. And yet, as the Great Bard reminds us in As You Like It . . . *"this, our life . . . finds . . . good in everything." Find whatever comfort you may in the world around you . . . until you come back to me.*

Lovingly Yours

Ellie walked a path about the Duke of Bentley's library. It had been a path she'd traveled many times before this one. Chiswick Hall had become one of her favorite places to be.

Unlike her earliest memories of her own childhood, where her ducal father had ruled with an iron fist and demanded everyone from his staff on to his children conduct themselves in a certain way, there'd been happiness in this duke's home.

From the moment Ellie had begun paying visits to her

brother's father- and mother-in-law, she'd noted the happy chatter and unrestrained laughter that filled the rooms, the easy, ready smiles worn by all.

In short, it had been a wholly foreign place, like some mythical land where unicorns flew and fairies danced.

That was not, however, what brought her here this day.

Now she'd come armed with the information she'd received from Mrs. Porter, in the hopes she could help him.

. . . All people benefit from someone whom they can freely communicate with; speaking about old hurts and fears and past suffering tends to bring a cathartic release . . .

"Do you ever intend to pick a damned book?"

Ellie gasped. The small leather collection of poems slipped from her fingers and sailed to the floor with a quiet *thwack*.

She'd known he was here. She'd deliberately sought out the library to see Wesley, but upon her arrival, she'd pretended to not notice him so that she might get up the courage to speak.

Her heart hammered at the unexpected change in his voice. It was harsher and graveled in ways it hadn't been before.

Ellie peered across the room, into the shadows. "Hullo," she called softly.

Her greeting went unanswered.

How very different he was from the man who'd indulged her as a young girl that long-ago day. She mourned that transformation. Even as she understood why he'd become this angry figure in a corner.

When first she'd met him, his dark hair had been snipped close to his ears. Now those loose waves had become overgrown like an ill-tended garden maze, and a wild growth upon his face matched the unruliness of his curls.

"You're in desperate need of a shave," she said, in a bid to get some reaction—any reaction—from him.

"What was that?" he asked, his voice low and ferocious.

Ellie cupped her hands around her mouth and spoke more loudly. "I said, it is as dark as a cave."

He growled. "No, you didn't."

"Fair enough. Either way, both statements hold true." She wandered a step closer, and curiosity pulled a question from her. "If you know what I said, then why did you ask?"

At last, she reached him, and another gasp exploded from her lips. Her stomach pitched, and her head grew fuzzy as she caught her first close-up glimpse of his leg. Twisted at an unnatural angle, the limb protruded at his left knee.

Wesley grinned, a feral, mocking, empty expression of mirth.

This silent, brooding man had replaced the charming, affable soldier of her younger years.

He was still the same man, she silently reminded herself of that. Somewhere inside. He'd just been changed by what he'd seen and done and suffered. Tragedy indelibly shaped them all. His tragedies had just proved greater than most.

Ellie ventured the remaining distance. "Captain Aud—"

"Don't call me that!" he hurled.

This time, she didn't falter in the face of his fury, a tactic intended to scare her away.

"What *should* I call you?"

"Nothing," he seethed. "You should call me nothing."

You treat him as you once did before he was changed...

"Well, that is silly." She forced as much levity as she could into those handful of words. "I cannot very well go about calling you 'Nothing.'"

"You should, because I don't want you here," he said, tiredly, as if the fight had been drained out of him. "I don't want anyone here."

Wesley slumped in his chair.

Once Captain Audley feels he can trust a person... once he can speak first casually about topics that are more mundane and easy, then he can eventually move on to talking about the hurts he suffered, or the horrors he witnessed...

Ellie's heart splintered and broke.

"I was teasing," Ellie said softly.

"Do I strike you as someone who wants to be teased?" he jeered.

He'd used to enjoy when she teased him. The chambers of her mind still echoed with the sounds of his laughter in that copse long ago when she'd pointed out all the many ways in which she was eminently more qualified and skilled as a fighter.

He sneered. "Do you think I *want* to talk to you?"

"I rather think you don't want to talk to anyone."

"Brava." He brought his hands together in a slow, mocking clap. "That is the first correct thing you've said since you came in here, madam."

Gathering her skirts, Ellie sank into a deep curtsy. "Why, thank you—"

"Would you stop," he thundered, slapping a fist down hard on the arm of his chair.

Ellie jumped, and her courage flagged as she was instantly transported back to a different library, where a different gentleman had raged at her. She closed her eyes tightly.

Perhaps I cannot do this, after all . . .

She opened her eyes and her gaze caught on Wesley. All the blood had drained from his face, leaving the skin not covered by his beard a sickly white. His body spasmed.

Her own fear forgotten, Ellie rushed the remaining way to him. "You've hurt yourself."

An animalistic laugh spilled from his lips, twisted and raw and bordering on the edge of madness, and she wanted to run all over again.

Instead, she dug in.

"Is there something I can do?" Ellie looked desperately to the doorway, because suddenly, in the moment, applying all Mrs. Porter's lessons seemed an impossibility.

Perfect in theory, but hopelessly flawed in reality. What good could she do Wesley?

"I should fetch the doctor or your father or—"

"No." He struck his fist a second time along the wood arm of his chair, this time gritting his teeth through the obvious pain his gesture inflicted. "How many times must I say it? I don't want anyone here. Who the hell are you, anyway?"

She started. The truth suddenly hit her with all the force of a blow her father had once delivered to her back.

Wesley had no recollection of who she was.

Ellie stared sadly at him—this lost and lonely and hurting man. It shouldn't surprise her. Time had changed her, but that was hardly the reason he'd not recognize her. He'd not, because to Wesley Audley she'd merely been the small girl he'd been instructing to fight . . . not anything more.

"Ellie," she said softly. "My name is Ellie."

Wesley's eyes looked blankly back at her.

"Ellie," he repeated dumbly.

"Ellie Balfour," she murmured, clarifying further for him. Reflexively, she dipped a curtsy, and it was the first time in the whole of her existence that the ladylike gesture served a functional purpose—it gave her some distracting action.

Wesley continued to stare with that vacant gaze.

It is essential for an affected person to surround themselves with people whom they love, people who are important to them . . .

She dampened her mouth. "I'm Courtland's sister. Cailin's sister-in-law."

Do you truly think you are the one to help him? a voice taunted. How could she do him any good if he didn't even remember who she was?

And then Wesley blinked several times.

"Ellie," he spoke her name in peculiarly flat tones. "Ellie," he said a second time, this time with a trace of recognition.

Ellie nodded enthusiastically.

Slumping in his chair, Wesley scrubbed his right hand across his eyes. "Forgive me," he said gruffly. "You shouldn't be here. Why are you here?"

"I was paying a visit with Cailin." *In the hopes I would see you . . .* "She and your father, the duke, wished to speak alone with her and Mr. Audley." She paused. "The other Mr. Audley. Your brother, Rafe."

Wesley looked at her like she'd popped a third eye.

Ellie made herself stop rambling. "I like to visit with His Grace and Her Grace," she finished.

"In *this* room?" he demanded between clenched teeth. "Did they send you?"

Ellie shook her head. Why would they have? She was nothing to Wesley, certainly not someone whose presence he'd seek, and certainly not a woman whom he'd look forward enough to seeing that he might step out of the shadows. Her heart hurt all over again.

"I was looking for a book," she said quietly.

Wesley slashed his right hand angrily her way. "Get one then and get out." He grunted. "Please."

He was still in there. That slight *please* tacked on pointed to the truth of it. He didn't want to be this way, but he didn't know any other way.

Ellie made herself look away from him and headed over to the nearest shelving unit. She squinted, attempting to make out the titles in the dim lighting.

"You know, the sun is out," she called back.

He cocked his head.

"What are you on about?" he barked, his voice hoarse, but less harsh.

"The sun," she repeated, crossing over to the curtains. "It has rained for days on end, and the day sky may as well have been the night sky."

Ellie caught the pale yellow velvet material and drew one of the panels back. "But no longer—"

"No!" Wesley threw a hand up, as if to ward off that light.

She stopped.

"I don't want any damned sunlight," he hissed.

Ellie tensed.

She'd been barked at before. By a man far meaner. But that had been a different man. One who'd hated Ellie for her many imperfections.

Before her, Ellie saw a man who hated the world at large.

"You're certain?" she asked. "The sun . . . it might do

you good. 'Yet this my comfort: when your words are done, My woes end likewise with the evening sun . . . '" She recited aloud those words she'd previously only penned in a letter to him.

Even with some ten paces between them, Ellie caught a flash of recognition.

Her heart picked up its beat.

He recognized it.

Ellie continued. "Still, I do have one comfort: when you stop speaking, my miseries will be gone like the setting sun." She paused. "It is Shakespeare," she said softly.

His entire body jolted. He went pale once more, and she tensed, waiting for him to lash out again, but then he slid his eyes away from hers.

"Get your book, Ellie."

This time, he did not snarl that order, and she took comfort in that.

Nor did he urge her to close that curtain. Keenly attuned to his gaze on her back as she moved throughout the room, Ellie tried to forget he stared at her. Instead, she made a show of perusing titles. Periodically she'd pluck one of the duke's volumes from the shelf, and then return it to its spot.

The clock ticked away the passing moments as Ellie slowly filled her arms with a small stack.

When she'd finished, she landed herself deliberately before Cailin's brother.

At some point, he'd shifted his focus away from Ellie and trained his attention on the hearth.

She cleared her throat. "Ahem."

When he remained engrossed, Ellie did so a second time. "Ahhhem."

Blinking slowly, Wesley looked over at her, and it was as though he'd only just recalled her presence, as if he were only seeing her for the first time.

"I have my book," she said, shrugging her shoulders, and highlighting the six books she'd gathered.

She set five down on a table beside him. "You needn't worry I'm going to filch them from your father. I'm going to leave these here for when I return, and when I do, I will swap them for the one I've read."

"You could burn them in the fire now, and I wouldn't care."

"Well, that would be quite a waste of the written word." She paused. "Particularly *these* written words." Ellie let that dangle in the air between them, deliberately enticing.

His chiseled facial muscles remained a perfect mask, cracking not the slightest with interest, feigned or real.

"I could read to y—"

"No," he interrupted sharply, and she tensed. Wesley sighed and swiped another palm over a bearded cheek. "That is, no . . . thank you. I prefer being alone."

She bowed her head. "As you wish, Mr. Audley."

As she went, Ellie held close to her chest the book she'd availed herself of from the duke's shelves and headed for the doorway.

"Ellie?" he called, and his voice boomed around the library and froze her in her tracks.

Holding her book close to her chest, Ellie faced him.

"Wesley . . . is fine. You may call me Wesley."

With the permission he'd granted her, Ellie tested his Christian name, tasting it upon her tongue.

"Wesley," she murmured, those two syllables rolling ever so softly. "Good day, Wesley."

He yanked his gaze away from hers and stared emptily back into those dancing flames before him.

Ellie let herself out.

Chapter 6

My dearest Wesley,

"Doubt thou the stars are fire. Doubt that the sun doth move, doubt truth to be a liar, but never doubt I love . . ."

Lovingly Yours

Wesley didn't know why he'd given Ellie Balfour permission to call him by his given name. Just as he'd not known why he'd read that stack of books she'd left for him.

But he had.

And it was as though Ellie had used his offer as an invitation, and in the days and weeks that passed, she sought him out.

Though, in fairness, she didn't really seek him out. She sought out the duke's libraries.

And knowing that, knowing her penchant for visiting that room of all rooms, he certainly could have stayed away— but, for reasons he couldn't understand, he didn't.

Mayhap it was because when she did enter the rooms, aside from the casual greeting, she swapped out whatever book she'd picked last time for another one of those that sat untouched on the table near the hearth.

She didn't attempt to coax him back to the living.

She didn't tiptoe around him.

She didn't ask if he'd read the books she left for him.

She just visited, sat, read, and then left.

Nay, that wasn't altogether true.

She came, sat, read, and occasionally laughed softly to herself at whatever words were written on the pages of whatever book she'd commandeered. And sigh. She did that, too.

And sniffle.

She did plenty of that, also. As if she were fighting tears.

It was enough to make a man wonder at what titles she'd selected and proved the *only* reason he availed himself of those works when she did leave them behind.

But somehow, some way, when she was near, Wesley forgot that he'd been broken. For a short while, his deformed leg wasn't his sole and only focus—rather, it was her.

Just then Ellie giggled. She was curled up on the low, tufted arm of the leather button sofa and she tried to catch the sound with her fingertips, but her efforts were futile, as it turned to an all-out snorting laugh.

And it appeared the war hadn't killed his curiosity, after all. Rather, he found himself entranced by the sound of her enjoyment. She reminded him that some people were capable of joy.

What made her laugh so?

Ellie glanced up and over from across the top of the pages to where Wesley sat in his wheelchair.

Her cheeks, already flushed a pretty red from her laughter, turned several shades deeper as she noted his stare.

"What is that?" he asked, annoyed with himself for caring, but unable to stop from asking.

The lady cocked her head. "Wesley?"

It was not the first time she'd spoken his name. Every time she did, it somehow filled him with warmth.

Then understanding dawned in the bluest eyes he'd ever before seen.

"Oh . . . you mean my book." Ellie turned around the book in her hands, facing the pages out toward Wesley. "Shakespeare."

Ellie enjoyed Shakespeare. He stared unblinking, unmoving, as she spoke. How many times had he read the words of the Great Bard shared by another woman, in letters that had been a light amidst the darkness of war.

"I am quite keen on *some* of his work," she said matter-of-factly, even as her words wrought reminders, different ones, still painful.

Wesley's eyes slid shut, as he replayed in his mind the inked letters he'd committed to memory.

"*. . . Someday, when you return, I shall rest my head upon your lap, and ask that you regale me with the words of Shakespeare. The funniest of ones, the most romantic ones. I want to feel every emotion roused with you . . . I want to experience . . .*"

"You like this one, do you not?"

Wesley's eyes flew open. "What?" he rasped, his breath coming harsh in his ears.

Undeterred by his sharp tone, Ellie extended the book toward him so he could better read the title, and then flipped it around and read aloud:

"*O, when she's angry, she is keen and shrewd!*
She was a vixen when she went to school; And though she be but little, she is fierce."

"It suits you well," he murmured.

Ellie cocked her head.

"The quote."

Her full lips parted, forming a surprised little circle. "Oh," she whispered.

And for a brief moment, she looked at him as though he were a complete, unbroken man, and for an even longer moment, he exulted in the feeling of being whole.

Only, he wasn't. He was shattered and useless.

Bitterness filled him.

Wesley wheeled the chair out from behind the hearth and propelled himself over to where Ellie sat. He ignored the way his muscles screamed in protest at his hasty movements and welcomed the fiery sting.

He stopped before her.

She smiled serenely back, and with the curtains drawn and the sun filtering into the room, up close, closer than he'd been to her in the light of day, he peered at her freckled face—a pert nose; lush, pink lips perpetually upturned; her eyes windows to her damned soul, and they revealed an untroubled soul—and it set his teeth on edge, being presented with this . . . this innocence.

"Why the hell do you insist on coming here?"

Ellie cocked her head, and one of the lady's hair combs failed in its job as several curls slipped out, bouncing at her shoulder.

"I don't—"

"To this library," he demanded.

"To read," she said simply.

"To *read*?"

She nodded.

Wesley fell back in his chair. "And you can't do that at home? St. James doesn't have a sea of books for you to read?" She had to come sit here and steal his solitude and make him think about . . . things that weren't the war, and loss?

"I've read those books."

"All of them?" he asked incredulously.

"All the ones I cared to." Ellie's features grew contemplative, and she leaned over and peered at his face. "Though, I suppose the better question is . . . why do you come here, Wesley? If not to read."

Why, indeed?

There was a challenge in her eyes.

Grabbing the cane that rested nearby, Wesley jabbed it unforgivingly hard into the Aubusson carpet and leveraged himself up, panting with the effort of his exertions, and hating himself for being as weak as a child.

"What are you saying? Are you thinking that I enjoy your company?" he taunted.

She laughed again. "I wouldn't presume to say *that*."

And it was that bright, cheerful laughter that pierced the darkest parts of a man's soul and reminded him that there was a place where light dwelled, a place Wesley never would again belong.

"Because I don't," he snarled. "I tolerate you. That is different." Did he seek to persuade her or himself?

Her laughter faded. The cheer died from her eyes, and he despised himself all over again. This is what he'd become? And yet, he knew no other way. He'd lost every part of himself that was good on those battlefields.

Wesley collapsed back into his chair. The cane slipped from his fingers and clattered upon the floor, mocking him as it clattered for his feebleness, and he closed his eyes. "Get out," he said, tiredly.

He waited for the rush of her delicate footfalls as she raced off.

He expected her to flee.

And yet, attuned as his ears were to both the invisible sounds inside his head and the ones in the waking world around him, he detected no trace of movement.

He forced his eyes open and found her staring back through thick, golden lashes.

Wesley growled, and then leaning in, he caught her interestingly squared jaw with his hand, daring her to pull away. She didn't.

"Why won't you just go?" he begged.

Ellie spoke quietly. "I like being here."

His ears sharpened on that pregnant pause.

"In the duke's library," she finished.

Of course it wasn't being here with him.

Why should she enjoy the company of a miserable cripple who couldn't even manage a smile, let alone to stand?

"Like being here, do you?" he jeered, and drew her onto his lap. "Enjoy keeping company with the beast?" he whispered harshly. He spoke those words aloud so as to remind himself of precisely what he'd become, and what his actions in this instant further leant prove to.

"You're no beast, Wesley," she said softly, so simply. She remained steady as if it were the most natural thing in the world for a man to handle her so.

Close as they were, the scent of her—delicate apple blossoms—filled his nostrils and conjured thoughts of innocent pastures and not ones slicked red with the blood of dying men.

Sweat popped up on his brow, and a groan started low in his chest. "Ah, but aren't I?"

And then, she touched her fingertips to his jaw, palming him. Her fingers grazed that jagged, still-healing mark that ran the length of his face from ear down to the underside of his neck.

"You are no monster," she said simply. "You are just a man."

Just a man.

How long had it been since he'd felt like that? A whole man? Fully intact from mind, body, and soul, and not this broken, battered, shattered shadow of what he'd used to be?

And for a moment, her words, and her touch, and just being here made him forget who he was—what he was. His gaze slid to her mouth. Her berry-red lips formed a perfect bow. They were lips made for all delicious types of sinning.

He dipped his head a fraction, closer to her mouth, wanting to taste of that flesh. Needing to. "Ellie," he whispered.

Ellie's lashes fluttered.

With shock? Horror? No doubt both.

Wesley wrenched away. "Just a man," he laughed coldly. "If you believe that, you're a damned fool," that whisper pulled from him. "Now get out."

Ellie hesitated.

"I said go!" he thundered.

She scrambled from his lap and raced from the room, leaving Wesley at last alone.

He ran a hand that trembled across his eyes.

Well, if nothing else, he'd scared her off and ensured

himself that she'd not return, and he'd not be saddled with her annoyingly chipper presence.

And yet, as he sat there, staring at the book she'd left behind, why did he feel something very close to regret at her being gone?

Chapter 7

My dearest Wesley,

As a girl, I never considered myself romantic. I never thought about or dreamed about love or falling in love. In fact, I wasn't even sure I was capable of loving . . . until you.

Lovingly Yours

Following Wesley's explosion, Ellie did something she had always excelled at—she ran.

As a girl, it had been a necessary skill she'd put to use for any number of reasons: When she and her siblings had been playing a game of chase or hide-and-seek. Or then there'd been the times when she'd actually been chased by her late father, and whatever cruel words he'd intended to speak, or inevitable slap or knock to the back of her head he ultimately delivered.

This, however, marked the first time she'd run as a young woman.

Her breath came quick as she raced along the Duke of Bentley's wide hallway corridors; her white skirts, like a flag whipping in the breeze, snapped noisily about her ankles as she went.

In all her life, Ellie had never thought she'd know a man's kiss, and she'd been fine with that truth.

Better than fine, really. Because she hated men.

Not *all* men. Her brothers she liked just fine. She loved them, even.

But her brothers were not all men.

Her father had shown her the ugliest side of a man's soul, and the fact that her brothers, who'd loved her as they did, had also been powerless to stop her from being hurt had taught her something early on: a man with absolute legal power over her ultimately could not be stopped.

When the miserable excuse of a monster had given up the ghost, it'd been a happy day, one that had freed her, and she'd absolutely no intention of ever, ever willingly trusting herself and her happiness in the hands of a husband—those fickle creatures.

Ellie came to an abrupt stop and caught the edge of a mahogany side table.

Though, in fairness, there'd been one man whom she'd entertained a future with.

That same man who, for a sliver of an instant, she'd thought intended to kiss her, and she'd desperately wanted that kiss.

She climbed her gaze above the cheerful arrangement of assorted colored roses overflowing from a silver urn to the gilded mirror that hung there.

Her visage stared damningly back: her cheeks flushed, her eyes glittering.

Absently, Ellie touched two fingers to her lips, and her hand trembled.

She'd never carried the romantic inclinations of her elder sisters, who'd dreamed of marriage. All Ellie had dreamed of were the ways to avoid that miserable state.

She'd never craved intimacy of any sort with any man.

And it was why she knew she would never, ever come back to this townhouse. At least, not by choice, and not unless there was some function being thrown by the duke and duchess that required her to be here. A pang struck at that loss; this home in many ways had become more of a home than her own family's household had ever been. Nor did her plan to not come back have anything to do with fearing Wesley—she didn't. Rather, she feared what he made her feel and dream of. Dreams about more kisses and embraces that she'd no place having.

What would it be like to feel his mouth on hers? Or his hands on her body?

He'd called her by her given name, whispering it in a husky baritone that had revealed a hungering. Her eyes slid shut and a sigh slipped out.

"Ellie . . ."

Ellie blinked.

Wait a moment.

That wasn't the echo of his imagined voice.

Coming to the moment, she looked at the tall, regal gentleman at the end of the hall now approaching.

A man who was very much not Wesley Audley, but nonetheless bore a familiar look, and whose powerful, long-legged strides were reminiscent of Wesley's from a time past. The duke.

He'd always treated her the way she'd wished to have a father treat her. She'd always looked forward to her visits with him.

Now, panic consumed her. The duke had come upon her woolgathering and dreaming about his son's kiss.

Oh, God. Did he know she'd been nearly kissing his son? He couldn't.

As he moved toward her with determined steps, she found her feet twitching with the need to run off in the opposite direction.

In a bid for nonchalance, she made herself call out a greeting. "Your Grace."

Belatedly, recalling she was still touching her mouth in

a telltale, damning way, Ellie dropped her arm swiftly back to her side, only standing as close to the table as she was, her knuckles collided with the wood.

She gasped as pain resonated along her fingers, and she reflexively drew her hand close to her belly.

The duke stopped before her. "Ellie, are you all right?" he asked, his voice laden with concern.

"Fine," she squeaked. "Nothing . . ." *Happened between Wesley and me.* "I . . ." And it was a moment before she registered his question wasn't about the kiss but about her hand. "I'm fine." It was a bald-faced lie. She wasn't certain she'd ever be fine again.

The duke searched his gaze over her face.

"You are flushed," he remarked softly.

Oh, God. He knew. He knew she'd been having wicked thoughts.

Stop it. He cannot possibly know that.

"I . . . was racing off."

The duke clasped his hands behind his back, and then rocked forward on his heels. "You were with my son."

"Your Grace?" Her voice emerged faintly squeaky.

"You were with Wesley," he clarified, though there'd really been no need for him *to* clarify.

Her heart paused mid-beat.

Oh, dear. The duke *did* know. He knew Ellie yearned for Wesley. Which meant Courtland would know and Cailin and then everyone.

A sad glimmer filled the duke's eyes. "He seemed to like you."

Her face went hot.

"Back when he returned from the war. The first time, that is . . . at the house party, the wedding."

And then it hit her—he didn't suspect anything at all. Relief filled her, leaving Ellie giddy inside.

The duke blinked several times, and gave her an odd look. "You are . . . certain you are all right?"

No. "Yes," she said with a calm she didn't feel.

Sadness glimmered in Bentley's eyes, ones that gleamed and hinted at tears. "He ran you off. I . . . heard his voice raised . . . moments ago when you were in the library. I am sorry he spoke to you so."

"You needn't apologize," she assured him quietly.

The duke drew his hands back; lowering them to his side, he glanced at the floor. "He's not the same, I know you know that."

"No," she said softly. He wasn't. "But how could he be?"

The duke's features spasmed, and he squeezed his eyes shut and sucked in a ragged breath that cut all the way through her.

"I should have never agreed to that commission. I should have insisted he remain here, safe and happy and—"

"He wished to go, Your Grace," she said gently, but with a firm insistence meant to penetrate his paternal guilt. "Mr. Audley was not one who would have allowed for anything different."

What must it be to have been so loved by one's father?

The ghost of a smile hovered on the duke's lips. "He's an obstinate one, isn't he?"

Obstinate in the love he carried for a woman who'd proven when she'd stopped writing him that she'd never deserved him. Obstinate in all ways.

"It is how I know he'll be fine," she said quietly. *Eventually.* Or as fine as he could be, given all the various different hurts he'd suffered.

The duke's smile faded. "I do not know if that is the case, Ellie, but he will live. I understand if you don't wish to return, but it is . . . a happier place when you are here. For Lydia and I."

She knew what he spoke of. Courtland and Cailin had become preoccupied new parents, whose visits to the duke and duchess came less. Rafe and Edwina had two babes, along with Edwina's thriving business helping young ladies making their debuts, which meant they'd even less time to visit.

"I am happy to be here, Your Grace," she said, taking one of his hands in hers and covering it with her opposite fingers.

For he'd been good to her, treating her far better than she deserved given the trouble she'd wrought for his daughter.

The duke covered the top of her hand with his palm and patted. "It is my hope that you will still visit with me and continue to use the library as you have. It might also do Wesley some good to see you about. You are always so bright and cheerful, and"—he waved a hand about, gesturing to the hall—"this household has been anything but since my son's return. However, there's a pall that now hangs here, and if you'd wish to avoid . . . coming, I more than understand."

He was allowing her an out.

And coward that she was, she wished to take it.

She wished to take the easy way and thank him for all the times over the years he'd allowed her to visit and make his home hers so that she needn't see Wesley and be reminded of the feelings she'd carried for him.

But she could not.

"I would be happy to return." And oddly, in a strange way, despite the fear she felt over this pull Wesley had over her, she found there was . . . truth to her words. "If you'll have me."

A smile wreathed His Grace's face, briefly transforming him to the carefree, happy father without real woes he'd been over the years. "I look forward to that very much," he said softly.

And as Ellie forced a smile, she could not help but feel a sense of dread mingled with relief at the thought of again running into Wesley.

Chapter 8

My dearest Wesley,

*I enjoy music, but only the cheerful types. There is
enough gloom in the world, is there not?*

Lovingly Yours

After Ellie Balfour had fled the library yesterday afternoon, Wesley had been certain it was the last he'd see
of her.

And he was glad for it. *More* than glad, in fact.

The last thing he needed about was a young lady who
blushed and kissed with innocent lips.

Not when she'd posed a temptation he'd been almost hopeless to resist. And not when, with her innocence, she reminded him of all the ways in which he was broken.

Only Ellie had come back.

And not only had she returned, but she'd done so day
after day, and he only knew it because he'd caught a glimpse
of her through the crack of the curtains in his windows that

overlooked the duke's grand gardens outside. Each afternoon, at the same time, he'd peel them back a fraction to find her there.

Sometimes alone.

Sometimes not.

When she wasn't, she was joined by her maid or Wesley's father.

And she always read.

It was a detail he'd not even known about Claire Sparrow, until she mentioned it in one of her notes. The times they'd been together were clandestine, stolen ones, where they'd hardly had time to share the most intimate parts of themselves.

Ellie, however, he'd come to discover, loved books. Day after day, she'd turn the stone bench into a desk, and the emerald grass into a makeshift bench. She always knelt there, alternately reading, and then pausing to make notes.

And it was only boredom that left him wondering as to what words she wrote.

Or why.

It was why, time and time again, he'd make the slow, painful walk across the room, forcing a limb that did not wish to move to do just that, so he could catch a glimpse of her, and try to figure out the answer of a puzzle he didn't understand.

Eventually she would snap her books closed, and then add them to a small basket, along with her portable inkwell and pen, hop to her feet with an agility he shamefully resented her for, and leave.

And that was when he knew it was safe to venture out of his rooms. That was how he knew beyond the assurance of a doubt that she'd gone, and there was no risk of running into her.

Standing at the floor-to-ceiling-length windows, Wesley stared out. Rain came in steady sheets, striking the window with angry drops.

Rain also kept her away, which he was glad for.

Oddly, though, it felt a touch like . . . regret, too.

"Regret?" he muttered to himself. "What shite is this?"

He didn't want her about or underfoot. He didn't want anyone. He was content to stay here, without having to suffer through inane conversations about things that didn't matter, when in his mind, a different world existed: one of fire and pain and destruction and death.

A jagged streak of lightning briefly illuminated the ominously dark afternoon sky, lighting up the gardens below.

The stone watering fountain erected at the center, overflowing from the deluge that had rained down since the early morn hours, spilled over the side, leaving puddles upon the grass.

Wesley had always despised the rain.

First as a boy who'd given chase over the Cheadle countryside, and then as a young man consigned to the fate of miner in a mining town. Those rainstorms had left the earth slick and dangerous with the risk of a landslide.

And he'd come to hate it even more as a soldier fighting on mud-slicked battlefields, the sting of cold as that rain had penetrated his garments and turned the earthen floor he and the other soldiers slept upon into a muddied mattress.

He hated it even more now for the memories it ushered in.

Rain pinged against the windowpanes in a steady staccato.

Plink-Plink-Plink

Pop-Pop-Pop-Pop

Sweat slicked his palms as in his mind, that ping of sharp rain melded and blended with the pop of thousands of bayonets exploding in rapid succession.

It was the Devil at play, gleefully reminding the men of their darkest, evilest deeds, and punishing them with the memory of the lives they'd taken and the things they had done in the name of survival.

Pop-Pop-Pop

Wesley clapped his hands hard over his ears in a bid to drown out the sound, but the imagery played in his mind, and he glanced over, beside him, looking for the soldier who'd been standing next to him.

He squeezed his eyes shut to ward it off, but the memory danced in anyway.

A soldier whose name he'd not known, whose mouth had formed a small circle of stunned surprise, and the hole left by a bullet that had marred the center of his head.

Before he'd collapsed sideways, knocking Wesley to the ground, and—

A tortured moan had climbed up his throat and gotten lodged there, choking him on the sound of his own misery. Haunted, he sought to knock the thoughts loose, banging his forehead against the panes, rattling them.

Pop-Pop-Pop

The gunshots kept coming.

Wesley gripped the long strands of his hair and tugged hard, sharply at his scalp.

Rain.

It was rain.

Wasn't it?

It was all mixed-up. *He* was all mixed-up.

He was cold, but not wet. How could that be? How, if he was in the midst of a raging battle, could he be dry?

No, that didn't make sense.

Think, man. Think.

It didn't make sense.

Because there was no battle, at least not one that he now fought in.

There were other battles still being waged, by the men who'd not yet been mowed down on those bloodied fields, but who eventually would be. But it wasn't Wesley.

I am here. In London.

With a desperate gasp of breath, Wesley managed to pull himself from the abyss of nightmares, and, yanking the curtains shut in a bid to blot out the ping of rain, he grabbed his cane and made a lurching beeline for the door.

He yanked the ornate oak panel open and stumbled into the hall.

A pair of servants carrying vases of bright, cheerful flowers let out matching startled gasps.

With a growl, he stalked past. His leg screamed in protest of the pace he'd set, but he welcomed both the distraction and also the reminder of his broken body.

He was mad, deserving to be locked up in some asylum for the nightmares haunting him and the thoughts he was powerless to control.

Wesley didn't stop until he reached the library.

Gasping for breath at the exertions his efforts cost him, he stumbled through the doors.

He did a search of the room.

The ragged rasp of his breath proved his only company.

Drawing the panel shut hard behind him, Wesley limped over to the fireplace; a toasty fire danced in those grates, and he sank into the folds of the leather winged chair positioned before it, and, resting his cane along the side of his seat, he closed his eyes.

He closed them so as to not see the fire, but instead welcomed the warmth of those flames upon his face: a reminder he was, in fact, here in London, in the comforts of the duke's home, and not trapped on a rainy battlefield, slicked wet with blood and mud.

Only . . .

Wesley opened his eyes and stared emptily out at the fire.

For there was guilt, too.

Guilt for all the men he'd left behind, who still fought. For what was worse, coward that he was, he didn't want to be back there. He didn't even want the memories of the time he'd spent fighting.

His lips formed a small, painfully rusty smile, one that strained the muscles which worked so very hard to make that once-easy expression of mirth.

For perhaps the madness that gripped him, day in and day out, was his punishment for wanting to forget; perhaps the Lord was no benevolent one, after all, but a vengeful one, set on punishing Wesley for the crimes he'd committed in the name of war, and Wesley's cowardly yearning to forget them.

What existed for a man such as he?

The arm where he'd taken a bullet throbbed, and he shifted in the folds of the seat to alleviate some of the pain; he concentrated on breathing in an attempt to distract himself until it had passed.

When he'd had the idea to go off and fight, he'd never given thought to a possibility of his returning anything less than whole, in both body and mind. He'd painted an entire scenario in his head, one that included Wesley being fully intact and possessed of money and an honorable reputation, all of which would see him worthy of Claire.

Only to have lost her before he returned.

Which was better off, really.

For the man he'd returned as wasn't worthy of any woman.

Click.

Wesley felt her before he saw her; without so much as a glance, he knew who'd entered the duke's libraries—*Ellie*.

Even so, he turned his head slightly to catch a look at her.

Ellie pushed the door shut.

Nay, not just Ellie.

This time, Ellie had come with a maid.

Smart girl.

Protection. Because even innocent as she was, she'd sensed how very close he'd come to doing the unthinkable—taking her in his arms and claiming her mouth in a kiss that would have been entirely too violent.

Her coming with a companion was certainly far better and safer for both of them. Even knowing that as he did, the idea of anyone intruding on his time with Ellie grated.

Rather, her arriving with a maid in tow was just one more reminder of the monster he'd become. That he'd scared not only a young lady, but his brother-in-law's sister, a girl who once upon a lifetime ago, he'd instructed how to fight, and teased, and who'd teased him in return.

The maid reached for the satchel Ellie had arrived with.

Ellie shook her head, and said something.

The girl nodded and then quit the rooms.

Some of the tension he'd been carrying left, because he'd been freed of one of their company.

Or is it because you prefer being alone with Ellie? Ellie who hadn't wept copious tears that day he'd been carried into his father's foyer and marched past the assembled line of Audleys and Balfours. She'd been pale and stricken, but she'd spoken to him, and she was the only one who really had said anything to him.

It made him feel . . . human.

He should announce himself.

And yet, as she continued her familiar stroll down the length of the library, perusing the titles and occasionally adding a book to her bag, he kept his silence.

To announce himself would send her fleeing. Strangely, he did not want her to go. It was an admission he'd never willingly own aloud, but one that he could silently acknowledge to himself.

He . . . liked her: He liked that she did normal things around him, like read and laugh and talk. He liked the way she didn't avert her gaze from his, staring up at the ceiling or floor, or wall, or anywhere that wasn't part of his broken body.

Ellie paused in her search, dusting her fingers down the length of the book spine she now studied.

"Are you going to say hello, or continue watching me in silence?"

Wesley blinked, his mind sluggish from his distracted thoughts of her, and then, wonder of wonder, even he, a battle-hardened soldier found himself capable of blushing. Grateful for the shroud of the shadows, he scowled.

Grabbing up his cane, he thumped it angrily against the floor. "I was not watching you," he snapped.

Another woman would have cowered; Ellie casually glanced up, and slanted a mischievous grin his way. "I was teasing." She winked.

It was a bold flutter of endlessly long, golden lashes that swept briefly down, and then up, and something odd shifted inside; thoughts—desirous ones—he'd no place having . . . of how very close his lips had come to tasting the pillowy-soft contours of hers.

"Oh," he said belatedly. She'd been teasing him. People didn't tease him. Not anymore.

"Perhaps if you weren't always so angry, they still would."

He blinked slowly and looked to Ellie.

Ellie, who'd since pulled a book from the shelf and who now directed that suggestion at whatever page she'd opened to. For a moment he wondered if he'd imagined her voice and her words, but then she glanced over and clarified.

"Tease you, that is. I was saying—"

"Why do you insist on coming here?" he demanded. With the aid of his cane, Wesley propelled himself to standing and stalked across the room to join her. Or he attempted a normal stride. His leg dragged slightly, his muscles still not recovering from the bayonet that had lanced through his flesh. "Why?" he repeated, furious with her and himself.

"We've already discussed this. I told you before, I like the libraries." Ellie tipped her head back, but made no attempt to run from him, as he had expected she would. "And what is it to you? You don't leave your rooms, anyway."

"I leave my rooms," he said defensively.

"Yes, you come and sit in here, and glare at the curtains, and stare at the shadows. But you can easily do that in your chambers."

He clenched his teeth. "God, you are audacious in your insolence."

"Yes, I heard as much from my father countless times."

"He was right!" he exclaimed, knowing he was being surly and boorish, and hopeless to stop himself.

"Oh, undoubtedly."

Ellie had dreaded seeing Wesley again.

And she'd hated that.

She'd hated it because he'd been someone whom it had been comfortable being around.

And it had all gone and changed, because she'd longed for him the way her elder sisters had sworn Ellie someday would. Ellie had been so smug and so confident, never believing she'd want a man in any way.

She took mercy on him. "You may rest assured, I've not come to intrude on your space today. I am here for my lessons."

He stared blankly at her.

"My etiquette lessons." Then, tipping her chin up a fraction, and holding her head perfectly aloft, she also sank into a curtsy the queen would have likely not even found fault with. "For my launch."

"Your launch?" he echoed. "What are you, a ship?"

A smile twitched at the corners of her lips. The light-hearted Wesley who'd returned for Cailin and Courtland's wedding those years ago and remained in the countryside with their families would have made a similarly teasing remark.

Only he would have joined her in grinning, and added a wink of his own.

Her smile faded.

Ellie sighed. "That's what it is like. A ship. Everyone wanting a pretty, perfect vessel to be sailed into the perfect crystal waters, so that someone might add that pretty bauble to their perfect shipyard." She grimaced. "Not that I'm saying I'm pretty," she said, her cheeks catching fire. "Rather, I'm making an analogy, as you did . . ."

At Wesley's odd look, Ellie let her words trail off. "I make my Come Out this Season. Edwina is coming to provide me with lessons."

"And she can't visit you at *your* home?"

Ellie winced. Only she would go falling for a man so very eager to have her gone.

He grunted.

"That is . . ." He swiped the hand not holding his cane in the air. "Forgive me," he said gruffly. "It was . . . just a question. Not a suggestion."

And perhaps she was pathetic, desperate and hopeful for any scrap of kindness from him, but warmth filled her chest.

"Edwina is so busy with her business that the times she's able to visit are infrequent. We meet here so that Henry can visit with the duke and duchess."

There was also the matter of her eldest sister getting so very sad-eyed at all the reminders that her youngest sibling would have her Come Out while she remained unwed.

"Henry?" Wesley said, drawing her attention back.

"Your . . . nephew," she clarified.

Something glinted in his eyes. "I . . . didn't know that about Edwina's visits."

Nay, because he'd shut his family out. He'd shut the whole world out.

She cleared her throat. "Yes, so as I was saying, I will not be in your way this morning. Today I'm merely claiming my books and headed to the parlor for my latest etiquette lessons."

"You don't need etiquette lessons."

Ellie peered up at his scowling face. Why . . . he almost . . . sounded angry on her behalf. More of that wonderful warmth continued spreading throughout.

"Yes, well . . ." She pointed a finger up toward the sky. "Everyone who must face Polite Society must be properly prepared."

The ghost of a smile danced on his lips. "Edwina?"

She nodded.

"That was a very good impression."

She leaned in conspiratorially and, cupping a palm around her mouth, whispered, "Oh, you should see my 'Courtland' one."

They shared a smile.

And Ellie's heart knocked wildly against her ribcage. Wesley was smiling. He was smiling again, and she knew she was grinning like a lackwit, but was hopeless to contain that joy.

Only, as quick as that glimpse of Wesley as he'd always used to be slipped in, it was gone. His expression went dark once more.

"I expect you've had lessons your entire life. That wasn't enough?"

"Oh, you are right on that score," she muttered.

"Which one?"

"Both that I've had them my entire life, and that it wasn't enough."

He froze, and then tossed his head back and laughed.

Startled at that unexpected, robust, and very real laugh, Ellie drew back, and then joined in.

When their mirth had faded, she smiled. "I was a terrible student as a child."

He scoffed. "I don't believe that."

And she went warm all over again at that bluntly matter-of-fact disavowal. The most precocious of the Balfour lot, she'd grown accustomed to everyone treating her as the recalcitrant child, and . . . well, she'd never really had anyone see her in the best possible light.

"You?" he persisted, and, shifting his weight over the head of his cane, he leaned toward her. "A duke's daughter?"

Matching his movements exactly, Ellie leaned in, shrinking the space between them even more.

"Alas, it is true." She dropped her voice again to a conspiratorial whisper. "Though, in fairness, I was a deliberately terrible student."

It'd been a small triumph to have over her father: not allowing him to shape her into what he expected and demanded that she be.

"Now, *that* I can believe."

She swatted his arm, and he drew it back playfully . . . only . . .

A sharp hiss exploded from his teeth, and his skin went ashen.

Ellie recoiled. "I've hurt you."

"I'm fine," he gritted out.

Only the muscles of his suddenly gray face spasmed, and his eyes glinted with pain.

Her heart turned over. "I'm so sor—"

"I said, I am fine," he barked, and her apology withered and wasted on her lips.

Ellie drew her books closer to her chest and hugged them tightly.

Wesley closed his eyes briefly and spoke between clenched teeth. "Forgive me."

"There's nothing to forgive," she said softly.

A laugh, all twisted up with grief and pain exploded from him, and she ached with every part of her soul for the previous sound of his laughter, the one that had been free of cynicism and suffering.

"There's everything to forgive. I'm a monster," he hissed, and then, stealing a glance about, he looked to her once more and dropped his voice. "I don't know how to be around people, and they don't know how to be around me, and with good reason." The words came tumbling out.

"I'm short-tempered, scarred, and surly." Each sentence rolled into another and another, and she didn't know if he even realized he spoke to her, just that he needed to speak, and she just listened, because it was what he needed.

"But I'm just so tired of it. So goddamned tired of the looks and the silence, and I'm tired of my body being broken and my mind—" His cheeks went red.

"And your mind?" she quietly urged him.

He gave his head a tight shake and continued with different enumerations. "The last time you were here, I scared you deliberately, because I wanted you gone."

And you thought he intended to kiss you . . .

She curled her fingers sharply into the book she'd taken from the duke's shelf, hugging it closer. "You didn't scare me."

The fight seemed to go out of him. "No," he murmured, passing his gaze over her face. "I don't think any man can."

He'd be wrong. Unnerved by Wesley's words and the intensity of his gaze, Ellie glanced away. She knew the evil men were capable of. But Wesley . . . he was not her father. He was just a man who was hurting.

Rough knuckles caressed the curve of her cheek, and she went still under that touch: coarse from the calluses upon his hands, and yet more tender than anyone had ever touched her.

"What is it?" he murmured, his low baritone a tender cascade of warmth that rolled over her and brought her eyes shut. "You've gone all sad-eyed and quiet."

He was a man hurting. Which was mayhap why he'd recognized a woman who'd been hurt.

"I was just thinking . . ." she began, before she could call the words back, desperately wishing to.

"I made you sad."

"You didn't—" She immediately clamped her lips shut. Only—

She felt his gaze sharpen on her face. "Who?" he murmured, relentlessly. "Who hurt you?"

Ellie tensed.

No one knew she was hurt. She wasn't hurt. She'd been hurt in the past, but all of that had come to an end with her father's passing. And none of that compared to what Wesley had endured.

"I didn't say anyone hurt me," she said evasively.

"You didn't have to," he murmured, continuing that slow, soft, quixotic caress, one that brought her lashes sliding shut, and set her heart to fluttering. "Not with your words, Ellie."

She drew in a deep breath and made herself draw away from that tender touch. "No one," she said flatly, determined to put a nail in the coffin of his questioning.

Click.

They looked over to the front of the room just as the door opened, and Ellie proved a coward for the great rush of relief she felt as Wesley's sister-in-law, Edwina Audley, sailed through.

The pretty, always-smiling woman's gaze went to Ellie. "Ellie!" she greeted happily. "There you—" Her gaze landed on Wesley beside Ellie. "Oh."

Ellie and Wesley immediately took damning steps away from one another—hers quick. His lurching.

It's only damning if Edwina knows you've carried feelings

for Wesley. It was a truth known by none. Ellie hadn't even committed it to the pages of the journal she'd kept all her secrets in as a young girl who'd been enamored of the dashing soldier who'd taught her to fight.

"I was just fetching several books," she said dumbly, and weakly lifted those books.

With her usual sunny smile restored, Edwina sailed over with gracefully perfect steps, greeting Ellie and then looking to her brother-in-law. "Hello, Wesley."

Only Edwina's eyes locked on his neck, and never quite met his eyes.

"Edwina," he said, in his gruff new normal tones.

And a pang struck.

This was what he'd been speaking of, how everyone . . . how both servants and his family were around him. Skirting him and avoiding his gaze. How awful it must be. Between that and the injuries he'd suffered, to his body and soul, was it a wonder he prowled the shadows and preferred his own company?

Edwina cleared her throat and returned her full focus to Ellie. "I thought we might begin our lessons this morning in the breakfast room."

Dining etiquette, again.

She resisted the urge to groan. "Splendid." At least there'd be chocolate biscuits.

"Splendid, indeed." Edwina gave a cheerful little clap of her hands and glanced once more at her brother-in-law. "Would you care to join us, Wesley?" she ventured, hesitantly.

Of course he didn't wish to join them.

Ellie didn't even wish to join herself on this.

"I would," he said.

It was hard to say who among their trio was most shocked by that capitulation.

Edwina's mouth opened and closed, with no words coming out after several tries, and then she beamed. "Splendid! That would be splendid."

And so it was, a short while later, Ellie and Edwina sat

beside one another at the duke's long breakfast table, with Wesley at the farthest, opposite end. He might as well have been in another room for as far as he'd sat himself from them.

Though, if Ellie were being truthful, she was grateful to not have him so close to the lesson she suffered through.

". . . Now, do remember the hostess takes her place at the head of the table, with the spot to the right of her as a seat of honor, always reserved for a gentleman . . . and in the case of the host, the place to the right of him is reserved for the . . ." Edwina stared expectantly at her.

"The lady who is the guest of honor," Ellie supplied.

"Splendid. Of course you know that. Now," Edwina went on, "as you might recall, dinner parties always begin with soup, which one must never refuse to eat. If you do not wish to eat it, you are encouraged to play with your soup—like so." Proceeding to dip the tip of her spoon into a bowl of clear broth, she made a show of toying with the fare.

Wesley snorted.

Edwina lowered her spoon to the corner of her porcelain plate and looked to Wesley, who sat scowling into the contents of his coffee cup.

"Is . . . there a problem, Wesley?" Edwina ventured cautiously.

Only Wesley ignored that query, and instead glared blackly into the contents of his drink.

"I don't know how to be around people, and they don't know how to be around me . . ."

Ellie recalled his pained words of a short while ago, and her heart pulled.

Out of what Ellie had come to recognize as misguided sympathy, Edwina slightly averted her gaze from Wesley.

And Ellie well knew what it was to have one's family avoid one's eyes, and . . . avoid one, altogether. And yet, also, neither was it the same. Her family had treated her differently following the deceitful role she'd played in getting Courtland and Cailin together. How the world now treated Wesley was a product of the scars he wore and the man he'd returned from war as.

Edwina cleared her throat. "Shall we continue?" Though, she didn't so much as pause, rather launching into the next portion of Ellie's lesson. Instructions flew rapid-fire from Edwina's lips. "Always eat your soup from the side of the spoon . . . never from the point of the spoon . . ."

And there'd been a time a lifetime ago, back when she'd been a girl delighting in making her governesses' existences miserable, when Ellie would have done just that. But with Edwina, she more carefully attended her lesson.

Liar, a voice jibed. *You know it's really a matter of Wesley watching you under hooded lashes.*

". . . take care not to slurp or make any other noises, as it is considered uncouth . . ." Edwina was saying.

Sluuurp.

From across the room, Wesley drank loudly of his coffee, bringing Edwina's lesson to another pause.

Ellie's lips twitched.

"This . . . this habit . . . that is . . ." Edwina's cheeks pinkened. "If *you* make that sound when you are eating . . . that is, the sound I'm speaking of, not the sound anyone is making in this room at this moment."

Sluuurp.

There came another noisy show from Wesley.

"So that sound Wesley is making is okay to make when eating?" Ellie asked in feigned innocence.

"No!" Edwina exclaimed. "Uh . . . shall we continue?" she asked, her voice slightly squeaky.

She motioned with a hand, and two dutiful footmen were instantly there, clearing away the barely touched broths as another two servants ventured forth with a plate of sausage links.

"Now, as it pertains to eating, one must always feed oneself with the fork." As if there was a question about the item of mention, Edwina held the appropriate utensil aloft. "A knife is only used as a divid—"

Her words trailed off for a second time as Wesley grabbed his knife, speared an entire link with the tip, and like some primitive pirate of yesteryear, took a larger-than-would-ever-be-polite bite of the breakfast meat.

Footfalls filled the corridor as a moment later, a young maid appeared. "Mrs. Audley, my apologies for interrupting, but Miss Rose is fussing for you—"

Edwina was instantly on her feet. "If you would excuse me for a moment?" she said to the room at large.

"Of course," Ellie said, the only one of her and Wesley's pair to pardon the young mother from her responsibilities.

Edwina took off quickly, with a relieved eagerness to her steps.

The moment she'd gone, and only he and Ellie remained, she gave him a pointed look. "You don't have to be rude."

"I wasn't being rude."

Ellie arched an eyebrow.

"Not intentionally."

She folded her arms at her chest and continued to stare pointedly his way. "You were not intentionally slurping your drink?"

He lifted his glass in a silent toast. "Oh, no. That was completely intentional."

Wesley grabbed his cane and propelled himself to his feet . . . to leave.

Only—

He headed the length of the room, and when he reached her, Wesley perched his hip at the corner of the table where Edwina's place setting remained untouched.

"And tell me?" he drawled, leaning forward, and her heart skittered as it always did at his nearness. "You weren't having fun at Edwina's expense, too."

Her cheeks warmed. "You are a terrible influence."

He grinned and leaned in a fraction closer. "You are correct on that score."

"You don't have to be so terrible to everyone, Wesley," she said quietly, and he stiffened.

Encouraged when he did not explode in anger, she carried on. "It is not their fault—"

"Yes?" he taunted, daring her with his gaze and tone to finish the thought.

She tipped her chin up a fraction. "It is not their fault you are hurting. They are hurting because you are, and want to—"

"I'm not hurting," he snarled, slapping a fist on the table. The plate near his fingers jumped and rattled as it fell back into place.

"They want to make it better for you," she finished quietly.

"Well, they can't. There is absolutely nothing they can do . . . nothing . . ." He drew in a raggedy breath through his teeth. "I am the man who I've become."

"You are the man you always were."

A pained-sounding laugh burst from his lips and ripped a hole inside her chest, as she longed instead for the brief levity that had come from him a short while ago, to now this pain.

"I'm not." And, stealing a glance at the footmen who'd melted into the shadows, Wesley returned his attention to her, and when he spoke, he did so in a furious whisper. "I'm angry and surly and fucking scarred inside and out."

"We're all scarred inside and out—"

"You aren't."

Ellie recoiled. What would he think . . . what would he say, if he knew the truth? Would he be as repulsed by her as he expected the world was by him?

Unnerved, Ellie jumped to her feet.

"Running away," he called as she gathered her books.

Yes. Actually, yes, she was.

For she'd accidentally stumbled very close into something she'd no wish to speak with him or anyone about.

"Good day, Wesley," she returned, her voice steady, her legs less so, and as she made her way from the dining room, she felt that intense gaze boring into her.

Chapter 9

My dearest Wesley,

Do you ever feel as if when you speak, no one is truly listening? The only time I feel as though anyone hears me is when I write my thoughts and feelings to you.

Lovingly Yours

C lick-click-click.

The errant tap of Ellie Balfour's pen touching a small inkpot filled the quiet of the library.

He'd hand it to Ellie Balfour.

Seated with his back to her, and facing the closed curtains, Wesley admitted there was something oddly calming about the rhythmic tap of her pen, each day she came. And she'd continued to come even after he'd been a damned bully to her.

Having been born into a mining family in Cheadle, over the course of his life, Wesley had known all number of women. His understanding and experience of ladies born to elevated stations, however, had proven limited.

There'd been Mrs. Crowley, the old villager who dressed her cat, and eventually drove the poor creature batty enough that various men in the mining town alternated whose job it was to rescue poor Mr. Bluebell Kittendoodle from the made-for-climbing old English walnut tree on her property.

Then there'd been the washerwomen, who were gruff and given to blunt speaking . . . and cursing.

And as for the young women of Cheadle, they'd done what every last family did in the mining village: they worked, but spent their handful of free moments at Sunday sermons casting hopeful glances at their would-be sweethearts.

No, there'd never been any shortage of colorful women in his life.

It was the fancy sort of women Wesley had little to no experience with.

In fact, until Wesley had approached his father, the closest Wesley had ever come to interacting with a higher-born woman had been Claire Sparrow; as beautiful as anyone he'd ever laid eyes upon, dainty, and given to averting her gaze and blushing, she'd been careful with everything from the looks she'd given him to the giggles that had never given way to robust, unrestrained laughter. He'd been endlessly intrigued by her. And desperate to win her affections, desperate enough to accept the scraps of even her measured affections.

But never before had he spent much time with a lady born to the nobility.

The one time he'd returned from fighting to visit Bentley's ducal seat, he'd enjoyed a fortnight with his family. Only Wesley had felt more out of place than in it, and had taken to avoiding the formal gatherings when he could. Instead, during those fourteen days, it'd been far easier, and far more enjoyable, keeping company with young Ellie, who'd become an eager pupil of his in how to brandish a weapon.

Ellie, however, was no longer that same small girl who donned breeches or hitched up her skirts to run freely.

She was all grown up, a proper lady.

Click-click-click . . .

There came a brief pause of that pen touching the ink-well, and for a moment he thought she was done for the day . . . with whatever it was she came in this room and did, but then she resumed writing.

Not that he cared.

He didn't.

Wesley glared at the thick, always-drawn curtains, the same curtains Ellie had attempted to draw open only that first day, and not again since.

How she spent her time . . . for that matter, how anyone spent their time, wasn't his affair. Not in the least.

It was merely that she was a peculiar woman.

Each day she arrived in the library to read, and aside from an always-cheerful greeting, she didn't say much to him . . . which was all good and fine with him, as he didn't have a goddamned idea what to speak about anymore with her or anyone. She'd pop open a journal and set herself up a little workstation, like some general with a field desk taking notes before battle.

Occasionally she spoke to herself. Or hummed. Sometimes she sang quietly, so quietly the murmured lyrics were impossible for him to make out. But she always wrote.

Click-click-click.

Muttering to himself, Wesley grabbed the wheels of the special rolling chair the duke had commissioned and turned his glare on the lady.

Of course, she would have had to be looking up from whatever it was that absorbed her every time she came to have noticed.

Instead, she remained fixed on her pages, her hand flying deftly as she scribbled—

"What are you doing?"

His voice emerged more of a demand. Misery and the nightmares a man kept after war had that effect. There were things a man didn't know before marching off to battle. That you'd forget the most basic way of how to be around people. Wesley rolled himself the rest of the way to her.

Instead of startling, however, Ellie continued scratching away with her pen before slowly lifting her head.

She blinked several times, as if having forgotten his presence, as if she was only just remembering she wasn't alone, and was surprised to discover at some point he'd joined her.

"Writing?"

There was a slight uptilt that leant that response the hint of a question.

"What exactly is it that you are writing every day you come here?" he clarified in curt tones, and the man he'd once been would have been capable of curiosity and not this surly edge that now emerged from the sparse words he spoke.

"Ahh," she said, setting down her pen. "Words."

He cocked his head and waited for her to elaborate.

Alas, the peculiar chit bent her head, picked up her pen, and proceeded to scribble away.

Frowning, Wesley rolled the rest of the way over to her. This time, however, as he neared, she looked up and smiled. "You again."

"Me again," he muttered. He jabbed a finger at the page. "What words are you writing?"

Understanding lit her pretty blues eyes. "Ahh." She set her pen down again. "Quotes."

"Quotes," he echoed dumbly.

She nodded.

It didn't matter either way, and yet, he found himself blurting, "Why?"

"I find it helpful."

He peered closely at her heart-shaped face, searching for some indication that she was being deliberately evasive. "Helpful in what way?"

"All different ways."

If he were capable of normal muscle movement, he would have thrown his arms up in exasperation.

Ellie took mercy and explained. "Whenever I am troubled by something, it helps me to copy down quotes."

He ignored the latter part of her confession in favor of the former. "What do you have to be upset about?" he demanded, his tone harsher than he intended, even as he was eager to know. What the hell was troubling her? Who was?

Ellie fiddled with her pen and stared down at her words. "I'll soon have my presentation before the queen."

Ah. The lady was making her debut.

So that's what this was about.

"You'll do fine," his said flatly, with a bluntness borne of his confidence in her and her grace.

"Your father and the duchess are throwing a soiree in my honor."

"And you want me to attend?" he said tightly. God, they were relentless.

Ellie stared at him oddly. "No. Why would I make you suffer through that when even I don't want to?"

Some of the tension slipped from him. Ellie had been merely stating a fact.

"Forgive me," he said gruffly, flustered by his outburst. "You were . . . speaking about your notes."

She shook her head. "No, I wasn't. You were." With that, she resumed that process of alternately reading and writing in her book.

He narrowed his eyes.

The minx.

She knew she'd intrigued him, and thought to leave him dangling, making him put any questions to her. Well, he'd enough restraint.

"And this helps you?" he asked tightly, and she lifted questioning eyes to his. Apparently, he did not have the restraint he'd credited himself with. He waved his hand at her and the pages of her book. "Writing . . . whatever it is you're writing?"

"Oh, yes. Do you want to know the story?"

It was on the tip of his tongue to say no, and yet something compelled him to keep that callous word back. He gave a tight nod.

"My handwriting was atrocious," she said, and he glanced briefly down at the elegant swooping lines and angles and arcs of her penmanship that marked hers a lady's writing.

She hovered a hand almost protectively over her work. "I said 'was.' At first my father insisted my governess rap my knuckles until I'd perfected my handwriting." He frowned, fury tightening his gut. How casually she spoke of that cruelty. "But that proved ineffective," she matter-of-factly explained. "And so, his next idea for her was to have me write all day, every day until I eventually improved the skill. It was miserable, and I said, if I was to be forced to do something that was miserable, then I might as well enjoy what I was writing, as a distraction."

Her father had been a miserable man. What he'd originally expected his own ducal father would have been like. Only Bentley wasn't anything like the cruel, heartless cur Ellie spoke so casually of.

"You should try it," she remarked, bringing his attention back to the present.

He stared questioningly at her, and Ellie clarified. "Searching for quotes that make you . . . feel better."

"That make me . . . feel better?" A sharp laugh tore from his throat, ragged and raspy and raw. If only words could heal, he wouldn't be dead inside, and ofttimes wishing he was altogether dead. Because certainly with an eternal sleep at last came peace from the mind and body's suffering in life.

Instead of taking offense, however, she stared at him with sad—he recoiled—and something worse, pitying eyes. "I don't need your pity," he said sharply.

"I don't pity you." Ellie spoke with such a perfect calm, the kind of tones adopted to placate, and for some reason that set his nerves on edge all the more.

He gritted his teeth together so hard they clinked noisily and rattled his jaw. "You think to compare some miserable handwriting exercises to what I did first in a coal mine and then in a war? You think growing up a duke's daughter with a comfortable life and some shitty governesses is in any way comparable?"

"I did not say that," she said tightly.

"Because words don't help," he rasped, knowing he was being a bastard in all the worst senses of that word but hopeless to help himself. "They don't. They're just a damned facade that makes a person feel better for a moment, but it doesn't erase all the real hurt. It doesn't erase any of it. It gives false hope,"—as Claire had done—"and even worse, false happiness."

It briefly distracted a man from all he'd seen and done and— The fight went out of him, and Wesley slid his eyes shut. *Just go.* He willed her to leave.

"'The web of our life is of a mingled yarn, good and ill together,'" she said softly, in dulcet tones, a slightly lyrical huskiness in her voice that proved a siren's sound for the way it pulled him out of the mire of despair. "Shakespeare." She tacked on that explanation as an afterthought.

"What is it with you women and Shakespeare?" he said tiredly, and yet, the ghost of a grin pulled painfully at the corner of his mouth, muscles that had long since grown stale of smiles.

"He's the Great Bard." She spoke with a shock that would have been better suited to the Great Bard's own mother's defense of him. "His works, Wesley, they teach us about human life and reveal how people live and feel and love, and he did it in a way that was original. In a way never before done."

His smile dipped. "Love," he repeated, bitterness coating that word.

Ellie hesitated. "Your Miss Sparrow."

His Miss Sparrow.

She knew of Claire. Which meant . . . "My family has been speaking of it."

Her cheeks pinkened. She didn't, however, deny it. "You love her." She paused. "I'm so very . . . sorry."

He shrugged and looked away. He didn't want to speak

about Claire with anyone. For some reason, he wanted to speak about her with Ellie even less.

Alas, Ellie proved tenacious. "It might help you to speak about it," she put forward.

"There is nothing to speak about," he said tiredly. "She . . ." *Wrote me letters that gave me purpose and a will and reason to live.* Even now, inside his jacket, the weight of one of those letters burned with a lifelike energy.

"Have you written to her since you returned?"

Since he'd returned broken?

"I'm not the man she loved. She knew I would change. It's why she stopped writing." She'd known she was better off without him.

Ellie sailed to her feet. "I do not believe that," she exclaimed. "There . . . was surely some other reason she stopped, but you are home and alive and I have to believe if she saw you now—"

A laugh exploded from him. "You believe if she saw me now, she'd . . . what? Rush into my arms and declare her undying love." And then frustration leant him a restless energy. He gripped his chair and proceeded to roll himself back and forth. "Yes, I'm certain I'm everything she dreamed of. An unkempt man with wild hair."

"Hair can be cut."

He continued over her interruption. "And an overgrown beard—"

"Which I find rather rugged. But it can be shaved."

"Shaved to reveal scars."

"They are part of you, and she would love them, for they represent who you are and what you had to do to survive."

God, she had an answer for everything.

Wesley slammed a fist down on the arm of his chair. "What do you know about what I had to do to survive?" he rasped.

Only Ellie stood calm in the face of his storm. "I don't," she acknowledged. "I do know, however, that for you to shut yourself away in this room, and away from the family you so very much love, it must have been awful, Wesley."

Vicious. Savage. Cruel. Everything he'd done and seen and witnessed.

Boys alternately begging for their mothers and death. Men with limbs severed, men with their heads taken clear off by a cannonball.

He squeezed his eyes shut and willed the parade of images to stop; all the while bile stung his throat and vomit threatened.

He opened his mouth to throw out mocking words steeped in life's cynicism, but managed to somehow stop himself, exercising a restraint he'd not believed himself capable of.

"You can't just . . . unsee that, Ellie," he said between tightly clenched teeth. "You can't just forget."

"I'm not saying to forget." There came the light tearing sound as she ripped a page from her journal. She slid it closer toward him, and he mutinously held her gaze, refusing to look at whatever it was she'd have him read. "I'm saying you can be a new version of yourself. You can return to living amongst the world and attempt to woo her."

Woo her?

As in . . . Claire.

It was a moment before he recalled that was who they'd been speaking of. "And I trust you expect to tell me just how I can win her back?" he snarled. "You? What do you know of it? What do you know of anything?"

A gasp filled the doorway, and as one, he and Ellie swung their gazes to the front of the room.

Cailin stood framed in the entrance, pale, and even across the length of the room, her eyes blazed shock and disappointment.

"Ellie, Courtland asked that I come get you, as we intend to leave."

Ellie inclined her head. "Of course," she murmured, collecting her materials. "Mr. Audley," she said stiffly.

Mr. Audley. Not Wesley.

That was for the best.

The use of one another's Christian names had been

entirely too familiar. Even if they were joined by the marriage of her brother to his sister. Any intimacy with Ellie Balfour was a dangerous one.

After she'd gathered up her things, she headed from the library.

Cailin stepped aside.

It was too much to hope she'd leave without comment.

"You were atrocious to her."

"I'm atrocious to everyone," he said wearily.

"But everyone else steers clear of you."

"Then she should, too," he spoke brusquely.

His sister stared at him with sad eyes.

Good. Sad eyes he was accustomed to. It was the only way anyone looked at him anymore.

That was, except Ellie. Ellie saw him, and somehow saw more man than beast. He didn't know how or why . . . but . . . it made him wonder—

Cailin spoke. "I love all of my brothers equally." She took a step forward, and then another, joining him where Ellie had last stood.

"You didn't try to be the father figure to me as Rafe did. And you had time for me in ways Hunter didn't because he was always trying to be the best miner in Cheadle."

Tears glistened in her eyes. "But you? You were always able to smile, and there was just an ease in being with you."

His sister sucked in a shuddery breath, a pained-sounding one that wrenched through his soul.

"You were never mean, and you were never cruel,"—she gave him a sharp look—"and certainly not to a young woman as you were just now with Ellie."

His sister patted her cheeks, and drew her shoulders back, and glared at him. "Ellie's books were sold, Wesley," she said flatly, and a vise gripped at his heart.

"Courtland's father was a wastrel, and he pissed it all away, and even though Courtland and I are improving the estates and using our funds to set it to rights, the library they once had is no more. So perhaps you might . . . spare Ellie some kindness."

Without another word, Cailin left, closing the door behind her with a quiet, damning click.

When she'd gone, Wesley let loose a stream of black curses which would have horrified even the most hardened soldier he'd fought alongside.

His gaze went to the page she'd ripped out and left behind.

"... *If men could be contented to be what they are, there were no fear in marriage ...*"

He froze.

I'm saying you can be a new version of yourself. You can return to living amongst the world and attempt to woo her ...

Claire aside ... could Wesley truly return to living amongst the world?

Chapter 10

My dearest Wesley,

I'm not much one for fripperies and fancy garments, but I do appreciate a good slipper. They make it all the easier to sneak about.

Lovingly Yours

A meeting had been called between the Audleys and Balfours.

Even Ellie had been included, to *some* degree.

At that precise moment, she sat more on the fringe of it all, an outsider looking in. Mayhap that was why she was the only one present who could see the wrongness in these families failing to include Wesley.

The Duke of Bentley paced back and forth beside the hearth, while Courtland stood almost as a sentry near the mantel.

Ellie stole a glance at the three women whispering across from her. Sandwiched between Edwina Audley and the

Duchess of Bentley, Cailin sat with her son on her lap. The women leaned in with their heads bent toward one another, putting Ellie in mind of military men seated around battlefield plans.

The trio stole the occasional furtive look at the doorway.

Ellie kept her features perfectly even, and even as she did, she leaned forward and strained to pick up on the thread across from her.

". . . so worried . . ." the older, gracefully aging duchess with the faintest touch of silver in dark hair was saying. ". . . doesn't leave the house, and now he'll be expected to . . ."

Ellie attempted to sharpen her ears on the discussion moving in and out of focus.

"Rafe is speaking with Wesley," Cailin murmured. "He has always had the greatest influence on him."

"But this is different," Edwina said quietly. "This will require Wesley to face the world."

Ellie could not take the not knowing anymore. "What is *happening*?"

The trio of women looked to Ellie.

"Wesley is to be granted a title, for his acts of bravery in battle," the duchess explained.

Ellie drew back and looked to the officious folded note she'd earlier dismissed lying in the middle of the low rose-inlaid mahogany table.

This was the reason for the family gathering. Wesley was to be honored by the king. He'd be presented at court.

His family, well-meaning though they might be, had all assembled to discuss the summons without consulting him.

It was . . . wrong on so many levels. It was precisely why he felt the way he did. People tiptoeing around him. His family afraid to look at him, or speak with him about anything—even matters that directly affected him.

And it felt like a betrayal of Wesley, like she were among the ranks of those people who treated him . . . differently.

The tread of quiet but powerful footfalls echoed in the corridors, and as one, Ellie and the other women looked over.

Rafe, joined closely by his father, the Duke of Bentley, entered.

A look passed among the pair and the women crammed alongside one another on the sofa.

"It is . . . not good," Rafe declared in somber tones to the room at large. "I don't know how to broach the topic with him."

Cailin's features spasmed and she clasped her fingertips to her mouth.

Ellie's patience snapped and she stormed to her feet. "You don't know how to broach the *subject* with him?" she asked the room at large. "My God, it directly affects him. It is his business."

The Audleys and the Balfours went quiet.

The Duke of Bentley stopped pacing.

Everyone looked at Ellie.

Even Hattie looked up from the book she'd been reading.

Ellie resisted the urge to squirm.

"Ellie," Courtland scolded.

Ellie ignored that warning and the quelling looks her siblings cast her way. "He's not a child. He's a grown man. You all mourn and weep over the fact that he doesn't leave his room, but my God, why would he want to when every single time he does, people tiptoe about him and avoid meeting his eyes and act melancholy. He was injured. He is not dead."

"Ellie," Courtland said again, this time, his tone sharper.

Ellie turned to Wesley's father. "He doesn't want to be treated differently. He doesn't want your pity. He simply wants people to speak to him like you would any other man."

"Ellie," Hattie said gently. "Everyone means well. His family loves him, and they just want to protect him—"

Ellie cut her sister off. "*Protect* him? Would *you* want to be protected?" she directed that at Courtland.

"This isn't about m—"

Ellie swung her focus to Rafe. "Would *you*?"

To his credit, Wesley's eldest brother answered truthfully. "No," he answered quietly. "I wouldn't."

"No," Ellie repeated. "And I can't imagine a single person here would take well to having a missive addressed to them opened by family members—no matter how well-meaning they may have been—and then discussed in a family meeting that you yourself were excluded from."

She stood there, her chest heaving from the force of her emotion.

Someone touched her hand, and Ellie started.

Cailin.

Wesley's sister lightly squeezed her fingers. "Thank you," she whispered.

And the fight went out of Ellie, and she felt exposed in ways she'd never been before. She wanted to run from the collection of stares upon her, and the questions in their eyes.

Courtland cleared his throat. "My apologies, Bentley. Ellie did not mean—"

"I very much meant everything I said," she said. "I'm the only one who seems willing to speak any truths here." And the irony of that wasn't lost on her.

Her eldest brother leveled a glare on her, and Ellie glared right back.

The older duke held up a hand, ending the rest of Courtland's apology for Ellie's outburst.

"No." Wesley's father spoke in solemn tones. "Ellie is right. I . . . it was long overdue we heard those words, from someone." He nodded. "I will speak to Wesley. I should have done so already."

Yes, he should have. All of his family owed him that.

Wesley's brother joined the duke. The two men proceeded to speak.

Her skin prickling, Ellie glanced down.

Hattie studied her with knowing eyes, and Ellie swiftly averted her gaze.

A wail sounded in the hall, saving Ellie from further probing.

A moment later, Laurence's nursemaid appeared, holding a squirming, crying boy in one arm, and in her other hand, the toy sword Ellie had gifted her nephew.

The young woman sank into a curtsy, an impressive feat given her arms were filled. "My apologies, Your Grace. He was inconsolable, asking to see you. I know you said . . ."

Cailin and Courtland were already across the room, taking the boy from the young woman.

"No apologies, Tess," Cailin said, bouncing the chubby-cheeked boy on her hip while Courtland spoke soothingly to him until their son stopped his tears.

Ellie stared on at the bucolic scene—devoted, loving parents and their cherished babe. How many times growing up had she longed to have that? She'd never given thought to a family of her own. She'd been so very adamant she didn't want a husband, which thereby meant there'd be no children. Something, however, tugged at her, a longing for a spirited boy with dark curls. A boy who, in her mind, bore a striking resemblance to Wesley Audley.

"Aunf Ellllie!" Laurence cried happily, waving a fist her way, and her cheeks warmed.

"Hi, sweet pea," Ellie said, wagging her fingers in return.

Her nephew squirmed to be set down. "I go Ellie."

Cailin dropped a kiss on her son's cheek and then set him down on his feet. "Run along, love."

The boy instantly lunged for the wood sword Ellie had gifted him, and, picking up the pretend weapon, he toddled over to Ellie, slashing the tip of his weapon as he went.

He launched himself against her legs, and she pretended to stagger under his slight weight.

She scooped the boy up, lifting him high in her arms, his little body soft and warm against her chest. "Goodness, you are big now," she said, making a show of breathing heavily.

Her nephew giggled, and she tickled him under his arms where he was most sensitive, until he was snorting and gasping for breath.

Laurence thumped her shoulder with the sword in his hand. "We explore!"

Ellie dropped her voice to a hushed whisper. "We shall

venture into uncharted territories. Let us go gather your cousins from the nursery. If it is all right with your mamas?"

Cailin scooped her son up for another kiss. "I would never dare interfere with two brave explorers' mission."

From where she stood speaking with Rafe and his father, Edwina smiled and gave a wave of her hand.

The moment Cailin set Laurence on his feet, the little boy took off. Ellie gathered up her bag and hastened after her nephew, eager to escape the room and her siblings' still-piercing gazes.

For the first time, without Ellie's influence, he'd asked a servant to draw the curtains open. Now, seated in the corner of the library, not in his wheelchair, but in a comfortable wingback sofa, Wesley stared out the windows at the streets below.

Sun streamed through the crystal panes, and oddly, that cheerful light no longer burned or blinded. Nor did he wish to squeeze his eyes closed and shut those rays out.

It felt . . . almost normal—such a simple, underappreciated aspect of his previous life that he'd found his way back to.

Aside from the envy that still burned in his chest at the easy strides of passersby and riders. He expected the agony of that loss would never, ever fully go away.

Wesley's ears pricked up.

After he'd been injured in battle and returned *home* to London, he'd learned he could tell most of what he needed to know without even opening his eyes.

From the groan of a floorboard to the slowing of carriage wheels outside the windows. And the echo of footfalls proved as clear as a calling card in knowing just who approached: The hesitant heavier ones belonged to his father. The hesitant light ones, to Cailin. The hesitant, even lighter ones, always paired with another, more resolute footfall, to Edwina and Rafe. The absent ones: Hunter.

Then there were Ellie's. Ellie's confused him most of all.

Really, they were the only ones that confused him. They were quick and sprightly and eager and as bold and unafraid as the lady herself. Strangely, they also proved to be the only ones he looked forward to.

And also not the ones that grew nearer.

He frowned. The ones he looked forward to? Where had *that* come from?

His father stopped outside the library door.

Rap. Rap.

Two solid but tentative knocks always followed.

In a rote manner, Wesley opened his mouth to tell him to get the hell away when he recalled a conversation he'd had with Ellie.

. . . You really should try to be more patient with him. He loves you so very much, and most people would trade both working arms for a father who loved them . . . I know you are hurting, but your family loves you, and they are hurting, too . . .

"Come in," he said.

The door opened. A moment later, his father entered the room, drew the panel shut behind them, and headed over to join Wesley.

His father stopped suddenly. Surprise flared in his features. "You've . . . shaved," he blurted.

Wesley felt exposed. He felt like a ghoul man who'd been caught trying to step out into the living. Never more had he longed for the beard that had shielded his now-hot cheeks.

"In fairness, the credit doesn't belong to me. I had help from my valet."

The duke's eyes glittered with tears, and he laughed softly. "Who among us doesn't? You look—"

"Human?"

"I was going to say 'good.'"

"I was jesting," Wesley said. He grimaced. "Or attempting to, anyway."

His father laughed.

The duke reached inside the front of his jacket and withdrew a five-inch-wide missive containing an elaborate wax seal—that had been broken.

"This arrived for you," his father said.

There'd only been one person whose notes he'd relished receiving. Ones that hadn't been melancholy and mournful, but filled with humor and stories and quotes that had seemed to speak directly to his soul, about his hopes, dreams, and wants after the war concluded.

"Given the state of it, I trust you can fill me in on the details."

His father's cheeks flushed. "Forgive me. I had no right to open your correspondence."

"No, you didn't." Either way, he didn't give two damns about the fancy-looking letter. "Leave it there." Wesley nudged his chin toward the mahogany table.

The duke stared at it a moment, but instead of doing as Wesley instructed, his father held the note out. "Wesley . . . you . . . need to read this."

"I don't have to do anything," he said tiredly. And worse, he couldn't do anything meaningfully anymore, not without struggling like a weakened pup.

"Normally, I wouldn't compel you—"

"Good, then don't."

"But this . . . this missive, it is different, Wesley. It is from the king," his father explained.

Wesley dragged a hand down his scarred cheek. "God himself could have penned that damn note, and I wouldn't care." Whatever words of thanks he'd had some palace aide pen changed nothing for Wesley.

"You might not care, but he is still your king, and no one, not even you, Wesley, is free to ignore his summons."

His summons?

Wesley frowned.

Snatching the thick ivory vellum from his father, Wesley tore into the pages and scanned the elegant scrawl. And with every word read, his horror grew and grew, spreading to every corner of his person. He swiftly crushed the summons with his right fist.

"Oh, God."

The duke's lips twitched in the first smile Wesley remembered seeing from him in years. "I remember feeling precisely the same way when I discovered my fate, too. Granted, I was a small child and had many years to come 'round to the idea of being a duke."

"I don't want a *bloody* title," he said between tightly clenched teeth.

"Be that as it may, His Majesty is granting you one."

And not just any one. That of a bloody duke.

"With it will come properties and monies and opportunities afforded your future children, Wesley."

"My future *children*?" A harsh laugh ripped from Wesley's chest.

The duke frowned. "Wesley, you are a young man. Eventually you will heal and marry, and when you do, this offering from the king will provide you with an even greater security, in ways not even I can offer you."

He sneered. "If you've some fantastical idea of my future, one with a duchess on my arm, and a passel of babes and hunting dogs at my feet, you are even madder than I am."

His father's features twisted. "You are not mad, Wesley."

Speaking those words aloud did not make them true. No doubt it was far easier for his father to convince himself of that. No doubt it was safer for him to never speak of the times Wesley's broken mind transported him back to battle and left him trapped in the throes of a nightmare, with his valet fetching His Grace.

The duke attempted a different approach. "What you did, Wesley, on those fields? Your actions were nothing short of heroic."

Heroic? The recent past and present blurred as his mind's eye conjured thoughts of enemy soldiers, no more than boys whose cheeks hadn't even yet begun to spring beards, with weapons entirely too big for their small frames, the terror and shock stamped in their faces as Wesley's bayonet cut through their narrow chests.

The duke rested a hand on Wesley's arm, and he reflexively recoiled.

His father hastily drew that touch back. "He wishes to recognize your bravery."

"My bravery? My *bravery*?" Wesley's voice pitched up, and he surrendered to a searing laugh that ripped square from his chest.

"What you did *was* brave."

What he'd done was murder men, men who'd either fought because they'd been without choice, or who'd possessed the same naïve, romantic views Wesley had gone into battle with. The fight went out of him.

"There is nothing brave about war," Wesley said, tired to his soul. "I did nothing less than any other man." And nothing more. Nothing more than kill in the name of the Crown. He'd sooner lose his left leg completely than be granted a title that would serve as a forever reminder of what he'd done.

He crushed the king's letter in his fist. "I don't want it."

The duke made no attempt to take the wrinkled sheet. "You don't have a choice, Wesley. The ceremony is in a fortnight."

Because that was the way of this world: a king commanded all, and did not ask favors or request anything. He made demands.

Sweat slicked Wesley's palms, and a new kind of fear, different than the recently acquired demons that plagued him, licked at the corner of his mind. "I . . ." He tried and failed to get the words out.

His father stared at him. "Yes?" he gently urged Wesley, as if Wesley were a damned child, and hell, with all the ways he'd been broken and left dependent on others, was he really that different?

"I can't walk!" he whispered. "I can't function in society." He bit his tongue to save what little pride he had and keep from saying there wasn't a damned thing he could do now, without assistance. He couldn't do anything. Not without a struggle. Not without falling on his damned arse or face or even without losing his goddamned breath. "Would you have me roll up in a goddamned chair?"

His father stretched a hand toward Wesley. "I'll be at your side." He spoke in an entreating way, which only heaped guilt upon Wesley's self-loathing. "Your brothers and sisters—"

"Get out," he rasped.

His father nodded. "We will speak more later—"

"Please, Father," Wesley begged, and this time, the duke hastily complied.

The moment he'd gone and shut the door behind him, Wesley slumped in his chair. Goddamn the world and all the people in it who thought they knew what he needed or wanted, and who'd tell him what he must do. As a soldier, taking orders meant the difference between life and death; as such, there were codes men adhered to, or else they were killed or worse. Only to return from war and find *different* directives given, ones always surrounding the inanities of people who'd no idea, absolutely no idea of the hell unfolding away from the comfortable townhouses and parlors they inhabited.

They awakened to a bright morning sun and saw only a day where one might stroll the neat London streets or ride in one of the meticulously manicured parks. They didn't know how the sweltering heat thrown by that golden sphere, there for their pleasures, baked and burned a man's skin. And when it rained, how the sodden wool garments raked one's flesh raw.

Slowly, he lightened his grip, unfolded his palm, and stared at the crinkled page. It was impossible enough for his family, those he loved, to see him pathetic and pitiable and weak. All he had left in his broken body was his pride, and now even that would be stripped from him. Now he'd be forced to put himself on display for the king . . . for the world to see . . .

A joy-filled laugh echoed from the corridor, joined with the giggles of another person, followed by more voices. The sound of unabashed mirth, so at odds with Wesley's tumult, knocked him briefly off-kilter.

There came the flurry of fast-moving footfalls, and then silence.

Wesley sat there for a moment, and then, feeling a bit like a moth to the flame, he grabbed his cane. Getting himself to his feet, Wesley limped toward those now-distant voices and laughs.

He hobbled his way from the library and down the corridor, until he reached the next hall and then stopped.

Ellie stood, surrounded by three children. The boys and lone girl stretched their arms high and jumped up and down. They all spoke rapidly, loudly, and over one another, and the din left Wesley momentarily muddled.

With her back to him, and his niece and nephews absorbed in whatever game they were about, Wesley used the moment to study her.

"I want to lead the charge," Rose cried.

"Girls do not lead charges," her elder brother, Henry, insisted.

"They most certainly do," she shot back. "Isn't that true, Ellie?"

"Oh, absolutely." Dropping to a knee, she motioned the children closer, and Wesley found himself taking a step closer, as enrapt as the little ones around her.

When they hurried nearer, Ellie spoke in a low whisper. "But we are all neglecting the most important rule of battle."

"What is that?"

"We must work together. Especially if we are to defeat the Green Knight."

Releasing battle cries, each child rushed forward to that imagined foe, with a zeal that pulled a smile from him. How many times had he played a similar game with his brothers? What it would be to go back to those far simpler times, before he'd found out firsthand the ugliness of actual war.

"Aunt Elllllie, help. Ellie, help," the smallest of the children yelled, making his tiny voice heard over the melee.

"Ellie does not have a sword, Laurence," Henry reminded the boy.

The boy's face fell, and he came to a stop, staring up at her forlornly.

Ellie dropped to her haunches and, touching her left index finger against the corner of her nose, whispered, "That is, I don't have a sword that one can see, Laurence."

His already saucer-big blue eyes went even more enormous as Ellie reached behind her shoulder and made a show of brandishing her invisible weapon.

Wesley found himself as interested as his youngest nephew.

How very good she was with Cailin's son, a child born when Wesley had been off fighting on the Peninsular. Not once since Wesley's return had he taken time to meet his nephew. He'd been too caught up with his own misery and regrets.

"Fiiiight!" Laurence yelled happily, as together, with Ellie leading the charge, they bore down on their imagined foes.

Even in her muslin skirts, she lunged with a speed and agility he was hard-pressed to not admire. "He is fierce," she shouted. "I cannot take him alone."

Wesley grinned again, when suddenly, Rafe's eldest son's gaze locked with his.

The boy nudged his sister. "Uncle Wesley."

All three children instantly stopped their play fighting and looked wide-eyed at Wesley.

"Yes," Ellie called, still fully engaged in her pretend battle. "He is the greatest warrior, but I shall help save the day."

Holding her imaginary sword high above her head, Ellie let out a war whoop and charged forward. She brandished her tip back and forth, hitting the armor at that place where a heart would have beat for the knight long ago who'd worn this silver suit, and then she made a show of striking him in that spot where armor would have met the man's neck.

"I believe you've quite killed him," he drawled.

Ellie gasped, spinning around so fast, her skirts got all tangled up with her ankles, and she came down on her buttocks.

Wesley limped as quickly as he was able down the hall and stopped when he reached her.

The man he'd been before would have easily helped her to her feet. The man he was now proved barely able to keep himself upright.

Ellie got to her feet.

And with his niece and nephews all staring on at him in silence, Wesley wished he'd never ventured over. He wished they'd not seen him.

Tensing, Wesley made to go, when Ellie's next words stayed him.

"I'll have you know, I'm quite skilled with a sword. I'm usually far more adept with my weapon."

Wesley froze, as their first meeting all those years ago whispered forward.

He found his voice. "I can see that. I observed you while you practiced."

Ellie's lips parted.

Was it a surprise that he recalled that day in the woods? Then, she smiled softly. "I didn't know you were there."

"No, you were very engrossed in your battle. Though I have it on the authority of one of the finest generals, a master never allows someone to catch one unawares."

And he may as well have placed the moon in her palms for the way she beamed.

When was the last time a woman had looked at him the way Ellie now did? Had anyone? Not even Claire. Odd, how often he thought of her. Perhaps that was because the time they'd had together had been so very short, nothing more than stolen moments, made all the more exciting for the furtiveness of them.

Small fingers twined with his, and tugged.

Wesley glanced down.

Laurence's big eyes stared back. "Who you?"

Who are you?

His own nephew didn't even know him. Wesley didn't even know the boy. Regret and shame filled him.

Ellie saved him from speaking. "This, Laurence, is your uncle Wesley," she said, making introductions between the two.

"You've boo boo," the boy said.

"Laurence," Rose whispered.

Wesley waved her off. "No, it is fine. Would you like to know how I received my boo boo?"

This time, even the elder children moved closer.

"I went to battle, as you are now, but I needed more lessons from your aunt Ellie," Wesley said.

"She *is* the best," Rose said, proudly.

"Your uncle is being modest," Ellie murmured. "He taught me everything I know."

And Wesley instantly regretted going along with this game.

All three children clamored closer. "Teach us!"

"Pweea, Unca Wesley," Laurence entreated.

"Yes, *pleaaaase*, Uncle Wesley!" Rose added her plea to the others.

Wesley's palms slicked with moisture, and he nearly lost his grip upon his cane. What had he gotten himself into? He cast a desperate look Ellie's way.

He couldn't—

"Your uncle would be more than happy to school you," Ellie said, making the decision for him.

He remained motionless for a long while. It'd been foolish coming here and intruding on their fun. It was too much, too fast.

"Is this part of it?" Rose whispered loudly to Ellie.

"Indeed," Ellie returned in a near-soundless voice. She touched a fingertip to her lips, and the little girl fell quiet.

Ellie looked to Wesley. *It'll be all right*, she mouthed, clearly enunciating each syllable.

Her eyes shone even brighter, and this time, it was not a fear of joining a gaggle of children in games of pretend that held him motionless, but rather, the entrancing glimmer in those cornflower-blue pools.

"Do we . . . stare at our opponent like that?" Rose ventured, snapping Wesley back from his musings.

Not for the first time that day, as his face went hot, Wesley mourned his missing beard.

He shifted all of his weight over onto his uninjured leg. "First," he began.

His niece and nephews leaned in.

"You must determine which is your dominant hand and hold your weapon accordingly. Who would like to be the first among you to demonstrate?"

As one, the children shot their hands up.

"Please."

"Please."

They all begged, speaking over one another for a chance at being his first pupil.

Wesley landed his gaze on Rose. "You."

Among the boys' groans, she squealed and rushed over.

"Now, we begin," Wesley said.

Chapter 11

My dearest Wesley,

You wonder at what books I enjoy reading. I never believed myself one for romantic titles . . . until I met you.

Lovingly Yours

For all the ways in which Wesley had changed, in all the ways that mattered, he remained the same.

Grinning as he once had, and cracking jests with Rose, Laurence, and Henry, one might think Ellie had merely imagined the somber, angry soldier alone in the shadows.

Only the slight strain at the corners of his mouth and eyes revealed the impact his exertions had upon him. Even so, he kept a smile in place for his captive audience.

Laying her back against the wall, Ellie smiled wistfully. She too had once been so dazzled by him.

Not much had changed.

"Lunge," he called, and even with the twisted bend in

his left leg, he managed to exude a warrior's grace as he demonstrated that movement for his niece and nephews.

"Disss?" Laurence asked his uncle.

"Perfect, Lieutenant," Wesley praised. "In fact, I daresay a promotion to major is in order."

The boy puffed out his small chest and made another adorable lunge.

Wesley's grin widened. "Bravo, Major!"

And standing there, on the fringe of it all, watching him play with those small children, Ellie fell completely, irrevocably in love with Wesley Audley—again.

"Well, I want to be a captain like Uncle Wesley," Henry said. "May I? Please."

"No," Rose cried. "I want to be the captain."

Wesley lowered his cane, and shifted his weight all the way over it, and took the break the children had unintentionally offered.

"I certainly was not the only captain in the King's Army. And I certainly expect two fine fighters as yourselves are both deserving of that title."

Cheers went up, and the three children resumed their pretend battle.

Wesley fell back, calling out commands and orders.

How very good he was with them. Sweet and patient as her eldest brother had been, and the opposite of how her own father had ever been with Ellie and her siblings.

One day, Wesley would realize he was whole in all the ways that mattered, and would make a lady the most lucky woman in the kingdom.

As if feeling her eyes, Wesley glanced her way, and his grin grew bashful, as if he were embarrassed to be caught playing so.

She smiled encouragingly. *It is perfect*, she silently mouthed.

You are perfect.

Wesley returned his attention to his niece and nephews.

Angling her head, Ellie watched them together once more.

He took their every question. He defused their bickering before it could become a full quarrel. And he treated each child, regardless of Laurence's tender years, or Rose's gender, exactly the same.

How many men would be so very tolerant with children? Certainly no more than a handful in Polite Society. They—

Wesley's features spasmed, contorting with pain.

Ellie sprang forward, motioning to the two nursemaids waiting in the wings.

"I do hate to interrupt your lesson," Ellie said, striding over. "But I fear that is all for this day."

The children lowered their swords and released a collective groan.

Ellie lifted a hand. "*Only* because I have it on authority that Cook has prepared meringues rempli and queen currant cakes, which will be waiting in the Ivory Parlor."

Cheers instantly erupted.

"Now, thank your uncle before you—"

"Thank you, Uncle Wesley," they all spoke as one, and then raced off with their nursemaids giving chase, until Wesley and Ellie were alone once more.

"Thank you," he said, the moment they'd gone. Removing a kerchief from his pocket, he wiped at his damp brow. "I'm not as smooth a fighter as I once was, I fear."

"Do you think Rose, Laurence, and Henry thought so?" Ellie asked, fetching a hall chair and dragging it over. "Because from where I stood observing your lesson, Wesley, they were thoroughly engrossed in every moment."

She pointed to the seat. "Now, sit."

"I'm a gentleman. I should be offering—"

"Sit," she repeated, and as he did, she dragged another over. "There," she said, after she'd positioned the seat near his.

The moment she sat, Wesley spoke. "I'm being made a duke."

"Yes, I . . . heard the news."

"A family meeting?" he asked dryly.

"Yes, or rather, it was . . . until I put an end to it."

He startled. "*You* did?"

"Oh, absolutely. Would you expect anything else?"

They shared a laugh.

"I merely pointed out how outrageous it was they'd opened your missive and discussed your future without your even being present," she said, after their mirth faded.

A sound of frustration escaped him. "I don't want a bloody title. I just want to live my life in peace, and yet, that is the one thing I am to be denied. I . . ."

His words trailed off as Ellie picked up her bag. "Here it is," she said, withdrawing the copy inside. She opened it reverently, smoothed her hand over the title page.

He nudged his chin toward that volume. "What is that?"

A wistful smile played on Ellie's lips. "There was a time, I would have traded my left littlest finger to even hold a copy of this book."

She turned it all the way around so he could read the title.

"Die Jungfrau von Orleans," he murmured.

Ellie dragged her chair closer. "You see, unlike Voltaire, who all but made a mockery of Joan of Arc and her accomplishments, Friedrich Schiller celebrated them," she explained. "He portrayed her as a romantic heroine and elevated her in a way in which women are not so very often elevated."

A memory slipped in of a long-ago day when he'd come upon Ellie in the forest, practicing her swordplay.

"Joan of Arc," he murmured. "Of course, you were fascinated with her."

Her heart tripped a beat. He *remembered* that? And here she'd believed only she recalled the details of that exchange.

Somehow, Ellie found her voice. "As you know, I had grand intentions of being the next Joan of Arc. Hattie, however, swore there'd come a time I read the books she herself loved."

"Which were?"

"Which *are*," she corrected. "Romantic ones. I laughed. How preposterous. They were utter rubbish. Beyond silly, and a girl with serious designs on becoming the next Joan of Arc would never dare read such drivel."

"I'd be remiss if I didn't point out Joan of Arc was burned at the stake."

A mischievous sparkle glimmered in her eyes. "Obviously, I'd every intention of being even *better* than Joan of Arc."

He grinned.

How much easier his smiles were coming now.

Ellie lowered her voice. "But then, one day, Hattie left one of her books in the library, and I plucked it up, and intended to tease her mightily for the drivel written there. Arming myself as only a master tactician might, I began scouring the pages for the most outrageous bits.

"Only the more I read," Ellie went on, "the more I realized. The words? They weren't so very ridiculous, after all. Despite how convinced I'd been that my sister read drivel and I was entirely too mature to read such nonsense, it was . . . really quite captivating."

Wesley stiffened.

"And the fictional worlds I'd had no intention of ever reading, ones that I couldn't imagine any good, were really not so very bad, after all. They were in fact quite . . . wonderful."

"Ellie," he said tiredly. "Joining Polite Society and enjoying the contents of a book are entirely different matters. Reading is a private pleasure one might enjoy in the comfort of their own company. The other? Being titled . . . it is the opposite of all that. The moment I become a duke, I will be thrust into a limelight that will turn me into a public object of fascination . . . and worse, ridicule and disgust."

"Perhaps," she allowed. "I would have also sworn no good could be found on those pages. Sometimes, Wesley, it's just a matter of focusing on the good."

Focus on the good, she said.

He'd not found a spot of anything even remotely positive since he'd fallen in battle.

That was, aside from this young slip of a lady before him.

He started. Where in hell had that come from? And yet, it proved the truth. When she was near, he didn't feel like a shell of a person.

"Wesley?" she gently prodded.

He gave his head a clearing shake.

"You are an optimist, Ellie." An innocent.

"Oh, no. I'm *very* much a realist."

And invariably, as he always did with her matter-of-factly spoken statements, Wesley managed a smile.

"If *I* had a title? I'd retire away to the country during the London Season."

"And miss all of the fun of the balls?"

She quirked a blond eyebrow. "Do *you* enjoy balls?"

"I'm not a young lady."

"Exactly. I am. As such, I do believe I'm more equipped than you to speak about what ladies do and don't enjoy."

"Touché."

She inclined her head.

"Very well. You say I should focus on *the good*," he said dryly. "What exactly is that?" Truly, he wished she could tell him, so that he could somehow remember.

"Well, first of all, you aren't a woman. I'd say that in and of itself is a spot of good luck for you."

His lips twitched again. "And it's so hard being a woman?"

She snorted. "Only a man could ask such a question. In two months' time, I will have my Come Out. I will be presented to the queen in a grand display, and then paraded before the *ton* until I at last make a match. Failure to do so will earn me society's condemnation. Success means I will begin the entire tedious process again and again, year after year, but only with a new name, and a useless husband to monitor my movements."

When she put it that way . . .

She wasn't done. "You, on the other hand? You'll get

your title and then be free to live your life. You can visit your clubs."

"I don't belong to clubs." And never would.

"But you *can*. You are also able to ride and hunt in the countryside without being expected to drag a poor maid about."

"I can't even walk, Ellie." That truth exploded from him.

"You can try, Wesley," she said simply.

"Try? Try for what purpose?" Gripping the wheels of his chair, he rolled himself the remaining distance over to Ellie. "So that people can feel better about the thought of men being sent to the slaughter?"

Suddenly, the fight went out of him. "People, they don't want the reality of war, Ellie," he said tiredly. "They want the heroes in their crimson uniforms, and not the knowledge that those dashing white trousers make a man overheat, and those gaiters cause bruises on their damned legs. People want to imagine a world where the soldiers are respected in life and die with dignity on the fields. Instead of knowing the truth—that most times there isn't enough water and too often the drink available makes men violently ill, soiling themselves like babes."

Any lady would have been horrified by those pieces he'd revealed. Particularly one as innocent and young as the big-eyed woman before him.

"You are right, Wesley," she said softly. "The world is content to see that which is on the surface and never look closer. No one wants to imagine the horrors that you or anyone else faced. But after you have your ceremony before the king and officially receive your title, then you can be finished with it all."

Even young as she might be, she knew that truth.

"Then, you are done with anything and everything else, so long as you wish."

With that, Ellie withdrew another book from her bag and placed it on his lap.

Wesley glanced down at the title.

Virtue Rewarded.

Distractedly, he flipped through the pages, landing on one. His gaze locked on the words there.

What the deuse do we men go to school for? If our wits were equal to women's, we might spare much time and pains in our education: for nature teaches your sex, what, in a long course of labour and study, ours can hardly attain to.

Wesley read them, over and over, comfortable and calm in the silence between him and Ellie.

He contemplated that passage . . . and the words Ellie had spoken.

Then, you are done with anything and everything else, so long as you wish.

It was all he wished. He didn't want to see people or interact with society. He didn't want to see the pity and horror in the eyes of both strangers and family. But for a short while . . . until that ceremony concluded, he'd be expected to put himself on display.

But then, after that, then it was done. Then he could retreat into one of those properties he'd inherit and shut himself away. And oddly, for the first time, there was something actually palatable about the prospect of a ridiculous title tacked on his name.

He would do this. As his father and Ellie pointed out, there was no other choice for him.

And when he was done, then he could be free.

Chapter 12

My dearest Wesley,

*I'm not much of a dancer. But I do believe for you, I'd be
willing to try my hand at it.*

Lovingly Yours

From the elevated dais in the middle of the Duke and
Duchess of Bentley's palatial ballroom, Ellie watched
over the latest of Wesley's sessions with the doctor. Over
the course of her eighteen years, she had herself suffered
through any number of miseries.

The one before her proved the absolute worst—which
was saying a good deal, indeed.

Wesley and the latest doctor attending him had been at
it some three days. Which was one day more than the previous ones had lasted. All the others had either quit or been
turned away following one or two failed sessions. Not a
single one of them had provided anything to remotely help
Wesley.

The windows, drawn open as they were, let in a cheerful sunshine, and those streaming rays illuminated the beads of perspiration dotting Wesley's brow as he remained standing with all his weight balanced on his uninjured leg.

Her heart constricted.

She knew the pain of being forced into a position, and being asked—nay, required—to hold that same miserable pose.

Sweat formed on her own palms.

Everyone likely believed a duke's daughter lived a charmed existence. One where those girls and then women were afforded respect and treated with dignity, if for no other reason than because of the station they'd been born to.

The world would also be wrong.

She'd learned early on, regardless of station, a girl was subject to the whims of merciless men. She still bore the marks upon her body as proof, testament of that hard-learned fact.

Even with the pain she'd endured from her furious father's riding crop or cane, nothing had prepared her for the level of agony on display before her.

"You must put your weight upon the other leg now," the prim, severe-looking doctor was saying. "The one you injured will never remember its function unless you provide the muscles with that memory."

Ellie grimaced. That was a horrendous idea. "The muscles aren't the problem," she said.

Neither man paid her any heed.

Wesley glared at the other man. "That seems like a bloody terrible idea."

Ellie quite agreed.

"Put your weight upon it, Mr. Audley," the doctor ordered.

His lower left leg twisted at an unnatural angle as it was, and looked one slight wrong movement away from snapping completely. Even so, he was going to do as the madman before them demanded.

Despite the imprudence of putting more weight upon

that crooked limb, Wesley would, because he was that desperate and driven.

This was really enough. She really needed to put a stop to this.

"You may curse, you know," she called out, halting him before he completed what might make that already debilitating injury permanent.

"I did," Wesley gritted out, his intensely focused gaze locked upon the marble floor he was being asked to put the weight of his busted leg upon.

Before he could attempt the latest mad feat the doctor was asking of him, Ellie cupped her hands around her mouth and yelled over. "Oh, no. 'Bloody' is a fine enough choice for ordinary circumstances. I, however, referred to one befitting the occasion."

Doctor and patient stared at her as if she'd sprung two heads. The bespectacled fellow, with disapproval etched in his aging features.

She didn't much care about the stern fellow's opinion, however.

Wesley lips turned up in the faintest ghost of a grin. He motioned to Ellie. "Well, go on."

The doctor pursed his mouth. "We do not have time for games. Furthermore, a young lady should not be present."

Ellie and Wesley both ignored him.

She sauntered over. "Might I recommend the more satisfying but frowned upon 'shite,' or 'bollocks.'"

The doctor gasped. "My lady!"

"Or," Ellie continued, despite his objections, "there is, of course, the eminently satisfying to say for how it rolls off the tongue: 'fuck.'"

Wesley laughed.

The doctor strangled on a cough, suffering what sounded to be the start of an apoplexy.

Ellie ignored the older gentleman. Her eyes remained locked on Wesley. His laugh was hoarse and yet full and real, and the first she'd heard from him since their first meeting all those years ago.

She smiled.

When the doctor had managed to get control of his choking, he turned a dismissive shoulder on Ellie. "Your injuries are serious, Mr. Audley, and the task you assigned me a great one. As such, we do not have time to be entertaining the distractions posed by an uncouth lady."

"Uncouth lady," she said, testing that new title out. "I rather like that."

Wesley's lips twitched at the corners.

The doctor's mouth merely tightened in a studiously satiric line. "I will not work as long as she's underfoot!"

"In fairness, what you're doing isn't really work," Ellie said. "You're asking Mr. Audley to further damage his leg."

The doctor's ruddy, plump cheeks went several shades redder. "I will *not* have my skills or methods questioned," he railed.

Ellie inclined her head. "That will be an easy feat."

Some of the tension eased from his gaunt, dissatisfied face.

"That will be an easy feat, considering you don't really have any skills to call into question."

The doctor's eyes bulged, and he dissolved into a second violent choking fit. "Why, I never," he stammered. Then, whipping on his heel, he stormed over, grabbed up his bag, and stomped out.

"I suspect you may have given the man an apoplexy," Wesley drawled.

"Over a curse word?" She scoffed. "The world is better off without him." She paused. "*You* are better off without him."

That rare hint of humor faded from his face, its scarred features only made more beautiful by their realness. He sank back in his chair.

"I needed him, Ellie," he said tiredly. "It was a struggle for my father to convince him to return the first time."

"You need *someone*," she agreed. "But you don't need him."

"That's the fourth doctor I've gone through. And among the best, sent by Prinny himself at my father's request."

"What does Prinny know of such injuries or how to cure them?" she countered.

"What do *you* know of them, little general?" His question, which wasn't really a question, came out more matter-of-fact than accusatory.

And Ellie was grateful when he limped over to the window and stared out at the London streets.

He asked what she knew about such injuries because he didn't know. Because, aside from the loyal, loving housekeeper who'd brought her to Mrs. Porter, no one really knew. Certainly not the world at large. Not even her own brothers or sisters knew of the various punishments she'd suffered through as a girl, which had provided Ellie with enough life experiences on the matter of gruesome injuries and how to help heal them.

It was something she'd no wish to ever talk about, and certainly not with this man or anyone.

They'd be bustling at this hour, with lords and ladies out for an afternoon stroll, and noblemen coming and going from Hyde Park. God, how she hated those London streets. How she longed for the freedom to be had in the countryside, away from people.

"The doctor was correct. You don't belong here, Ellie," he said, directing his words at the square crystal panes.

Taking that as an invitation, Ellie joined him across the room.

"I want to be here," she said simply.

He cast a brief look over his shoulder. His expression said he thought her mad, even when he spoke not a word.

"I do," she insisted, the truth of that making those two words slip out so very easily.

"Why?" he asked.

"Why?" she echoed dumbly.

Her mind went blank to anything but the real truth: it was because of him. She'd fallen in love with him at that house party all those years ago, when he'd been the only one to see her and truly speak to her, and to do so without the recrimination she'd deserved at the time. And she'd fallen more in love with him after every letter he'd sent, that had revealed the whole of his soul—secrets that she'd had no right being privy to, and that had only been secured through her deception of him.

Wesley leaned over the head of his cane. White lines at the corners of his hard mouth revealed the pain his exertions had brought him, and her heart wrenched as it always did at his suffering.

He peered at her face. His sapphire eyes seared her with their intensity. That piercing blue gaze had the manner of one that could see into a person's soul, and pluck forth her secrets.

Ellie remained motionless under his scrutiny. For the secrets she carried about him and what she'd done were entirely too great, and worse, unforgivable.

With his spare hand, Wesley dusted his thumb along the curve of her cheek, in a touch so very fleeting, so very gentle, Ellie bit her cheek.

For she'd not known a man's touch could be so very gentle. At least, that she herself would ever *know* such a kind caress.

"So soft," he murmured, more to himself. "So smooth. Untouched. Unbroken by life."

An almost-painful laugh built in her chest at that naïvete. Ultimately, all women, of every station, were broken. For most of them, the scars they carried were invisible. That way, the men who ruled the world weren't faced with tangible reminders of the suffering wrought by those they shared their power with.

Wesley paused that delicate glide of his callused finger. He moved his gaze over her face in a searching way. He was a man who now looked too close and, she feared, saw too much.

Ellie's breath stuck sharply in her lungs.

"Any young lady on the cusp of having her Season would have only thoughts of preparing for that momentous time in her life, and yet you'd prefer to be stuck away with me, here. Why is that, Ellie?"

Her mind went blank to everything and anything but her two absolute truths: she couldn't bring herself to marry a man who'd be a stranger to her, and over the years, she'd fallen in love with him.

She forced a breeziness into her tone. "Does being trussed up in big white lace ruffles and paraded before the queen with even bigger feathers sticking from one's hair strike *you* as a grand time?"

His lips didn't so much as twitch in an attempt at a smile. Rather, Wesley continued to study her in that unnerving way.

"No. A woman such as you would despise everything about that," he said with a quiet contemplativeness. "It doesn't escape me, however, that you didn't answer my question, Ellie."

Ellie glanced down briefly at the toes of her slippers and gave him the first truth in a very long while. "It's easier to be here," she said softly.

"It must be deuced awful for you, Ellie, that you'd prefer it here."

Ellie lifted her gaze back to Wesley's. "It's more that it's wonderful here." *With you.*

He snorted. "Wonderful with my father and his wife tiptoeing about lest they run into me and have to make conversation with me?"

In this, they were kindred spirits in yet another way. "That is how it is for me, too."

"Ellie, I'm a monster. You are not."

"You are no monster. You were a man who went to war and bears the marks of battles fought. Furthermore, I do not believe they think me a monster. But neither am I someone whose company my siblings necessarily crave."

The deficits of her character, after all, were what had made it so very easy for her father to put his hands upon her in violence.

Wesley made a sound of protest, but she spoke over him.

"First, it was my brothers, who really couldn't look at

me the same after what I'd done trapping Courtland and Cailin in marriage."

"It's been years, Ellie," he gently reminded her. "As I told you that day in my father's woods, they're hopelessly in love. Even more so than they were then."

"Yes," she said, willing him to understand. "Just because time has passed, it doesn't undo what I did. I revealed a side of myself they cannot be expected to unsee." After that day, her relationship with her brothers had been forever altered.

And then, all the words came tumbling out, and it felt so very good, so very freeing to just share how very lonely she'd felt these years.

"And then my sisters? They have always looked to me as their baby sister."

"You wish for them to see you in a different light?" he gathered.

She shook her head. "If it were that, it would be simpler. With my impending debut, Hattie is being reminded of the fact that she will be out now with her youngest sister, while she enters whatever Season she remains on as an unmarried spinster."

Wesley shifted his weight. "You don't know that, Ellie."

"I heard them," she said, reflexively taking him by his elbow. Ellie helped him back into his chair. With him seated, their eyes met almost perfectly. "They were discussing it when they didn't realize I was on the window seat, with the curtains drawn," she explained.

"Oh."

"Yes. Oh." She wrinkled her nose. "I suppose I should have announced myself. Alas,"—she struck a pose—"you know what they say about eavesdropping."

He shook his head. "What is that?"

"I don't know. I've been unable to find specific quotes on the subject, but I trust there's something to be said for not doing it, and the peril of what one might discover if they do."

Another smile ghosted his lips, and this one bore the traces of how it once had been, and how she so very much wished for it to be again—for him.

He brushed his knuckles over her jawline in a touch that stirred a wonderful warmth in her breast.

"You cannot help how other people view you, Ellie."

She bit the inside of her lower lip, lost in his husky murmur and his tenderest of touches.

"Nor do I trust anyone would judge you for your actions as a child," he said, his gaze still locked with hers. "As for your sisters? Those problems they may have with you? Those belong to them. You are who you are, and you shouldn't make apologies for it."

"That is wonderful advice, Wesley," she said softly, her senses dazed from his distracted back-and-forth caress. "For both of us."

He stilled, and she knew the moment he knew the purpose behind her telling.

"Ellie, I'm a broken man," he whispered.

"You can heal," she said softly.

The time had come, and yet, she struggled still. Because sharing Mrs. Porter with him—with *anyone*—would mean bringing them close to the truth of how she knew of the bonesetter.

"There is a place . . . I discovered," she said.

"A place," he repeated, eyeing her warily.

Ellie nodded. "I have done some . . . research about people who specialize in dealing with injuries such as yours." It was a lie that slipped out all too easily.

He eyed her warily again. "These doctors—"

She shook her head. "She is not a doctor."

"She?"

Ellie edged her chin up a notch. "Do you have a problem trusting a woman with your care?"

His lips quirked up at the right corner, in a devastatingly handsome half grin. "Ellie, if Satan himself were capable of fixing me, I'd see him."

"Well, fortunate for you, you'll not need to travel those

far distances to visit with Mrs. Porter." Though, at the time Ellie had her arm manipulated, she'd not been so sure the woman inflicting that excruciating pain upon her wasn't the Devil incarnate there to further torture Ellie for her wickedness.

Wesley continued to study her under thick, sooty lashes. "Where is this Mrs. Porter?"

"Between Northumberland and Craven Streets." She paused. "Just at the entry of Charing Cross."

"Charing Cross," he echoed.

Yes, given the dubious history of that area in East London, where violent crime and thefts of all sorts were committed, anyone would be skeptical of trusting a person in those parts—particularly entrusting one's care over to someone in those notoriously violent streets.

"I know Mrs. Porter can help you, Wesley." The older woman had saved Ellie from being permanently disabled. "I will accompany you." She took a step closer to him. "Either way, I know, even when your leg is healed, the demons will always be with you. But if you let yourself, you can smile again and laugh and—"

"Christ, Ellie!" A curse exploded from his lips, and she flinched from the suddenness of it. "You speak about my leg being healed as if it is a secondary thing to"—he waved a hand, gesturing angrily to his head—"I have many wounds, Ellie. So goddamned many." He proceeded to roll his chair back and forth in a neat line, pacing in his chair. "Now, I'm to be presented in a fortnight. I'll be in display before Prinny himself, my family, and worse, countless goddamned noblemen. There have been four doctors who've come and not one of them has helped me, and this latest was my best and only option."

"He was your best option at never walking again."

"And this Mrs. Potts—"

"Mrs. Porter—"

"Some quack in the Rookeries is capable?"

She nodded. "If anyone can help you, Mrs. Porter c—"

"*If*? Moments ago, you said she could."

Her face tightened with frustration. "What I am saying—"

"What exactly is it you're saying, Ellie?" he raged. He slashed his cane at the air. "What do you know of this?" he bellowed, as he limped with an uneven gait toward her. "You speak about rainbows and sunshine, without ever having known the rain. You come here convinced that I can be healed and be whole."

Ellie went silent and stared over the top of his head, to the prism made by the crystal chandelier. Her father's explosions had come fast, always startling for the unexpectedness of them. This, Wesley's rage, was an unfamiliar anger, but no less unnerving.

He stopped before her, and she planted her feet to the floor as she'd always done, refusing to be cowed.

"I know more than you think I do, Wesley," she said quietly.

His eyes blazed with hurt and fury and frustration. His long, dark hair hung in a tangle over his face, giving him the look of a black lion set to feast on those who'd roused his displeasure.

She'd been foolish to think she could help him. Just as she'd been mad to pen him those notes while he'd been away fighting.

Wordlessly, Ellie fetched her bag.

She turned to go. "If you wish to see Mrs. Porter, I will make the arrangements." With that, she headed for the door.

My God, who was he even? Wesley had become a monster he no longer recognized. A man too easily upset, but helpless to control his frustration at his lot.

She was leaving. As she should. That'd been his hope these many weeks now.

As such, he should let her go—for both of their sakes.

"Ellie," he called, for a moment thinking she'd continue her march to that exit. Nor would he blame her.

She halted in her tracks and kept her back presented to him. She remained silent as he made a long, slow, painful march that she'd made look so very easy with her graceful strides.

Wesley stopped just beyond her proudly squared shoulders. "You . . . think this woman can help me?"

Ellie faced him. "I do." She spoke easily and calmly, as if not even moments ago, he'd not been raging at her.

He was undeserving of her friendship.

Wesley scrubbed a hand over his bearded jawline and contemplated Ellie's offer of both help and to accompany him. It'd be mad to either ask or expect innocent Ellie Balfour, his brother-in-law's young sister, to journey to the Rookeries. Perhaps it was the fact that where his family pitied him, Ellie oddly understood the desperate measures he'd go to in order to be a whole man again. She understood so very well that she herself had done the research she had to discover this place she urged him to visit.

Wesley dropped his arm to his side. "You will make the arrangements?"

"You need just tell me when you wish to go and I will meet—"

"Tomorrow," he interrupted. "At dawn."

She nodded, gave him the address, and turned to go.

Wesley stayed her a second time. "Ellie? I've been an arse."

"Yes," she said instantly, which made him smile.

Smiles which he'd thought would never come again, did, and because of this spirited, sassy young lady.

His grin died. "I'm going to humiliate myself," he said. "And I absolutely despise the idea of being stared at as some object of horror or pity, but that does not give me leave to treat you—the one person who treats me as if I'm still the same man I was—unkindly. For that, I beg your forgiveness."

Ellie eyed him with a deserved wariness, and yet, also one that caused a pang.

After a slight stretch, she nodded. "There is nothing to forgive."

"You're more gracious than I deserve," he murmured,

eyeing the thick blond coil that fell over the curve of her
cheek.

At some point in his absence, those short, cropped curls
had grown. Her voluminous gleaming golden curls were held
in place by a set of butterfly combs that appeared strained
under the futile task of restraining that massive amount of
heavy-looking tresses.

Something in the air shifted.

Wesley dipped his head, and Ellie did not shift away.
Instead, she raised her head a fraction.

Her lashes fluttered, and then her eyes closed.

Wesley lowered his nose close to the delicate shell of her
ear and breathed in the intoxicating scent of her: a sweet,
subtle hint of apple blossoms, as he at last understood the
sin which had so tempted Adam.

Wesley's eyes slid shut as he inhaled more deeply of her,
wanting to consume the woman before him.

"You should go," he whispered hoarsely.

Her mouth trembled. How had he spent all this time
with her and resisted tasting that lush, pouty flesh?

"I don't want to leave," Ellie said, her voice breathless.

Wesley tamped down a groan. She didn't know what she
said. She was too innocent to understand the implications
of her remaining here, or the sudden surge of lust he'd no
place feeling for this woman.

"Ellie," he entreated. "You need to go. I cannot—"

Ellie tipped her head up, and touched her lips to his,
stunning him with the unexpectedness of her kiss—and he
was lost.

He kissed her madly, desperately, and deeply. He kissed
her with a ferocity better suited a woman with decades of
experience in bed, and not an innocent who tasted of apples
and cinnamon and smelled of violets. And gripping him by
his sleeves, she leaned up and in, and kissed him with a like
passion.

And he proved himself the monster he insisted he was,
because his hungering was only fueled by her innocence.
He was helpless to set her from him.

Wesley's leg ached from the chore standing had become for him, and even that vicious pain paled against the heady, intoxicating feel of her pillow-soft lips under his.

He looped an arm around her closer, and she went so very easily into his arms, following where he led. Not breaking contact with her mouth, Wesley seated himself on the pretty settee along the wall, and Ellie tumbled freely onto his lap.

The little satchel she always came with tipped over, and a book tumbled out, the forgotten volume falling with a *thump*.

Wesley angled her nape so he could better avail himself of her mouth. He slanted his lips over hers again and again, in hungry, desperate slashes.

She moaned and parted her lips, and he swept inside to consume her as he longed to.

His shaft stirred, and she moved innocently, instinctually against him.

Wesley groaned and grew harder.

He sank his other hand into the delicate curve of her hips, pressing himself against her, wanting to lose himself in something other than the misery that had made itself his constant companion; he wanted to drown out the sounds of suffering with the soft sighs of this woman's desire. And he wanted to feel whole again. With Ellie, he remembered what it was to be whole and unbroken and—

Broken.

That was precisely what he was.

His actions in this instant were proof enough of that.

His body went cold, and Wesley wrenched his head away, shattering that contact.

Ellie remained suspended there, her face hovering where last he'd kissed her. Her eyelashes fluttered, and then at last, she opened her eyes fully.

Desire filled their sky-blue depths. Desire he'd stirred her to, and it enlivened him. For all the ways he was broken, he was still a man, capable of bringing a woman pleasure.

A woman who is the absolute last person you had any place touching.

Suddenly, reality intruded, and along with it, a rapidly growing horror.

"Oh, God," he whispered. "What have I done."

Ellie traced her fingertips along the scar on his left cheek. "I wanted your kiss," she said softly, confirming he'd spoken aloud.

She'd wanted his kiss. That bold admission, and the breathy desire in her voice as she uttered that admission aloud, sent another wave of forbidden hunger through him, and he felt himself weakening once more.

He recoiled. What madness was this?

With alacrity, he set her away from him, guiding her quickly to her feet. "This was a mistake," he said hoarsely.

She blinked slowly, and then at last a belated but deserved horror filled her eyes. "Oh," she said weakly, when she'd only ever been strong and bold and spirited in Wesley's presence.

And the sight of her rendered this way because of liberties he'd taken ravaged him. "Go," he ordered harshly, hating himself for altogether new reasons.

Ellie bolted, and he stared at her as she raced from the ballroom.

He'd known he was a monster. That'd never been in doubt. Kissing his brother-in-law's youngest sister was just further proof of the degree of Wesley's depravity.

With a curse, Wesley ran a hand that trembled across his eyes.

He should be grateful he'd scared her off. He didn't like having people about.

And yet, as he rescued the book she left behind and stared at the title, he could not shake an emotion that felt remarkably like . . . regret.

Chapter 13

My dearest Wesley,

*One time, when I was a girl, I hurt my arm most
dreadfully. I've never cried more tears or known greater
hurt. I'd endure it all over again if I could be promised
you'd not be hurt in battle. Please, be safe.*

Lovingly Yours

The following morning, with a damp London fog swirl-
ing over the dirt-slickened cobblestones, a silent Ellie
stood between the intersection of Northumberland and Craven. From within the enormous velvet-lined hood she'd
donned as she left her family's household, Ellie watched as
a pair of the Duke of Bentley's strapping footmen hastened
down from their perches upon the gleaming black carriage.

There'd been a time when even the thought of visiting
Ole Mrs. Porter's had left her gut churning and her body
slick with sweat. It'd been a place that haunted her sleeping

and waking thoughts, until Ellie, at last, managed to banish them to the furthest recesses of her mind.

Last night, she'd been unable to sleep. She'd not slept so much as a wink. Only, her restlessness stemmed from having to again visit Mrs. Porter and all the oldest, darkest memories associated with that place.

Yesterday, she'd had a taste of something she'd never thought to know, and in honesty, and something she'd not at all cared about knowing—her first kiss. The memories of Wesley's kiss stole all possibility of sleep: the feel of his mouth on hers, the sharp rasp of his breathing, the scrape of his bearded cheek against her smooth one.

Her sisters were romantics.

Ellie? Ellie was practical and logical. She didn't dream of a dashing suitor or marriage or babes of her own. Rather, she'd dreamed of avoiding all of those expectations society had for women.

Then, in an instant, in Wesley's arms, she'd at last understood why women woolgathered and sighed and swooned. She'd loved him for having been a man so very kind to her, when no one else had been. She'd loved him for serving in the King's Army when any other duke's son would have opted for the lavish, comfortable life his father had offered.

As the two servants reached inside the conveyance to help Wesley disembark from the carriage, Ellie rubbed her gloved palms together restlessly, to ward off the tremble in those digits—a quaking that had nothing to do with the cold.

The pair of footmen handed Wesley down, onto the uneven cobblestones, and the driver rushed forward to hand Wesley his cane.

Accepting it with a word of thanks, Wesley glanced about, doing a sweep of the streets.

Then his gaze landed on Ellie. He said something else to the servants. Those young men nodded and fell back into the shadows of the conveyance.

Using his cane for support, Wesley began a long, slow path toward her. All the while, his focus remained locked her way.

Ellie's breath quickened.

And then Wesley reached her.

She dampened her mouth, glad for the shroud of her cloak, which prevented him from seeing that telltale generous of her insecurity.

How did one act around a man who'd given one their first taste of passion? A man who'd been so very clear in his regret? A fact that hurt still—a fact that would never *not* hurt. What did she say to him? More, what would he say to her?

"You came," he said quietly.

Ellie countered with a question. "Did you think I wouldn't?"

"You would have been within your rights," he murmured.

"I said I would be here, and I am a woman of my word, Wesley."

She managed to get those words out, speaking them matter-of-factly, even as a physical pain so acute stabbed at her breast. Ellie shifted to escape that unbearably unpleasant sensation. How ridiculous and selfish she was to fixate on the complete one-sidedness of yesterday's magic. Given the nature of their meeting today, she should think only of the upcoming visit with Mrs. Porter, and yet, she proved hopeless to stop the flood of regrets.

"I owe you an apology," he said quietly.

She tensed.

"For . . . for my behavior at our last meeting," he murmured. "I greatly regret how I conducted myself with you, and I . . . You have my assurance it will not happen again."

He regretted their embrace. That single most magical moment of her entire life, he'd wished had never happened.

Of course he does, you silly ninny. His heart belongs to another, and you are just Ellie.

His eyes darkened, and he passed his gaze over her face. "Ellie?"

"It is nothing at all," she blurted.

It was a lie. His embrace had been everything. It had

been passion, and the feeling of touching the sun, and—he regretted it.

Wesley took a step closer, and spoke in quieter tones. "It was not nothing," he insisted. "It was shameful"—his every word was a lance upon her heart—"and wrong and—"

"And we really need not speak of it again." She cut him off, self-preservation lending a desperate thread to that question.

Wesley's high-chiseled cheeks went flush. "Of course not. I . . . You are correct. That is for the best."

For the best.

Ellie had the sudden urge to weep. She . . . a woman who did not cry.

Wesley lingered his gaze upon her hood, and then without another word, motioned for Ellie to lead the way.

Mindful of his injury, Ellie took care to keep a slower pace so that Wesley could match her small, measured strides.

Ancient, largely windowless medieval buildings stood out as relics of life a long time ago that'd been worn down by time, and were now sandwiched between newer, more cheaply made structures.

As they walked, she caught Wesley passing his gaze over the dung-filled streets and rotted carcasses that had been hastily thrown out.

His eyes revealed no hint of what he thought of the sordid and poverty-stricken place she'd brought him.

She herself couldn't recollect her own initial thoughts of visiting this place. The agony had been so excruciating, she'd been reduced to focusing on that pain and only that.

The slight *click-click-click* of his cane echoed eerily upon the cobblestones. Somewhere near, two dogs engaged in a battle, snarled and barked. Otherwise, the streets were as still and silent as when Ellie had visited Mrs. Porter all those weeks ago. And with every step that brought her closer, the past mingled and melded with her present, twisting the two divergent times up in a confused knot inside her head.

Her distant screams came creeping in. Sweat beaded at her brow. Vomit burned her throat.

"You're killing me . . ."

"Look at me."

Look at me . . . I don't kill people . . . though there are any number of miserable men I'd like to. But certainly not girls . . . I'm a helper, not a hurter . . . Look at me, girl . . .

"Ellie. *Ellie.*"

Wesley's sharp query yanked her from the past.

She blinked dumbly.

What was happening? Where was she? And then Ellie came whirring to the moment. "Wesley," she said, speaking his name to remind herself she was here, with him. She wasn't a young girl, and her father was dead and buried, unable to hurt her anymore.

He shifted, angling his body so he shielded her from the streets. "Are you all right?" he asked quietly.

She managed a nod. "I'm fine."

"You're a deuced bad liar, Ellie Balfour." He glanced about. "This was a terrible idea. You should not be here." Wesley took her by the elbow and steered her back toward the carriage.

"There was never a need for you to come."

Ellie dug her heels in, grinding her booted feet to a stop.

He gave her a questioning look.

"I want to be here, Wesley."

He opened his mouth to protest, but she cut him off.

"I *should* be here. I am the one who discovered this place."

And there was some truth to that admission. She did want to be here . . . but she wished to be here for him.

"Very well," he said.

Together, they made their way to Mrs. Porter's. At her side, Ellie felt Wesley's palpable skepticism. To his credit, however, as they approached the ramshackle establishment, he gave no outward reaction. He took in the cracked windowpanes and unevenly hung sign with crudely painted letters.

Ellie knocked once, and then let them in.

They were greeted by Mrs. Porter. "My lady." She spoke

to Ellie with a familiarity. "You convinced him to come, did you?"

"I did."

Ellie felt Wesley's eyes on them, taking in their exchange.

The bonesetter finally turned her focus on Wesley. "Are you ready to begin?"

Was he ready to begin? Wesley wasn't quite certain what exactly she did.

"Mrs. Porter is a bonesetter," Ellie explained.

Wesley stiffened. "A bonesetter."

The women nodded.

"Is the process as horrific as your title sounds?" he said in a bid for levity.

Only Ellie's features blanched, and Mrs. Porter stared grimly back.

"I will not lie to you. The process is not a pleasant one."

"It is awful," Ellie whispered, her voice weak, and Wesley briefly shifted his attention from the older woman speaking.

"I've endured a good deal of pain during battle," he said softly, seeking to assure her.

Ellie hugged herself. "Not like this . . . I expect," she added on a rush.

Wesley returned his focus to Mrs. Porter. "What does it entail?"

"First, I will assess the injury. Whether it is a severe dislocation and not in fact a break." She spoke methodically. "If it is a dislocation, I'll need to identify the place of injury, and whether I'm able to manipulate those particular bones. If I am, I will then adjust the affected ones, shifting them back into their proper place."

Wesley's stomach turned, and he forced a laugh. "That is a good number of 'ifs,' Mrs. Porter, with the end outcome sounding anything but enjoyable."

"If it is broken, I'd advise you to have it amputated," she said, no-nonsense.

Wesley dragged a hand through his hair. The options he

had were few. This was his last chance, and his only hope. Even so, what the woman proposed was ghastly in nature.

Unbidden, he looked to Ellie.

Ellie, who at some point had taken his hand in her own and offered him silent support.

"You don't have to do this, Wesley," she said.

"I do, Ellie. You know that."

She didn't feed him a second lie.

Before his courage deserted him, Wesley nodded to Mrs. Porter. "Very well."

"I'll begin with the examination." She motioned to a nearby door, and then, giving him a moment, headed for that room.

Wesley waited until Mrs. Porter had gone before speaking. "I don't want you here for this, Ellie."

Ellie was already shaking her head. "I'm not leaving, Wesley."

"You don't need to—"

"I'm not leaving," she repeated, lifting her chin at a pugnacious angle.

Fiery resolve glittered in her eyes.

Wesley waged a different kind of war—this one with himself. "As she said, she may not even be able to save the limb."

"She'll be able to save it, Wesley. Go . . . let her examine your leg."

Clutching his cane harder, he turned to go.

"Wait." Going up on tiptoe, Ellie pressed a kiss against his scarred cheek. "It will be all right, Wesley. Whatever it is."

He managed a nod, and then, quitting her side, Wesley made his way into the room where Mrs. Porter had begun the preparations for his procedure. She didn't even look up at his approach.

While she worked, he did a quick sweep of the space. Small but tidy, with a bed at the center of the room and a handful of amateurish drawings upon the wall, there was nothing that would give a person pause . . . until one took in the oak armoire Mrs. Porter stood before.

She assessed the belts and boards inside, and then reached for something.

Wesley stiffened, but she merely turned around, and returned with a blanket and a flask.

He waved off the drink.

The bonesetter lifted it his way once more. "Have some."

He hesitated a moment, and this time, so as to not be rude to the peculiar woman whose help he sought, Wesley accepted the flask. He took a small sip.

She grunted her approval. "Take another."

Then it occurred to him: no different than when soldiers' injuries were tended under a battlefield tent, the bonesetter sought to get him foxed.

He managed a smile. "I thought you needed to assess my injury first," he said, after he'd seated himself on the edge of the bed. "I may not even require your services."

"Then consider a good sousing a lucky gift of our meeting."

He managed a smile.

"Here." She held out a blanket. "Unless you require help, I'll step out so you can remove your trousers."

Wesley forced himself to release the tension. "You may cut them." Ellie insisted on being present through this appointment, and he'd not have her present while he sat bare-arsed.

The woman started. "If I do so, it may be for naught and you'll surely attract looks when you—"

"I attract looks enough with my leg," he gently interrupted.

She instantly ceased her protestations. "As you wish," she demurred.

A short while later, positioned on the table, Wesley lay there while she cut his trousers just above his knee.

Snip-snip-snip.

There came a slight tug.

While she prodded at the deformed flesh, Wesley remained still, and his eyes closed.

At last, she finished.

"Well?" he asked, tension radiating through him.

The break before she answered him proved interminable, a different kind of agonizing.

"It can be set," she said.

A prayer slipped from his lips.

"Remember that relief you are feeling in a few moments," she advised. "Now, drink."

This time, when she went about gathering items for the procedure, he didn't protest. Wesley sat there a long while, drinking, until a smooth, welcome heat spread through him, and he briefly closed his eyes.

"How did you come to know Ellie?" he asked, his voice languid, as the spirits he'd consumed continued to warm him.

"I don't discuss how I meet the people who come to my offices," she replied with a vagueness that frustrated him. "I suspect by the quality of your speech it is time."

"Time," he echoed, slurring that single syllable so it rolled into two.

While she went to collect Ellie, Wesley helped himself to another deep swallow.

The moment Ellie appeared, it was like a bright light amidst the darkness that had dogged him for so long. He lifted his nearly empty flask in salute. "She can fix meeee, Ellieee. You were riiight."

"Are you certain you wish to remain, my lady?" Mrs. Porter asked.

"I'm stay—"

"Elllllie neeeever leaves me," Wesley interrupted. "Isn't that right, Ellllie-girl?"

"That is right, Wesley. I'll never leave you."

"You look saaaad," he slurred. "I haaate when you're sad."

"Yes, well, that makes two of us, as I hate when you are, too."

"Well, I'm about to be verrry happy. Isn't that riiiiiiight?" he turned that question to Mrs. Porter.

Her lips tightened.

"You looook grim." He angled his head toward Ellie. "Sheee looks grim, dusun she?"

"Somber." Ellie laid her hand over his, twining their fingers together. "She is somber, Wesley."

"Are you ready?" Mrs. Porter asked, even as she fastened Wesley's arms and uninjured leg.

Wesley grinned. "Never more revy." Anything would be worth being set to rights again.

She held a stick near his mouth. "To bite," she said, and he clamped his teeth down. "I'm going to begin by pulling the muscles and stretching them so I can place the bone in its natural position."

He chuckled. "That doesn't sound so—" A pained hiss spilled from his lips. He lost his grip on the biting block. "Chrissst." He'd never been one for praying, but in this instance, the Lord's name slipped out as just that.

He dimly registered Ellie placing the stick back between his lips and murmuring supportive words as she did.

Mrs. Porter continued her manipulation.

Wesley whimpered. He didn't want her to see him like this. "G-get outttt," he gritted out around the stick.

"I'm staying with you. It is going to be all right, Wesley," Ellie whispered, placing a kiss against his damp brow.

He squeezed his eyes shut. "Liiiiar."

Did that mewling voice belong to him?

"Think of something that makes you happy," Ellie pleaded, her voice the only thing keeping him from descending into total madness.

Mrs. Porter pulled his leg harder.

Wesley cried out, and this time he thrashed his head when Ellie attempted to give him the block to bite on.

Think of something that made him happy? "Therrre's nothi—ahhhhh."

"There has to be something."

"Letttters," he keened. "The lettttters." Those notes he'd not pulled out once since he'd returned home.

"Are you almost done?" Ellie's pleading question reached through his suffering.

"There's a bit more, my lady."

Mrs. Porter rotated his thigh, twisting it with an impressive strength for one her size, and this time, Wesley wept. He fought and twisted against his restraints, pleading and begging for her to finish. Mayhap he'd landed himself in hell, and all along, sweet, smiling, steadfast Ellie had really been the Devil disguised as an angel to lead him to this place and put him through his penance for all the lives he'd taken in the name of war.

"Throwww up," he moaned piteously. "Gonnnna be sick."

"That is normal," Mrs. Porter said. Even so, the bonesetter paused and ensured he didn't vomit before returning to her work.

"Breathe, Wesley. Breathe," Ellie guided him through his suffering.

The bonesetter manipulated his leg the opposite way.

Her tortured touch was too much, and Wesley, like a poor, pitiable child, wet himself.

All the while, Ellie's tears ran over his face, and somehow she remained there with him, through the mortification of his greatest indignity. There was only one certainty: when—if—he survived this, Wesley would never be able to look her in the eye again.

Suddenly, the maniacal twisting stopped.

"It is done, sir." Mrs. Porter's quiet murmur cut through his shame and pain.

It was done.

Quiet sobbing filled the room. His and Ellie's grief and pain joined together.

Inky blackness pulled him under, and then, mercifully, Wesley remembered no more.

Part Two

They stand in Awe of her, knowing her to
be a Gentlewoman born, tho' she has had
Misfortunes.

—*Virtue Rewarded,*
Samuel Richardson

Chapter 14

My dearest Wesley,

I am quite adept at faro, whist, and hazard. One day, we must play together.

Lovingly Yours

Seated at his tables in London's notorious gaming hall Blackmantel's, playing cards with his recent friend, the Marquess of Brackley, Wesley spent the night as he'd spent so many others that had come before it.

Here in a place where men were too focused on their own vices, and drunk with spirits, no one looked too close at Wesley, and it made this place the perfect one for him.

Or it usually did.

This evening appeared to be the exception.

Distracted, Wesley tossed down a card and followed his eldest brother's approach. Rafe's features were set in a hard mask, the one he'd always donned when lecturing men in the mines for various infractions.

"Bloody splendid," he muttered.

"Indeed, that was a bad hand on your part," Brackley said, from around the cheroot clenched between his teeth. He scraped over his earnings, and then tamped out the stub. "Another round?"

The marquess had already proceeded to deal.

The last thing Wesley wanted or needed was a lecture from his big brother.

Alas . . .

Rafe reached his table. He looked Wesley over, lingering his gaze on the light growth on Wesley's unshaved cheeks, then the half-empty bottle near Wesley's fingers and the empty glass still in his hand. And then Rafe briefly settled a disapproving gaze on the Marquess of Brackley, who didn't so much as glance up from the deck of cards he shuffled.

Wesley added several fingerfuls to the snifter and lifted the spirits in salute. "Brother," he greeted. "What an unexpected pleasure. This is not your usual haunt. Care to join Brackley and I for a game of faro?"

Neither Rafe nor the marquess so much as acknowledged each other.

Rafe's mouth tightened. "I've not come to partake in cards."

Wesley nodded to Brackley and the gentleman proceeded to deal the deck. "A drink, then." He shot a hand up, and a voluptuous beauty instantly materialized, with a silver tray rested on her bare shoulder.

"Looking for company, Your Grace?" she purred.

"Perhaps later, sweet." He handed her several coins, softening that rejection. "Alas, my big brother requires a snifter."

Rafe shook his head, declining the server's attempt. "That won't be necessary."

The girl shrugged and then slipped off to a table filled with far more receptive gentlemen.

The moment she'd gone, Rafe looked to Lord Brackley. "Would you excuse us a moment?"

The marquess looped his thumbs in the waist of his

white wool trousers, kicked back on the legs of his chair, and glanced Wesley's way.

From the corner of his eye, Wesley caught the way Rafe's entire body tensed. Nay, his brother wouldn't like any part of this exchange. Since Rafe had been head of the Cheadle mines, and was accustomed to everyone and anyone heeding his wishes and orders, Brackley deferring to Wesley would have only grated.

But it was *also* how Wesley knew even if he declined Rafe's *request*, his eldest sibling would set up a permanent place at Wesley's table until he had his way.

Wesley nodded.

In an instant, Lord Brackley settled all four legs of his chair on the floor once more and got up. "I'll leave you to your *company*."

"We won't be long," Wesley assured the other man. Rafe's lips tensed in that now all too familiar sign of perpetual displeasure.

The moment the other man had gone, Rafe grabbed a chair and finally seated himself.

"You look like hell," Rafe said quietly.

Wesley cradled his snifter between his palms and grinned lazily at Rafe. "It is so very good to see you, brother," he drawled, lifting his crystal glass in another salute.

When Rafe simply sat staring at him with more of that quiet condemnation, he added, "What? Isn't it good to see me, too, big brother?"

"Not like this." Rafe scraped another disapproving stare over him, and then, when he met Wesley's eyes, Wesley tensed.

Pity. It glittered and glimmered as fresh and raw as it had been the last time he'd seen Rafe, at that damned ceremony when Wesley had been made a duke.

Wesley's fingers tightened reflexively on his glass, hard enough to shatter, and he forced himself to lighten his hold. He took a sip. "And how exactly am I?"

"Drunk."

"I'm not drunk." Yet. He was getting there, though.

"Stinking of a whore's cheap perfume."

From the serving wenches who availed themselves to his lap in a bid for coin. "I'll have you know the women at Blackmantel's are of the highest quality and wouldn't dare dab their skin with anything other than the finest French fragrance."

Sadness settled in Rafe's features, and oddly, this proved somehow worse than the pitying. "Is everything a joke to you now? Is there nothing you take seriously?"

Unable to meet his gaze, Wesley stared morosely into the contents of his glass. Rafe asked whether Wesley took anything seriously? He'd done just that and only that for the whole of his miserable existence. From back to his days as a miner, to his brief relationship with Claire Sparrow, and then his days as a soldier. Ultimately, aside from more heartbreak, what had any of that gotten him?

His brother must have seen a weakening, for he dragged his chair closer and dropped his arms on the table. Leaning in, Rafe spoke earnestly. "You haven't seen Edwina, or your nephew Colin, or me—"

"I saw you just last week," he protested.

"That was last month."

He started. Had it been that long? Surely not.

"It has been," Rafe said, interpreting Wesley's unspoken thoughts as only an older brother could.

"I've been otherwise occupied." Focused on avoiding that bucolic family. Focused on avoiding all bucolic families, in fact.

Rafe glanced about the club, giving a pointed look to the whores on the laps of drunken patrons, and the crowds of dissolute gentlemen surrounding the velvet-covered gaming tables. "I *see* how busy you've been."

"Are we d—"

"You haven't seen Cailin in even longer."

"Apparently we *aren't* done with this," he muttered. "Cailin has a family of her own. The last thing she wants is her older brother hanging about."

"If you believe that, if you believe she doesn't want her son to know his uncle, then you don't know our sister," Rafe said sadly.

Wesley continued to stare into the amber contents of his glass. The thing of it was, his brother had hit the nail on the mark. Wesley no longer felt as though he knew *anyone*. He'd gone off to war and seen grisly things, and worse, done horrific things in the name of war, that no man should do, but that he and others had to in order to survive. And once a man partook in that evil—even if it had been with the intent of stopping a madman bent on world domination—one couldn't unsee those sides of his soul.

"Father has hopes that you will join society."

"I have joined society," Wesley said, gesturing with his glass about the room.

"Polite Society."

"Is this something *you* wanted?" Wesley shot back, the muscles of his right thigh straining from the length of time he'd been on his feet. "Something you want now for yourself?"

"It . . . isn't all bad," Rafe said quietly. "Yes, there are aspects that are tedious, but the people here aren't all unkind and I think it might do you some good to try fitting into the duke's world."

Wesley recoiled, and then swiftly found his footing. "I've no wish to fit into the *duke's world*."

"Yes, well, I'll remind you that you now possess a title. As such, you belong to this world, whether you like it or not."

So much had changed in Wesley's absence.

Wesley looked at his brother, truly seeing Rafe for the first time in a long time. From his blue sapphire jacket on to his fawn breeches and gleaming black books, Rafe was immaculately attired in finer garments than any member of their family had previously worn.

His brother, his once best friend, was now . . . a stranger.

They all were.

"Father misses you," Rafe said quietly.

He tensed.

"Father, is he now?" Wesley flashed a mocking smile. "How touching."

A hard fury blazed to life in his eldest brother's eyes. "Need I remind you that *you* were the one who opened that door to us."

"And how easily you stepped on through, on the heels of my efforts."

Had it been Hunter here, Wesley would have gotten the rise out of him that he now sought with Rafe.

Rafe, however, proved unflappable. Instead, he sat back in his chair like one settling in for a long chat. "I'm not here to fight with you."

"Then why don't you say what it is you want?" Then they could be done with this and Wesley could go back to drinking his spirits and playing his cards and dulling the thoughts that refused to stay buried.

"Ellie has made her debut and Lord and Lady Davenport are holding an affair this evening in her honor."

Ellie. A memory slid in of Ellie holding him as he wept and wet himself like a babe. He cringed inside all over again.

"What does that have to do with me, Rafe?"

"Given your previous exchanges with the girl and the time she kept your miserable person company, I expect the least you could do is put in an appearance for her benefit."

"In other words, pay back the favor."

His brother didn't take the bait.

"If that's how you wish to see it? Then, yes."

"Cailin sent you."

"Yes."

Rafe didn't even attempt to deny it.

"Ellie doesn't need me about."

His brother scoffed. "Come, Wesley. When was the last time you thought about what anyone other than yourself needed or wanted? Don't be disingenuous. Simply say that you don't wish to go and support the girl because you'd rather be getting soused and bedding your whores and playing your cards."

Wesley flashed a crooked grin. "Goodness, why don't you tell me what you really think, brother?"

A sound of disgust escaped Rafe.

At last, Wesley had managed to penetrate that impervious wall. Oddly, it didn't bring him the sense of triumph he'd thought it would.

Rafe stood. "I won't bother you again with this request. Either way, it was Cailin's idea. I never had any such illusion that you could be bothered to take part in affairs that didn't in some way indulge your own wicked proclivities. I merely promised her that I'd speak to you."

He paused, looking as if he wished to say more. "Wesley," he said, and then took his leave.

Wesley followed Rafe's retreating frame with his eyes. His brother moved with a decisive speed, making a determined march through the den of iniquity.

"Big brother is gone."

Wesley looked up at Brackley and the two women he'd returned with.

The gentleman availed himself to his previous seat and helped the blond-haired beauty onto his lap. The marquess said something to the titian-haired woman, and she started across the table.

Wesley held up a hand, politely declining that offer.

Brackley grinned. "More for me," he said, urging the prostitute back over. She took up a place behind him and proceeded to massage his shoulders. With that, the marquess gathered up the cards and proceeded to set up the gameplay.

Absently, Wesley played several more long hands against the marquess.

Perhaps another person would have probed. That wasn't the relationship he had with Brackley. Two men who'd fought Boney's forces, in different regiments, but the same conflict, they understood one another. They knew the ways war had changed them and they didn't feel compelled to speak about their experiences. Nay, they neither of them wished to speak about what they'd seen or done.

Then there was his brother. His brother who'd arrived on behalf of Cailin and asked Wesley, of all people, to attend some frivolous affair for Ellie.

Ellie would hate that. Not that he'd be invited, but that an affair had been thrown in her honor, and she couldn't skip out herself.

A wistful smile pulled at his lips.

She'd despise absolutely everything about her Season. She'd spoken freely with him about her dread. And now, she'd face that hated affair . . . alone.

To banish thoughts of a miserable Ellie from his head, he picked up his snifter and stared into the contents.

It didn't help.

Thoughts of her remained. Ellie had seen the worst of him. She'd seen him at his lowest, first stuck in that chair, and then humbled and humiliated as, like a babe finding his legs for the first time, he'd learned to walk again. She'd heard his snarled curses, ones that would have made jaded men blush.

Wesley tugged out his timepiece and cursed.

From around the beauty nuzzling at his neck, Brackley stared concernedly back.

Wesley pushed back his chair and, gathering his cane, stood. "I'm afraid I've recalled another commitment this evening."

Limping through the crowded floors of Blackmantel's, Wesley made his way to the elaborate front entrance.

When everyone else had feared him, Ellie had come freely to visit. She'd been the one who'd brought him to the woman who'd healed his leg. Through all that, Ellie had asked for nothing in return. She'd simply been there, helping Wesley through his darkest time.

Putting in an appearance here and there, standing beside her in support at a London Season she'd not at all wanted was the very least he could do for the lady.

And then that debt to her was paid, and he'd be free to live his dissolute life without any sense that he owed any person a damned thing.

A short while later, Wesley entered the Baron and Baroness Davenport's lavish ball. The moment he did, every woman swung their alternately greedy and horrified gazes his way. Since he'd had a duke title affixed to his name, people's sick fascination with the injuries he'd forever wear on his face had morphed into something else—interest.

Any lady and her greedy mama and papa could overlook a scarred monster—even an illegitimate one—with that vaunted title, so long as he might make their daughter a duchess.

Suddenly, a commotion near the back center of the ballroom briefly called his attention.

A swell of dandies, fops, and even some of London's most resolute bachelors had taken up a place around whatever lady had been deemed the Diamond of the Season. Dismissing the scene, Wesley resumed his search for Ellie.

"You actually came," a familiar voice drawled from over Wesley's shoulder.

He stiffened and turned to face his brother Rafe, who stood with Cailin and Courtland at his side.

"Yes, well, I'd it on authority that I could attend and also enjoy my usual libations," he drawled, and to bait his big brother, Wesley rescued a champagne flute from a passing servant, toasted Rafe, and then took a long swallow.

His brother scowled in return.

"Oh, hush." Their sister Cailin shot Rafe a look before turning a radiant smile on Wesley. "What our dear brother *meant* to say is, it is so very good to see you." Tears glittered in her eyes.

Cailin's husband instantly collected her hand in his.

"It truly is," Courtland added with a like solemnity, which earned a nod from an always-stoic Rafe.

"No," Rafe said, with a somber gaze. "Cailin is not wrong."

"Which also means, Cailin is right," their sister drawled,

slipping an arm through Rafe's and making an attempt for Wesley's in a move that would unite the three siblings, but she came up short as her gaze moved between the cane he held in one hand and the drink he cradled in the other.

Unnerved by his family's show of emotion, Wesley tightened his hold on the head of his cane, and with his other, took another much-needed drink.

Ellie stared a long moment at his glass.

"Ellie will be so very happy to see you again," his sister confided, and then proceeded to speak in hushed tones about Ellie's first Season.

She needn't have bothered. The hum of voices and laughter from the crowd leant a din that made a man strain to hear the person next to him. The sound proved deafening, a swirl of blurred noise in his head that harkened back to a different pandemonium.

Sweat slicked his palms, and his belly churned with the same nausea that beset him on the eve of every battle, and in an instant Wesley was transported.

The bright orange glow cast by the enormous crystal chandelier merged with another, as the smooth marble floor shifted, turning to a muddied earth, slicked with blood.

The demons licked at the corners of his mind, sucking him back, pulling him in, and Wesley inhaled sharply through his nose.

"Wesley?"

Someone tugged his sleeve, and all his muscles tightened. They had him.

"Wesley?"

Except . . .

Wesley.

Not Audley.

Not Lieutenant Audley. Nor Captain Audley.

He came whirring to the present to find his siblings and Courtland staring at him with confused eyes.

"Have you heard a single word I said?" Cailin ventured hesitantly.

Concern filled Rafe's and Courtland's usually carefree eyes.

Wesley tossed back the remaining contents of his drink. "I heard you," he lied. Lying was far easier than admitting the truth—he'd lost his mind, and there was no getting it back.

Fortunately, Courtland filled Wesley in on the bulk of what he'd missed. "Ellie's really quite miserable, you know."

"Actually, given he's only shown up to this one respectable event, he probably *doesn't*," Rafe remarked, pulling a laugh from Courtland.

Cailin shot both men a dark look; her husband's features grew instantly contrite.

She turned her displeasure on Rafe, and gave him a light pinch on the arm.

With a scowl, Rafe rubbed at the offended flesh. "I was speaking matter-of-fact," he muttered under his breath.

Their older brother only had one way and knew one way.

"Sometimes matter-of-fact is rude," their sister pointed out.

In fairness, Wesley wasn't deserving of Cailin's defense. If he were a decent man and as good a friend to Ellie as she'd been to him, he would have known long before now that the lady's Season had been a dismal failure. Even as he'd never admit as much aloud, Rafe had been right in that the very least Wesley could do was attend and put in a show of support for her.

"As Courtland was saying," Cailin said, returning her attention to Wesley. "She is miserable . . . even more so than *I* was."

Which was saying a good deal indeed.

Wesley glanced out at the crush of dance partners vying for a scrap of space on the too-crowded ballroom floor.

"I expect she would be," he murmured. Ellie, who fenced and climbed trees and engaged in pretend wars, would hate *all* of this.

He looked to the two neat rows of chairs set up at the

corner of the room and searched for her among those ladies deemed wallflowers, their companions, and the elderly ones favoring a nap.

"You won't find her there," Cailin remarked, having correctly identified the purpose of his search.

Courtland stepped in to help. "She's there, near my other sister Hattie."

Wesley followed his brother-in-law's discreet point across the room, drawing Wesley's attention to a lady with bounteous blond tresses. A vision in pale blue silk, she possessed a golden beauty that would have put Athena to shame, and yet, it was the ease with which she spoke that held Wesley— and her legion of suitors—enthralled.

Ellie?

Her neckline, embroidered with white flower accents, didn't plunge as the widows and unhappy wives who always had a look for Wesley. Rather, the lady's bodice provided only the subtlest attention to her slightly olive-hued flesh. Her playful translucent sleeves teased a man, encouraging him to look, and Wesley drank his fill of her.

It was a transformation he'd no place noting, but then, in his ungodly existence, he'd committed far greater transgressions than looking where he oughtn't.

Ellie moved her arms and smiled wide as she spoke. Hers was an imp's smile Wesley knew all too well, revealing flawless porcelain-white teeth, and a grin big enough to rival her even bigger corkscrew curls.

At that precise moment, she said something that roused her admirers to like amusement, and damned if Wesley didn't have a sudden interest in knowing what words she'd just uttered.

She sat surrounded by a bevy of swains, and yet, of all those gentlemen, just one of them, a tall, not-at-all-foppish fellow, stood closer to her than the others. To anyone else staring on, the lord bore a relaxed air.

Wesley, however, wasn't just anyone else.

He thinned his eyes on the unscarred, and more-handsome-than-Wesley-cared-to-admit gentleman, a gentleman who hovered close enough to send a message to the other chaps—he'd a claim to Ellie.

A muscle pulsed at the corner of Wesley's eye.

Only a fool would believe spirited, clever Ellie Balfour was a woman to be claimed.

As if she felt Wesley's gaze, the lady paused. Her enormous smile dimpled her cheeks. It remained frozen on her face. From across the way, her eyes locked with his. Their stares collided.

The gentleman at her side said something that pulled Ellie's focus away from Wesley.

A growl formed in his throat. "Who is he?"

"Ah," Cailin said. "That is the Duke of Stenton. He is very devoted in his courtship of Ellie."

"A duke," he muttered. "Is *every* man in London a blasted duke?"

The *other* young duke beside Wesley laughed.

But then, with the way Prinny had gone about conferring titles since he'd been granted that power, even giving one over to bastard-born Wesley, it certainly appeared as if there'd be a whole Marriage Mart brimming with those titled fellows.

This particular duke—Stenton—however, hadn't been born on the wrong side of the blanket, and had an abundance of charm and unmarred skin. And Wesley hated him with a dangerously hot vitriol.

"Dear husband, perhaps you might go see to your sister's rescue," Cailin said, mistaking the reason for his annoyance.

As her husband dashed off, Wesley marveled at the preposterous idea that Ellie needed rescuing from *anyone*.

His brother had insisted Wesley support Ellie Balfour during her Come Out. Wesley had incorrectly assumed the young lady had been bereft and found herself a wallflower and in need of support.

The slender young lady with all those artfully arranged, gloriously blond curls that went on forever wasn't in need of *anyone's* support—and certainly not a broken Wesley's. The glow of the chandeliers played with the endless shades of gold in her hair, which was held in place by diamond combs that struggled with their task, giving her an ethereal look.

The moment Cailin's husband reached Ellie, she instantly brightened.

Like a queen addressing her lowly subjects, Ellie inclined her head at a regal angle. Whatever let-down she'd given the lot of those unworthy lords earned boisterous laughs from those suitors.

Yes, that had always been Ellie's way. She'd possessed a sharp wit, and a clever tongue.

Wesley tightened his already-tense mouth.

Never before had he witnessed her wielding that skill upon a sea of ardent admirers she'd accumulated, and some strange and nasty sentiment filled his chest. With a palpable reluctance, the crowd of gentlemen dissolved. That tall fellow with his possessive stare lingered at Ellie's side until the last dandy had gone before following suit.

Courtland said something to Ellie. Brother and sister exchanged furtive looks.

The lady leaned up on tiptoe and brushed a kiss against her brother's cheek. Then, the duke placed himself between Ellie and the ballroom, affording the young lady cover to slip off unnoticed.

Wesley followed her graceful flight. Even in that elegant gown, she moved with the same speed and agility she always had.

As Ellie fled, Wesley narrowed his eyes on his brother-in-law. What in blazes was the other man thinking, letting her go alone?

Depositing his glass on the tray of a passing servant, Wesley made his excuses and started after a No Longer Little Ellie Balfour.

Laying her arms on the terrace ledge that overlooked the Baroness of Davenport's gardens, Ellie rested her cheek on the smooth limestone and stared out. The fingernail moon hanging upon the star-studded sky barely provided a sliver of light. Yet, the rich aroma of irises mingled with the sweet, citrusy scent of daylilies and permeated the air.

On the eve of their debut, most young ladies feared they'd find themselves wallflowers, without the benefit of a single suitor's attention.

For Ellie, *that* had been the dream. What had greeted her upon her Come Out, on the other hand, was her greatest nightmare.

After all, it was a good deal easier escaping the literal and figurative bonds of matrimony when one failed to receive anyone's notice.

Oh, it wasn't that she believed her brother would ever dare force Ellie into a match she didn't want. Rather, Ellie's continual refusals would invariably lead to questions from her family, questions she didn't want, which would lead her to things she didn't wish to talk about or share with anyone.

On the eve of her debut, Ellie had wanted to run and hide. After all, every woman knew what that momentous event signified—the impending end of what little freedom a lady enjoyed.

The only thing that had made the moment bearable, the only solace she'd taken, was in knowing Wesley would be there.

Only, he'd not come.

Not when she'd been presented to the queen.

Not to Almack's.

Not even the ball thrown by his own father, the Duke of Bentley, and the Duchess of Bentley.

The last she'd seen him had been that day they'd left Mrs. Porter's. They'd boarded different carriages and never saw one another again. Instead, the only hint she'd caught of him had been among the scandal sheets. Those pages were constantly splashed with the exploits of the newly minted duke who spent his time not at *ton* events but naughty clubs . . . and she wasn't naïve. For that matter, her own brother had been a notorious rogue. She'd seen more than a sister would care to see about a sibling's exploits on the gossip pages. It was why she knew precisely what Wesley was undoubtedly doing when he attended those haunts.

Until, after weeks of her London Season, she'd stopped looking for him at the entrances of ballrooms.

Not that she could blame him. She didn't. The offer of friendship she'd extended him had not been granted with any thought of reciprocity on her part. No, the truth remained: given both the deception she'd committed when she'd sent Wesley letters, bearing the name and mark of another, and the decision she'd made to stop writing him, she certainly owed Wesley more than he ever would or could owe her.

She had been hard-pressed to find anyone else who wished to be in this particular ballroom less than her.

Until she'd caught a glimpse of Wesley, who but for the rumpled plum cravat had been attired in all black. In an instant, she'd identified a kindred spirit.

Click-click-click

Ellie stilled. Her ears caught the tap of his cane and the shuffle of his slight limp the moment he entered the grounds.

"Forced you to come, did they?" She directed that greeting out to the baroness's hydrangeas.

"No," he said with an automaticity that should have suggested it had been borne of truth.

Alas, she'd come to know this man well enough to recognize a lie when she heard one.

Straightening, Ellie turned and rested her lower back against the terrace ledge. With a pace far slower than when they'd first met, but even smoother and quicker than those days she'd come visiting, Wesley reached her.

He leaned against the terrace ledge, borrowing obvious support from that limestone structure, and there was a tangible easing of the always-tense muscles of his face.

"You're a liar, Wesley Audley."

"And you are a success, little general."

Little general. Not many years ago, she'd have preened with pride at such a compliment.

"It all depends on one's definition of 'a success,'" she said pertly.

Reaching inside his jacket, Wesley fished out a silver flask, uncorked it, and toasted Ellie.

She studied him as he took a long drink, and then sniffed the air to convey her displeasure.

He merely flashed a crooked grin, one that did wicked things to her heart's rhythm.

"And I'll have you know, I no longer entertain thoughts of enlisting," she informed him.

Wesley set his flask down near her fingers and, shifting his weight over the head of his cane, leaned close. "And why should you, Ellie? You've got legions of suitors tripping over themselves to get you a glass of lemonade. They are yours to command."

"I don't like lemonade. It's tepid."

"Your would-be beaus would likely fetch you whatever drink you sent them questing for."

Ellie turned her lips up in a forced-feeling smile. "You and I have different views of what qualifies as a 'success,' Your Grace."

He scowled. "Your Gracing me, now, too, are you?"

"Well, you *are* a duke."

"Tell me, Ellie. Why would you hide away out here, even as it will break all those gentlemen's hearts?"

She snorted. "You're making a gross assumption that the gentlemen back there are in possession of that organ."

"Yes, it's all a fallacy, isn't it," he murmured, more to himself. His hard lips formed an even harder line. "That ridiculous illusion of love."

Because of his Miss Sparrow.

And Ellie despised in equal parts that woman who'd been undeserving of him and that her breast should tighten so at the evidence of just how very much he still loved the lady anyway.

"It isn't all an illusion, you know," she said softly.

As if only just recalling her presence, Wesley blinked and looked over.

"My brother is *very* much in love with Cailin, and your father? There can be no doubting he's head over toes in love with his duchess. So I do know it is real." It just wasn't real for her.

Wesley lightly cuffed her on the chin. "Given your inclination toward a romantic nature, one should expect you'd be less cynical in judging the affections of the potential suitors who are even now certain to be looking for you."

She stared past Wesley's broad shoulder. "Hunting me," she said. "Those men are hunting me."

Having been the property of a man who'd been more predator than father, she was in no rush to enter into a hasty union with a stranger whom she'd no reason to trust.

Despite the warmth of the spring night, a chill rippled through her, and reflexively Ellie hugged herself, rubbing at her arms to ease the cold within.

Long, deft fingers touched her chin.

Wesley angled her face back to his. "Considering your belief in that emotion called love, one should think you would be in favor of accumulating all those potential hearts from the vying swains, as one among them might *surely* possess an organ that beats, and therefore, be capable of the sentiment."

Ellie drew herself up on the ledge so she could more comfortably meet Wesley's eyes.

"Ah," she lifted a finger. "But a man capable of love would never declare his affections and bestow his attentions so ardently because of nothing more than a woman's looks."

Wesley moved his eyes over her. He lingered his focus on the diamond hair combs that had been a gift from Cailin and then moved his focus to her mouth, and then lower, to the neckline of her gown. His gaze burned like an intimate caress.

Ellie's heart thumped a wild beat.

He lifted his eyes to hers. "But every relationship,"—he spoke in the husky tones of a rogue, which she'd vowed never to fall for or be swayed by—"it always begins with physical attraction, Ellie."

Hers hadn't. Granted, she didn't have a physical relationship with this man. She'd *wanted* one. Which was altogether different . . . and worse, given the fact how very one-sided her affections had always been.

Until now. For in an instant, in this instance, she could almost believe the desire in his smooth baritone was reserved for her.

And then Wesley flashed a rakish half grin, following it with a wink, and the moment was shattered, as there could be no doubting he'd merely been teasing her with that feigned interest.

Rolling her eyes, Ellie thumped him lightly on the chest.

Ellie hopped down and started for the terrace doors.

"You might like it, you know, Ellie," he called out, staying her in her tracks. "You might revel in a man's touch."

She knew she'd revel in *his* touch. The memory of his kiss lingered in her mind still. It always would.

Ellie, however, had witnessed firsthand the worst aspects of a man's touch, and knew just how easily they could bring violence and pain.

A chill crept in.

She briefly closed her eyes. "Perhaps," she said noncommittally.

"Ah, because you can't imagine there is something so very wonderful," he murmured.

Actually, this time, he'd landed on the mark.

Ellie said nothing.

He lowered his mouth close to her ear, and a delicious little shiver radiated from where that soft sough caressed her skin to her belly.

"Do you know what I think, Ellie?" he whispered, and her eyes slid closed.

She managed a brief, uneven shake of her head.

"I believe a woman like you would revel in the taste of passion." He brought his lips close to her shoulder, and as he spoke, his mouth lightly brushed hers in an accidental kiss. "You'd not only come to crave it, you'd love it."

She bit her lower lip hard; an unfamiliar, wicked ache settled between her legs.

A low chuckle rumbled in his chest.

The haze he'd wrought over her senses lifted.

Ellie faced him. Angling her chin up several notches, Ellie managed her greatest accomplishment to date—feigned indifference. "But then, you know I did enjoy your embrace."

Color filled his cheeks.

He was still capable of blushing. Imagine that.

"Anyway, it will take a good deal more than the seductive words of a rogue to win my heart, Wesley."

"What will it take?"

"Are you throwing your hat into the ring?"

He inclined his head. "I wouldn't dare when there's an entire army of more suitable, deserving fellows."

He used that teasing tone he'd adopted since the war.

Only . . .

Ellie moved her eyes over the harsh angles of his face, the vicious scar that ran from the lobe of his left ear up to the very corner of his left eye. It spoke to the violence he'd confronted, and just how very close he'd come to losing not only that eye, but his life, as well.

He frowned. "What is it?"

"I believe you mean that, Wesley," she murmured. "I suspect you find yourself somehow undeserving and unworthy of any number of gifts or pleasures."

Wesley caught her lightly but firmly by the wrist, locking her in place beside him.

"And what are you suggesting, Ellie?" he asked, his voice harsh and sharp as it'd been upon his return, when he'd been lashing out at her. "That *you* are some treasure I should seek to attain?"

In a bid to protect himself, he sought to hurt her. She knew as much.

Even understanding that did little to ease the lance of pain.

Refusing to be cowed by anyone—including this man—Ellie edged her chin up a notch. "I wasn't suggesting anything. I'm no treasure and I'm *certainly* not looking to be

attained by any man, and that includes you, Your Grace."
She gave a pointed look to where he held her.

Wesley immediately released her.

"What I did state was a flat-out truth: *you* are the one
who finds yourself wanting. It is you who finds yourself
somehow unworthy or flawed. And until you learn to love
yourself and accept you as you are, you will only be this
shallow, empty shell of a man."

With that quiet pronouncement, Ellie collected her skirts,
and left.

Chapter 15

My dearest Wesley,

My favorite hour of the day is early dawn, before the whole world rises. There is such peace in the quiet to be had.

Lovingly Yours

The moment he'd returned home, he'd shut himself away in his offices and helped himself to the many papers stacked neatly on his desk that he'd never bothered to touch, and sought out what information he could about Ellie.

Hours later, with a snifter of brandy nearby, Wesley remained there, poring through the stack of newspapers and gossip pages. He flipped through them, searching and finding. Over and over again.

He'd always been a bastard. Last evening on the Lord and Lady Davenport's stone terrace, Wesley had lived up to that title, in every ugly sense of the word. Ellie had been right in every charge she'd leveled at him. He had been a lousy friend. He had cut her out. And he hated himself for it.

Wesley scanned another gossip column.

Society is left to wonder which gentleman the Diamond will choose. All signs point to the illustrious Duke of S, who has since given up his roguish ways. Alas, love has that effect upon—

With a growl, Wesley tossed those pages over the front of his desk, and read the next.

Lady E, the Diamond and Darling of this Season, is rumored to be days away from accepting an offer from the Duke of S. This person would be hard-pressed to find a more striking, a more perfectly matched couple than—

Wesley hurled those sheets onto the floor, to join the others he'd already read and promptly discarded. This was how he learned of what she'd been up to? Through the words and speculation written by another.

Ellie was right. Wesley was a deuced lousy friend.

In fact, she deserved a paragon such as Stenton, who'd the sense to put her on the pedestal as she deserved. She might resent Wesley for having disappeared these past months, but he'd done her a favor.

Hadn't he?

Restless, he picked up his half-empty brandy and wandered to the floor-to-ceiling-length windows that overlooked the quiet Mayfair streets below. The crystal panes reflected back his scarred visage, as in the early dawn hours, Ellie's charges played over and over inside his head.

. . . Until you learn to love yourself and accept you as you are, you will only be this shallow, empty shell of a man . . .

Grimacing, Wesley raised his glass to down another

drink—and suddenly stopped. His gaze locked on the topaz contents.

What had he become?

He despised the men in Cheadle who'd lost themselves in drink at the local tavern. He'd never understood what made them so very weak that they'd surrender their pride and honor to the bottom of a glass. All the while, he'd failed to consider just what demons had driven them to seek solace in whatever way they could. And in the end, he'd become them.

Ellie had been right to call him out as she had.

He'd been boorish and rude and crass. She'd gotten him through those darkest days and joined him in sessions that had left him humbled and sweating and near tears. And how had he repaid those gifts? By treating her like some common trollop.

Wesley winced. It wasn't every day that a man was confronted with what he'd become. He didn't much like himself.

And he didn't want to be this contemptible man, one whom he didn't recognize.

Wesley set his half-empty glass down on a nearby side table, and, quitting his offices, he bypassed the bellpull to summon servants and headed to the stables to clear his head. The moment he entered, the servants who'd already risen and begun their day's work instantly stopped.

The head groom, Harold, rushed over. "Your Grace. Is there anything I can help you with?"

"I was coming to saddle my horse," he said.

The crimson-clad servant looked to one of the younger grooms and motioned for him to see to that task.

Wesley stayed them with a hand. "I'll see to it."

He may as well have stated his intentions to sack the lot of them and turn them out for the shock and horror that greeted Wesley's pronouncement.

"But . . . Your Grace." Harold spoke haltingly. "Is there something wrong with the work we'd been doing thus far with your mou—"

"It is not that, at all," Wesley assured him. "I—"

Want to go back to a point and time when I was just a man, doing normal tasks that average people do.

"I merely wish to see to the task myself," he finished.

He headed for the stall that housed Mine. As Wesley strode the graveled path, the servants parted to either side of the stables and bowed as he passed.

Wesley reached Mine's stall, and the midnight horse, purchased as a gift by the duke when Wesley had first enlisted, pawed the floor.

Shrugging out of his jacket, Wesley rested the wool garment on a nearby hay bale and let himself inside.

"Someone is happy to see me," he murmured softly, scratching the gleaming black mount on his withers. "Not that I can understand why," he added.

Mine tossed his head.

A short while later, after he'd brushed and saddled the horse, Wesley guided him on to the closest feeling thing to the hills of Staffordshire. Entering Hyde Park, Wesley urged Mine into a canter. The minute the mount's hooves hit the riding trail, Wesley shortened the reins, and holding his own way over the back of the horse, he turned Mine over to a full gallop, freeing the beautiful creature.

Wesley became one with Mine's strides. The pounding of his horse's hooves and the churn of gravel filled Wesley's ears. The sounds of them, soothing for their ordinariness. They weren't the screams and wails of agony that haunted his waking and sleeping thoughts. Nor the entreaties and shouts, mingling in different tongues, from men who'd made a last plea to live before their opponent's bayonet blade found its mark.

In this instant, the Peninsular melted away, as Mine's heavy breathing melded with Wesley's increased respirations. The cool air hit his heated face, and he welcomed the soothing balm. In this instant, one with a horse and alone in the park, he could almost forget all his greatest transgressions and sins—sins that were not exclusive to the things he'd done in the name of war, but also his actions upon returning.

He'd kissed Ellie Balfour, and last night, on Lord Davenport's terrace, he'd wanted to take her in his arms again.

He'd wanted to run his hands all over her and lose himself in her.

And then, as if he'd conjured her of his own sinful hungering, she was there in the distance.

Alone, without the benefit of even a maid or groom, like some fairy creature, she led her white mount through the morning mist.

She paused to loop her reins about a hitching post, and then, stroking the animal between the eyes, she collected her parasol and headed for the slight outcrop of woods.

Wesley followed her with his gaze until she disappeared, lost to the morning fog and swallowed by those tall oaks, so that he wondered if he'd in fact dreamed her up this day.

He should leave, and yet . . .

Once more, she was alone, without a chaperone. Any number of harmful scenarios might befall her. That was the only reason Wesley found himself tying his own horse to a nearby post and setting after Ellie.

Chapter 16

My dearest Wesley,

*I despise crowds. I very much prefer the solace and
peace to be had beside a lake, without anyone else
about. Someday, I would find a hidden part of earth that
is only ours, and we can live in a world no one else
knows.*

Lovingly Yours

Seated in the wooden copse on the side of the Serpentine,
Ellie chucked a rock at her visage reflected back in the
placid, glass-like surface of the lake. Her stone landed with
a *plunk* and sent ripples fanning over the water, until her
image reappeared smooth and intact.

After Wesley's leg had been healed by Mrs. Porter, Ellie
hadn't known what she'd expected. Perhaps that he'd be less
bitter, and less cynical, and more like the man whom she'd
fallen in love with years earlier. But he hadn't been.

Instead, he'd disappeared from her life, and the only

glimpses she'd caught of him were in vague mentions of which club he was attending from the gossip pages.

Her own life experience should have taught her that while wounds on the surface heal, the ones inside prove greater and longer-lasting. Foolishly, with all the time she'd spent with him, she'd thought she might mean more to him. That he might come to care for her even a little. But he hadn't. Nothing had changed.

That was, aside from the cynical fellow he'd since shaped himself into.

But for one instant last night, when she'd first caught Wesley standing there, she'd believed that he'd come for her.

Ellie stared at her own slender visage, and with a sound of disgust, kicked the bottom of her heel at the edge of the water, disrupting the glass-like surface, and briefly erasing her own image from it.

She should have known better. Wesley had never seen her in that light. She'd just . . . hoped that he might have come to view her as more than just Little Ellie, the girl he'd played make-believe with.

She tossed the last large rock in her hand at the lake, and it hit with a big, satisfying splash, sending little droplets raining down on the surface around it. Ellie stared as she dusted her gloveless palms together.

The trees overhead rustled, sending the leaves upon their branches dancing in the wind of an impending storm.

Crack.

She stiffened at that snap of brush, and then a shiver of awareness moved along her spine as she felt him.

Ellie cast a glance over her shoulder. "Spying on me, are you?"

A ghost of a smile hovered on Wesley's lips. "I had it on the authority of my sister that you spent many mornings here." He glanced about at their surroundings. "Hiding in the bushes, are you, little general?"

She gave her head a little toss. "I'll have you know," she said archly in return, "it is a time-honored strategy that goes back hundreds of hundreds of years. The Goths, Van-

dals, Scythians, and Huns all used the shroud of their surroundings to fight the Persian and Roman Empires."

"Then you are at war with someone, little general?"

There was a smile in his voice—the light, teasing, un-
cynical one that had existed years before.

"I'm at war with a whole number of someones," she muttered. The sea of suitors hounding her, looking for that which
she'd never give them—marriage.

Wesley touched his index finger to the lobe of his ear.
"What was that?"

"You don't need that anymore, you know," she said. "Your
cane."

"That is not what you said."

"If you know, then why ask?"

"But I shall allow you your prevarication, my lady."

"As for the cane," he said as, strolling over with his
smooth-once-more strides, he joined her, "it lends me a
dashing air." He twirled that cane—a new one, gold and
ornate and different than that wooden one he'd used upon
his return—at his shoulder. "Does it not?"

Ellie looked Wesley up and then down. "If one prefers a
purely affected gentleman, who goes about with props."

"Ah, but that is what all the papers are saying about the
cane, anyway."

"We are now taking the London gossip rags as an authority on anything?" she drawled. "If that is the case, you
might wish to add a monocle to your collection, *Your Grace*."

Amusement danced in his eyes, and Ellie hated that her
heart should flutter so, still with this jaded, harder version
of the man she'd once known.

Wesley leaned over the head of that article that had
sparked their current debate. "Tell me, do ladies find old,
monocle-wearing dukes appealing, little general?"

He'd managed to add a layer of mockery into what had
once been an endearment.

"We find sincere men who don't flaunt their wealth and
title appealing."

Ellie scooped up a pile of rocks, returned her attention

to the lake, and proceeded to toss them into the smooth waters.

He chuckled, and then as easily as he'd once done years ago, dropped onto the ground beside her.

Ellie gave him a look and edged her skirts away.

Surprise filled his features. "You're annoyed by my company."

"A gentleman like you would be surprised by that," she muttered.

"'A gentleman like me,' you say? I wasn't aware I was a type of gentleman."

"Yes, well, you are, and I do not mean that in a good way, Your Grace. Since your return, you've used your new status for nothing but your own pleasures."

He chuckled.

The lout. Only Wesley Audley would find amusement with that set-down.

She wrinkled her nose and he tweaked the end of it. Only he lingered, brushing the pad of his finger over the tip, and then, with a movement so slight she could have taken it for accidental, he slid that digit a hint lower to the top of her lip.

The teasing faded from his eyes, replaced with a more serious, heated spark. "Tell me, little general. Whose pleasures should I consider?"

Her chest hitched in a noiseless inhale at the soft seductiveness of that gentle caress and the less than subtle innuendo within his query.

Thunder rumbled, with the earth under her feet trembling from the impending storm, a warning sent her way from the heavens about this man and her feelings for him.

"You can use your wealth and power to help others who may need it. Orphans. The disabled. Street beggars."

"Ah, and here I thought you were referring to yourself."

"As I said last evening, I've no interest in being some rogue's conquest, and that includes you, Wesley," she said quietly.

He smiled lazily. "Ah, but you're different, Ellie-girl."

But for that "Ellie-girl," another might have taken Wesley's admission for a promise of something more. She knew him all too well. She knew all the affection he might show anyone—herself included—was purely feigned. She knew it because she'd witnessed firsthand what a true interest and regard looked like from this man, when he'd bestowed it upon his Miss Sparrow.

"Nothing to say," Wesley murmured, removing a flask from inside his jacket.

Uncorking the silver bottle, he availed himself of a sip. "I'll have you know, any number of women would be all too eager to receive such a compliment."

"As you yourself pointed out, I'm different." She gave him an arch look. "It will take a good deal more to snare my notice than such a flippant endearment."

"Flippant, is it?" he drawled.

"Indeed. I've had gentlemen call me their 'greatest heart's desire,' 'dear heart,' 'light of my life.'"

"And yet, none of those gentlemen with those lavish compliments managed to win you or woo you."

Ellie wrinkled her nose. Drat him for being on the mark. She quickly recovered. "Not *yet*," she said. Not ever.

His eyes instantly hardened, the teasing glimmer going out, and Ellie could almost believe in that moment he was bothered by the thought of her with another, which was of course preposterous. He'd never cared about Ellie in that way. He'd only ever seen her as a friend, and nothing more.

"And who will this paragon of a suitor be, Ellie?" he asked.

"The man who would earn my affections would not be one to lose himself in drink and spending his night with various paramours or one who'd simply cut me from his life." As Wesley had.

She'd expected so much more of him, and she hated that her heart should hurt so at the realization of not only how little she'd mattered to him, but whom he'd ultimately become.

Ellie gave a toss of her head, and, gathering her parasol, she stood, popped open that white lace article at her shoulder, and made to leave.

Good. She was leaving. She'd formed the same ill opinion as his family and society on the whole. It was better that way. He was better without someone pure and good and there to remind him that he was anything but anymore.

Before he could stop himself, Wesley called after her retreating form. "I didn't cut you from my life."

He raked a hand through his hair. "At least, not . . . deliberately."

She continued her forward stride without a hitch in her movement, and then ever so slowly, stopped.

She turned around, facing him. "You accidentally cut me out of your life, then?"

Hurt bled from her question and her eyes, and each hint of her pain hit him like a blow to the chest.

She thumped a fist against her breast. "I thought you were my friend."

"You were. We are."

"Friends don't just disappear, Wesley," she cried. "They stay with someone through the darkest times, and the good ones, too."

"If it is any consolation, there's been no good ones since you, Ellie-girl."

She shook her head and took a step to leave.

"I'm serious," he called, staying her. "I . . . did enjoy our time together. That is no lie."

"Then why—?"

"Because I hate that you saw me how I was!" he exclaimed. "I couldn't face you after that. How could I?"

Her features softened. "Wesley, there was no shame in your response to such horror."

Wesley swiped a hand over his face. "For me, there was. I . . . I wet myself," he dropped his voice to an agony-laced whisper.

"Any person would."

"But I did. And seeing you, Ellie . . . reminded me of the moment I'd been at my absolute lowest. And so I did not know how to face you." He lifted an arm. "There you have it. I'm a bloody coward."

"You're no coward," she said softly. Opening her parasol, she rested it at her left shoulder.

Sadness filled her eyes once more. "None of that changes the fact of who . . . what you've become."

A rake.

He'd faced bloody skirmishes and deadly battles he'd prefer to being exposed before her in this way.

"There haven't been any women, Ellie." Somehow, for reasons he couldn't quite understand, it seemed suddenly important she know that.

Ellie angled her parasol back a fraction and eyed him warily.

"I've read the papers, Wesley. They write quite freely about your conquests."

"They also write quite freely about you and the Duke of Stenton. Are they correct in saying you're days away from accepting his offer?"

It was rumored the gentleman had set aside his roguish ways the minute Ellie Balfour made her Come Out, and that he'd been undeterred thus far in trying to woo Society's diamond of the first waters. Wesley had despised him on mention and hated him last evening on sight.

"Hmm?" he asked, when Ellie remained blasted silent, neither confirming, nor worse, denying that connection.

"He is charming," she said. "Exceedingly handsome."

Exceedingly handsome. The Duke of Stenton was tall, strappingly put together, and without a scar upon his olive-hued visage. Wesley's fingers curled reflexively upon the smooth head of his cane.

Ellie wasn't done.

"He's clever and tells a fine joke."

There'd once been a time Wesley had always been ready with a jest.

"I could certainly do far worse than marrying the duke," she said.

And something that felt very much like jealousy ran hot through his veins.

"He sounds like a regular ole paragon," he said between gritted teeth.

Jealousy? This visceral rage merely stemmed from the fact he'd known Ellie since she'd been a girl, and felt a sense of obligation where she was concerned.

"Well, he doesn't go about pulling a flask from his pocket in the middle of our conversations together. So there is that."

"It doesn't escape me that you've not answered my question. Are the papers right about you and Stenton?" he murmured.

She hesitated.

"No, they aren't," she muttered, glancing over at the waters.

Her admission sent an odd, welcome lightness to his chest. Only because Ellie deserved more than a pompous, roguish duke—even if the gent was dashing in all the ways she'd said, and seemingly reformed.

"Not Stenton, then," he murmured, more pleased than he ought be at that truth. "What of your army of suitors?"

"What of them?"

"Surely one among them has snagged your affections, Ellie?"

"I'm not marrying."

He stared confusedly at her.

"Ever," she clarified. "I've no desire to marry."

He rocked back on his heels. "Impossible."

She flashed a wry grin. "Do you have a desire to marry?"

"I did, but no longer." His mouth pulled. "That's different."

"It's not. Not really. Men decide all the time for all manner of reasons that they wish to remain bachelors."

Ellie nibbled at her lower lip, inadvertently bringing his

attention to the flesh he'd tasted just once, and secretly—shamefully—thought of too many times after.

"You are saying what they write about you is . . . just gossip, too?" she ventured.

He tried to make sense of the almost hopeful quality to her question and failed.

"When I went to war, I left behind a sweetheart."

"Claire," she supplied softly.

Surprise brought his eyebrows up. "You heard of her, then."

Color filled her cheeks. "I . . ."

"Of course our families would have spoken of her," he murmured. "Yes, she is the one I was speaking of. I was faithful to her the entire time I served, and when I returned . . ." He grimaced. "Well, you saw what I'd become."

"I saw you were a man who returned from battle, bearing marks of your honor, courage, and strength."

A bitter laugh bubbled past his lips. "Honor, courage, strength," he spat out that naïve list of compliments.

"The papers are correct to an extent, Ellie. I do drink entirely too much and I enjoy cards more than I once had, but as for the string of widows warming my bed?" His frustration mounted. "What do you want me to say?" he whispered harshly, striding over. "Do you want me to tell you how my body is riddled with scars and I cannot bear to expose them to anyone?"

"Oh, Wesley," she whispered, that sound so pitying, it set his teeth on edge.

"The thing of it is, Ellie, I thought if my leg had not been damaged, and as grotesquely as it had been, that I could have had a normal life. That I could return and go for Claire and fight her father for her, as I'd been unable to do before I left. I'd be whole, and I'd proven myself."

He briefly closed his eyes.

"I was so fixed on the damage done to my leg that I didn't even give a proper thought to all the worse ways in which

I'd been broken. Ways that can't be fixed," he finished on a ragged whisper. His mind. His mind was thoroughly ravaged, with no hope of healing.

Soft fingers touched his sleeve, and Wesley stiffened.

"If she loves you, she will love you for who you are *now*," Ellie said softly. "She will hold you through your nightmares and build with you newer, joy-filled memories to fill the places where only the dark ones now dwell."

She, this woman before him, painted an image so very real—of Wesley adding new stories to his life. Stories that were not shrouded in darkness and horror and the ugliness of war. In his mind's eye, he tried to drag forth the image of Claire beside him in it, and yet, her face remained amorphous, shadowy, and incomplete.

Because Wesley knew his fate. That was why. Strangely, when he imagined a future, it wasn't one with Claire Sparrow in it. Perhaps this was another way war had left him numb and unfeeling. He expected the finality of the ending of his relationship with Claire Sparrow should hurt more than it did. That it should hurt, at all.

"You can still have a future with her, Wesley," Ellie said, following so very close to where his thoughts had been, as only she'd been able to since his return.

Ellie continued. "Because you are scarred, you think you are somehow unworthy of her."

Only it wasn't Claire he thought of.

"I know I'm hideous," he said tiredly. "I know precisely what I look like, and the idea of baring those marks for *anyone* to see?" Wesley shook his head.

He couldn't do it.

Ellie stared at him for a long while, and he wanted her to say something, anything, rather than leaving them in this tense silence, exposed, with all his insecurities on full display before her.

Then she lowered her parasol, dropping it beside her, where it landed with a little *thwack* upon old, dried brush. And then, with her solemn eyes locked with his, Ellie touched the delicate fabric of her sheer puff sleeve and slowly tugged at first one pale blue silk organza, and then the next.

Like those sirens of lore, Ellie edged the bodice of her silk dress down. Lower. Ever lower.

His mouth went dry.

"Ellie." Her name was a hoarse prayer. An entreaty for her to stop warred with a far greater plea for her to continue baring herself before him.

And there proved to be a God after all, for she pushed the dress down about her waist. Her chemise followed suit.

A powerful, raw wave of lust bolted through him, and Wesley's eyes slid briefly closed. When he opened them once more, he devoured the sight of the proud, regal woman before him. He worked his gaze over her, lingering his eyes on the delicate pink tips of high-set breasts. The small pea-sized brown birthmark on the left swell, a flawless cream mound the perfect size for his palm. Her smooth skin was a warm shade of olive as if she played naked in the summer sun, and wore the remnants of those games still.

And there in that copse, as she revealed herself before him, Wesley confronted the shameful truth he'd long buried and had, until this very moment, fought himself on: he wanted her.

Long before he'd kissed her, but after his return from war, and certainly longer than could ever be deemed appropriate, he'd hungered for Ellie Balfour.

With all the noble bearing of a queen, Ellie held his gaze, her directness better suited to a woman two decades her senior.

Then, she turned.

Wesley went motionless.

His body, previously hot, now went cold, and his desire withered on the sinful vine of which it had previously flourished. All the air trapped in his lungs escaped him on a whispery hiss, as through Wesley's shock came a fierce and bestial rage, far darker and more volatile than any he'd known in the heart of battle.

Thin white scars marred the expanse of Ellie's bared back, in a crisscross of uneven flesh. Someone had put a lash to her skin and left their marks forever upon her, this spirited, clever, joy-filled woman.

When Wesley learned the name of the one who'd done this to her, when he found the monster who'd dared touch her, he'd kill him with his bare hands, then bring him back to life so that he could kill him all over again.

"Who?" His voice emerged on a steely whisper.

"My father," she murmured. "Knowing me as you do, you can probably imagine the manner of child I was."

She'd have been spirited and spritely and joy-filled.

Ellie pulled her chemise back into place. "I was *very* stubborn and found myself in all sorts of mischief. I ran through a number of governesses before I landed on one particularly stern, nasty woman who reported frequently to my father and declared the only way to cure me of my unruly behavior was that I be beaten regularly. He oversaw the task himself."

How very matter-of-factly she spoke. As if they discussed the rainy weather they'd been having or the latest book she'd plucked from the duke's library and not the marks made upon her by her father.

"When I secretly wished for a father to be involved in my life, I assure you that is *not* what I had in mind." She laughed, that sound strained and slightly pitched, so that it hovered in a place where amusement ended and tears began.

Wesley turned to stone as a hideous thought whispered forward.

His tongue grew thick, and his mouth heavy, making it impossible to form words.

Because to ask the question he already knew the answer to would make every horror in his head true. It would mean the agony he'd known just recently, as a grown man in the bonesetter's office, had been one Ellie had suffered through, and as a small child at that.

Somehow he found the will to ask. "That is how you knew of Mrs. Porter, isn't it?"

She hesitated, and then nodded. "One time, the duke shoved me into a wall, and my shoulder popped right out. The duke said he was of a mind to leave me deformed as a reminder of my sins, except it would mean no man would ever marry me, and make me completely useless to him."

Rage, furious and bestial, roared to life inside of Wesley.

How many times had he gone about bemoaning his fate? He'd simply assumed based on nothing that Ellie couldn't possibly know a hint of the strife he had. What a bloody, stupid, self-absorbed arse he'd been. When all along, she'd endured far more, far worse, and when she'd been far younger.

"Oh, Ellie," he whispered, his voice hoarse, his soul ravaged. He stretched a hand to her, needing to touch her, and yet afraid to do so.

Ellie ignored that offering, and Wesley let his arm fall uselessly back to his side.

"He used to pull me by my hair." She touched that mass of curls piled atop her head. "And so one day, I took a pair of garden shears and just chopped it all off."

She smiled a big, dimpled grin.

"That is why you wore your hair short."

She nodded. "That way, he couldn't grab it. If he wanted to put his hands upon me, to hell with him. I'd have some control over myself."

Oh, god. He wouldn't survive this. A vise caught about Wesley's heart and squeezed. Every single part of him, inside and out, hurt.

"This is why you don't wish to marry," he said.

Ellie nodded, and Wesley stared on, achingly, as she struggled to right her dress.

Wordlessly, he went over, crossing that slight divide she'd put between them.

"Here," he murmured, and then stopped, refusing to touch her without permission. "May I help you?"

Ellie nodded slowly, and then wordlessly, he helped guide her arms into those delicate sleeves.

All the while, he considered what she'd revealed this

day. At last, her insistence that she'd never marry made all the sense in the world. It was why and how she spoke so easily of remaining unwed. Given she'd been so cruelly treated at the hands of the one man who, above all else and all others, should have loved her and protected her, why should she trust any man?

Wesley drew the silk top into place until she was fully covered once more.

"They are hideous," Ellie said.

He gripped her gently by the shoulders. "You are beautiful," he said sharply, willing her to see that. To understand that.

Wesley softened his tone and touch even more, running the pads of his thumbs in small circles along the skin exposed just under her sleeve.

"They are marks of your strength and spirit, Ellie."

"My strength?" She scoffed. "If I'd been strong, I'd not wear the marks I do. It was my spirit that got me into that trouble, and my spirit that kept me there."

Another wave of fury coursed through him, and something else, something more—a deep admiration for this woman before him.

"Any other person would have become a shadow under such abuse, Ellie. You not only survived, you did so while managing to somehow smile. You never allowed him to crush your spirit."

Ellie shrugged. "I know precisely what I look like, and the idea of baring those marks for *anyone* to see?"

He opened his mouth to fight her on that point, and suddenly stopped.

His words. Those were his words she now spoke.

"It is different, Ellie," he said, releasing her.

"It's only different in one way. You earned yours for heroics upon a battlefield. I? I wear the scars of my misdeeds. Any husband who saw such marks would ultimately wonder what wickedness lives in my soul and punish me mightily, as he sees fit."

"I'd kill him."

"There won't be a 'him.'" She gave a dismissive little wave of her hand. "Do you think me hideous?" she asked instead.

"No!" That denial exploded from him, that adamancy born of truth.

She smiled. "They certainly aren't beautiful."

They were, because they were part of her and the story of her triumph over darkness and evil. He knew this woman enough to know she'd dismiss all his protestations.

Ellie caught his hands in hers and lightly squeezed. "But I do believe you do not judge me for what happened, and you accept me, scars and all . . . and so, mayhap not Claire, but another woman? She will accept you and love you as you are, too."

Something again shifted in the air all around them, charged from the impending storm and the tumult that had been unleashed in this wooded sanctuary.

His and Ellie's eyes locked, and then slowly, as if moving in a like rhythm, he dipped his head lower as she tipped her head up. They paused, hovering a fraction, before each shifting closer another inch.

The sweet, fragrant hint of violets filled his senses, and he breathed deeply of it—and of her.

Ellie's lashes fluttered.

The slow pitter of rain striking the leaves overhead filled the copse, and then it was as if gates were opened, and the sky opened up, that deluge shattering the moment.

Wesley hurried to retrieve Ellie's parasol. The moment he had it in hand, he popped the article open and held it over the two of them. The water ran in rivulets down the sides of the small tent they shared.

"Your maid?" he shouted over the raging storm.

"She is nearby, with an umbrella of her own," Ellie called.

As if on cue, there came a distant shout. "My lady?"

Wesley and Ellie looked toward that approaching voice.

They could not be discovered here. Not without raising questions, and worse, a potential scandal for Ellie. He swiftly ducked out from under the umbrella. Their siblings might be joined by marriage, but Ellie was still an unwed lady, and Wesley a bachelor.

Ellie gave him a long look, and, collecting her hems in one hand, she bolted.

Then came her voice from some ten or so yards away. "I'm here, Eloise!"

Wesley remained rooted to the spot long after she'd left. The rain battered his garments and sent water running in rivulets down his face, until his eyes were blurred from that steady stream of drops. All the while, he played each word Ellie had shared over and over in his mind; he let the rage, the agony, and the regret for all she'd endured batter at his soul.

How many times had he spoken to Ellie about his own pain, all the while oblivious to the suffering she'd endured? He'd lamented over *his* losses and even outright accused her of knowing nothing about pain, when all along, the hell he'd suffered had come from a decision he'd made. He'd set out on a quest for greatness and had seen the military as his way to rise up from his meager station and establish his own worth in the world.

Ellie? The demons that surely haunted her still were ones from no fault of her own.

She swore she'd never marry.

And secretly, shamefully, Wesley was glad for it. In large part, because no man was good enough for her. In larger part, for reasons that were entirely selfish. The idea of her in another man's arms drove him to a madness greater than any demons that haunted him upon the battlefield.

Chapter 17

My dearest Wesley,

I have never understood the fascination with spirits or lemonade. They're both vile in their own right. One too weak. One too strong. I daresay I'd far rather they melt frozen ices so that people might drink something truly delectable.

Lovingly Yours

From where she sat in the Duke of Mowbray's ballroom, surrounded by a sea of swains, Ellie did a search for Wesley.

He was sure to be here. Though Wesley avoided respectable events held by the *ton*, he'd not miss one thrown by his father's dearest friends.

It'd been two days since Ellie had revealed her scars—and story—to Wesley. She'd never believed there could be or would be another she'd feel safe sharing those truths with.

Until Wesley.

And now . . . she didn't know how to be around him.

Mayhap you won't have to worry about it . . .

After all, he'd made no attempt to seek her out after their last meeting. Why should he? There'd been nothing for him to say.

The gentleman at her shoulder spoke, pulling Ellie from her musings of Wesley. "You are quiet this evening."

Ellie glanced over at the Duke of Stenton. Tall, blond, charming, and exceedingly handsome, any lady would have been grateful for his attentions. Ellie, however, would have been grateful had he been content to remain nothing more than a dear friend who managed to make her smile, and whom she managed to make smile in return.

He stared at her from under thick, long golden eyelashes most ladies would have sold their souls for.

Ellie touched a hand to her throat. "I'm afraid I am parched, and my throat—"

She'd no sooner spoken the words than the ten or so gentlemen hanging about her bolted for the Duke and Duchess of Bentley's refreshments table, leaving Ellie and the young duke alone.

"That is convenient, is it not?" the duke drawled, eyeing the men scrambling toward the lemonade.

"Convenient because I'm likely to find myself with ten glasses of lemonade, Your Grace?"

"We can split them, five each."

She snorted. "And here I thought you were a serious suitor. A serious suitor would have heroically offered to down all ten glasses of the tepid, watered-down drinks himself."

His Grace tossed his head back, shouting his laughter at the muraled ceiling overhead.

She'd learned from her father that one could tell much about a person by the manner of lines they wore in their face. The late duke's mouth had been set to a perpetual scowl that had left him with harsh lines at the corners of his lips. The duke before her had crinkles of mirth at the corners of his eyes. As such, he should at the very least be a gentleman whose suit she considered.

But she couldn't bring herself around to the idea of marrying him or anyone.

Suddenly, the duke's features grew serious. "If I thought drinking tepid lemonade would earn me even a smidgeon of your affections, I'd down the entire punch bowl, lady mine."

Lady mine. It was the boldest of the endearments and compliments that had been affixed to her by any of the gentlemen vying for her attention. But then, he was a duke, and dukes were afforded liberties and luxuries that others—aside from the king and queen—were not.

He caught her hand in his, in a touch that was bold, familiar, and also gentle.

"You don't really know me, Your Grace."

"I know you tell jokes when you're uncomfortable as a way to release your tension." Retaining his hold on her, the duke shifted closer. "I know you've two dimples that only make an appearance when you're *truly* smiling, and not merely feigning amusement."

Unnerved, Ellie glanced at the immaculate folds of his white cravat peeking out from his dark tapestry waistcoat.

And then, she felt him. Shivers tripped along her spine, a delicious energy that moved quickly through her being.

Every set of eyes in the ballroom went to the entrance, because the powerful figure standing there possessed the manner of aura that made a person stop and stare, and Ellie found herself included among those ranks.

Wesley strode through the crowded room, moving past a sea of guests who parted for him.

All the while, Wesley moved his gaze over the guests, as if he were searching for someone.

Me. He is searching for me.

As soon as that thought whispered forward, a taunting voice at the back of her mind reminded her that if that were the case, he'd have sought her out one of these two days prior.

Then Wesley's stare landed on her, and everything melted away: The boisterous laughter from the crowd became a distant tinkling. The whiny hum of the violins' strings faded into a dull background noise. And everyone, but for him, melted away, dissolving into the shadows.

Even with the length between them, his piercing eyes burned her, warming her inside and out as she'd previously thought only that hottest of summer suns could.

Ellie's heart quickened.

Suddenly, he shifted his focus the tiniest fraction to a point and person just at her shoulder.

Wesley's eyes narrowed into thin, hard, and dangerous slits.

"Lady Ellie? *Ellie?*"

Ellie came whirring to the present, and she jerked her attention back toward the Duke of Stenton, an *actual* suitor who did seek her out. One who now stared concernedly back at Ellie.

"Forgive me," she said on a rush.

"Never tell me: your throat continues to ail you." As he spoke, the young duke shifted his attention to someone across the way. "Or perhaps there is another source behind your . . . silence."

She both heard in his tone and saw in his eyes that he no sooner believed a sore throat had been the source of her distraction, but rather the gentleman whom he now studied in a way that only a rival competitor could.

Ellie balled her hands.

Suddenly, a small stampeding army bearing down with glasses converged upon Ellie and the duke, and it marked the first time in the whole of her miserable Season she found herself grateful for that attention. For their arrival saved her from the Duke of Stenton's bold line of questioning.

If there'd ever been a doubt as to Stenton's feelings, it'd died when the wiry-built lord caught Wesley's focus on Ellie.

The other man's eyes had narrowed on Wesley, and his jawline hardened, only softening once more when he directed his attention to Ellie—where it had since remained. Even with the sea of suitors surrounding them, the gentleman had staked a clear claim and position above the lot.

An unpleasant emotion slithered within Wesley, a redhot, fiery fury that felt a good deal like jealousy—which was preposterous. Of course he wasn't jealous of the other man's interest.

Nay, it was more a matter that Ellie would hate the seriousness of that suitor's intentions, and after all she'd shared in those private woods in Hyde Park, he well understood why.

Wesley looked to his sister and brother-in-law, who stood nearby, supposedly guarding over Ellie. The happily married couple, however, remained engrossed in private discussion. Courtland whispered something into Cailin's ear that immediately raised a blush.

What the hell were they doing? Flirting with one another instead of watching over Ellie and that crush of courters.

Annoyance tightened in his belly as he returned his study to Ellie.

Ellie and the dapper fellow without a single scar upon his unblemished, entirely too-handsome face. That same gentleman who just then took Ellie's gloved hand in his and raised it to his lips for a k—

A pair of guests stepped between Wesley and Ellie and that ardent admirer, and a growl of frustration rumbled in his chest—until he registered the entirely too-amused person who'd blocked his view.

"Rafe," he said dumbly, and then swiftly recovered, with a greeting for his sister-in-law. "Edwina."

The always-cheerful woman clapped her hands. "It is so very wonderful to see you here."

Rafe flashed a crooked grin. "What my wife is really saying is it's *unexpected* seeing you here."

"Yes, that." As if realizing what she'd admitted to, Edwina blinked her big eyes quickly. "*And* wonderful, of course."

"Of course," Wesley drawled.

"You must forgive our surprise," Rafe said. "For here I

thought I'd be more likely to see a hog fly then find you at a *respectable ton* event."

"In case I needed to remind you, I previously *attended* such an event," he felt inclined to point out.

The first having been when he'd caught sight of Ellie in all her pale-blue silk glory and noted for the first time the siren she'd in fact become, and he'd not been right in the head since.

"Ah, but that one was coerced."

"Do behave." Rafe's always-smiling wife, Edwina, gave her husband's arm a light pinch.

Rafe merely grinned at her in return.

"Who is misbehaving?"

Wesley, Rafe, and Edwina looked to the arrival of Cailin and Courtland.

As one, Wesley and Rafe pointed at one another. Edwina, however, had an index finger fixed firmly on each brother.

"Now, that makes sense," Cailin drawled, and then coming forward, she went up on tiptoe and kissed Wesley's cheek. "You came!" she said happily.

"He wouldn't have missed a respectable ball for the world," Rafe said dryly.

Edwina sighed. "You are not going to behave, are you?"

Rafe's grin widened. "Never."

"I'm taking this one to dance," Edwina said to their group, and then, catching her husband by the hand, pulled him along to the floor just assembling for the latest set.

"Thank you," Wesley called after his sister-in-law, earning a more familiar scowl from his brother.

Rafe's groan faded as he and Edwina dissolved into the crowd.

Wesley stared at the pair. There'd once been a time when he'd dreamed of that close relationship for himself. Given Claire's relationship to the head of Cheadle mines, they hadn't been free to share in anything that would have earned notice. The time they'd snatched had been clandestine and quick. After his return from battle, he'd simply resigned himself to the fact that he'd never have that which he'd longed for.

His gaze moved of its own will, and he looked to Ellie.

Ellie, who at that moment also happened to pull her attention from the Golden Swain, and over to Wesley.

Their stares locked, and even with the length of the room, a magnetized heat radiated between them.

"It's hard to believe," Cailin said, breaking that connection.

Heat climbed his neck as he looked questioningly over at his sister.

She gestured to Rafe and Edwina. "Our brother dancing and doing so happily."

She'd assumed he'd been looking somewhere other than where he had been. Relieved, Wesley studied Rafe and Edwina twirling through the steps of a waltz with an effortless grace. "The change is unexpected."

It was hard to reconcile his once-scowling, grumpy brother with this teasing, smiling fellow.

Which only recalled his thoughts to a different teasing, smiling fellow.

He turned a glare on his brother-in-law. "Don't you have other responsibilities to see to?"

St. James didn't blink. "Er . . . uh . . ."

Er? Uh?

"Your sister," Wesley gritted out.

"Ellie assured us we might excuse ourselves a moment and come greet you," Cailin explained.

Well, he'd have rather they stayed and kept an eye on Stenton. Only a damned cherub would have locks that blond, and with the bold, possessive way he watched Ellie, the man was no damned angel.

He gritted his teeth.

"You may get back to it," he said to his sister and brother-in-law.

As if Wesley had been telling a hilarious jest, and not been absolutely deadly serious, Cailin laughed.

"Either way," Cailin said, when her amusement faded. "She is with Hattie."

As in the eldest of Courtland's sisters. Unwed and seated on a nearby chair, so engrossed in the book she was buried behind she'd wouldn't have known if the room had caught fire around her. Or, say, the Duke of Stenton breaking all rules of propriety by sitting next to the Balfour sisters and the other women seated there.

"Yes, she seems like quite a reliable companion," he said dryly.

St. James inclined his head. "Indeed."

He was apparently unable to pick out sarcasm.

Wesley slid his focus back across the ballroom, and fury mounted in his belly.

The Golden Swain had her blasted hand in his once more. Weren't there bloody rules of propriety on that matter? And worse, why was Ellie allowing that damned familiar touch?

"Who does the fellow think he is?" That query ripped from his chest in a harsh, sharp tone that brought Cailin and her brother up short.

"Uh?" St. James shook his head and glanced to his wife for help.

Cailin stared confusedly up at Wesley.

Wesley clarified. "The Golden Swain who is entirely too familiar with Ellie," he said between gritted teeth.

Husband and wife followed Wesley's discreet gesture.

"What is his story?" Wesley asked Cailin.

"He's wealthy and was something of a rogue—"

"Was?" Wesley didn't bother to hide his drollness. "He's suddenly transformed?"

"It can happen," his sister said defensively.

St. James piped in. "It *does* happen," he reminded his wife, and one of those intimate looks passed between the besotted pair.

"Oh, for the saints in heaven," Wesley muttered, retrieving a much-needed glass of champagne from the tray of a passing servant.

The color drained from Cailin's cheeks, leaving her a sickly white. "Oh, God."

Even as St. James Wesley stiffened and glanced toward Ellie and whichever bounder who'd triggered that horrified response.

"Miss Sparrow," his sister whispered.

Miss Sparrow?

Cailin gestured, and he followed that discreet point.

And then, he froze.

She stood at the top of the stairway, hovering like an uncertain bird prepared to take flight. Aside from that hesitancy, she was as majestic as she'd ever been; a vision in emerald-green satin, and with her golden-blond hair twisted like a coronet about her head, she was even more beautiful than she'd been all those years ago.

He studied her, expecting to feel a great rush of emotion: Desire. Longing. Regret. Resentment. Something. *Anything.*

Oddly, he stared on with a sense of detachedness, as if he stared at a stranger, and mayhap she was. Perhaps that was all they'd ever been.

Wesley moved his gaze from that woman from his past, over to another.

He narrowed his eyes. This one blond where the other was dark. Widely smiling where the other had always been more measured in her mirth.

And at that precise moment, she bestowed that smile upon the Golden Swain.

Wesley swigged the rest of his drink and set his champagne glass down hard on a passing tray.

"Wesley?" his sister asked, concern in her voice. "Are you all right?"

"Never better," Wesley lied through gritted teeth, and as he started across the ballroom, he'd wager it was an altogether different lady his sister thought he was fuming over.

The crowd of suitors eyed Wesley warily, and hastily stepped out of his path, until he reached her.

Or rather . . . them—the pair at the center of the circle.

Ellie and her duke.

A roguish duke, who didn't wear scars on his face and who'd been born to his station, unlike Wesley, who'd always wear a miner's work on his soul and skin.

The Duke of Stenton's words trailed off. He immediately sized Wesley up. "Smith," he drawled, a layer of ice within that greeting.

Wesley ignored him, all his focus on Ellie, Ellie who stared wide-eyed at Wesley as though shocked or annoyed at his interruption.

"Lady Ellie," he snapped.

She wrinkled her nose. "Your Grace."

"Dance with me," he said, reaching for her hand, that boldness earning gasps from the suitors around them.

Except for Stenton. The duke narrowed his eyes dangerously and made to position himself between Ellie and Wesley.

"Gentlemen, if you will excuse me," she said, with a lightness that instantly defused the tension. "His Grace is determined to discover once and for all what most of you already have—that I'm a rotten dancer."

A series of protests went up, with calls of her accolades trailing after her and Wesley.

"You're not a rotten dancer," he muttered, as they took their place on the dance floor. "You've always been a good enough dancer."

"La, you'll turn my head."

"You've never been one to go fishing for compliments."

She stomped his toe. "And you've never been surly."

"I've been plenty surly."

"Fair enough. I'll have you know," she said, and they twined their fingers, "I do not dance well in L-London."

Her voice trembled slightly as he settled his hand at her waist.

"Just in London?"

Ellie remained laconic. Laconic when previously she'd been chatting happily with Stenton.

The orchestra plucked the strains of the waltz, and he guided them through the sweeping steps.

She remained stiff in his arms.

"Miss Sparrow is here," he said quietly.

Ellie missed a step.

Wesley caught her.

"Your . . . Miss Sparrow?" she whispered.

He nodded, and leading her into another turn, he faced them toward where Claire stood, baldly staring.

Nay, stricken. The lady appeared stricken.

Wesley hardened his jaw and whisked Ellie about. "What grounds does she have to feel stricken?"

"Wesley?" Ellie ventured, and damned if her eyes weren't sad, too.

God, how he despised when she was sad. He lightened his hold and softened his features.

"At least look as though you are enjoying yourself," he gently teased.

"I'm not."

"You're fabulous for a fellow's ego."

"Fellows shouldn't have egos. They have should have self-esteem."

"Fine, that then. And mine is taking a beating under your toes." He winced. "You're doing that on purpose."

"Yes." She smiled and added another impressive stomp.

Wesley's lips twitched. She'd always managed to make him smile, and even this instant, on display before Claire Sparrow and the whole of the London *ton*, proved no exception.

"That is good," he said, his lips barely moving. "Look at me less like you are annoyed by me."

The music came to a stop, and they lingered on the dance floor, he with his arms about her waist, and her fingers in his.

They moved their gazes over one another.

The sudden applause brought them apart, and Wesley and Ellie joined in clapping.

Wesley escorted her from the floor, and being the petty, selfish bastard he was, Wesley guided her away from where the Duke of Stenton waited with the other suitors for her, and steered her over to Courtland and Cailin instead.

Wesley bent over her hand.

"Meet me on the terrace," she whispered, her voice the faintest, softest whisper that froze him briefly as he straightened. "The end of the next set."

Wesley recovered and quickly schooled his features. He remained chatting with Cailin and Courtland several minutes after Ellie claimed she was going to find Hattie.

"If you'll excuse me," he said to Cailin and St. James.

Making his goodbyes, Wesley abandoned his glass on a nearby walnut tripod table and made his way along the perimeter of the ballroom. A short while later, he found his way to his host's gardens, where he found Ellie perched on the wall.

She pumped her legs back and forth in a way reminiscent of when she'd done so on the wooden swing at his father's country estate in Kent.

"You," she greeted.

And he tried to make something out of that single syllable. "Me."

He reached Ellie and rested an elbow on the stone ledge she'd made her bench, and an ugly thought entered his head.

"Do you make it a habit of meeting gentlemen out on the terrace?" he asked, unable to keep the tightness from his question.

Ellie stopped swinging her legs and gave him an odd look. "Which gentleman would I be meeting other than you?"

"Oh, I don't know," he said, in an attempt at being blasé. "The Golden Swain, perhaps."

"The Golden Sw—" Ellie's words trailed off, and then understanding lit her expressive eyes. "The Duke of Stenton."

She'd gathered whom he'd been speaking about.

He gritted his teeth. "That one."

Ellie jumped down, and her satin skirts settled in a quiet *whoosh* about her ankles.

"Meet *him*?" She rolled her eyes. "I'm avoiding him, Wesley."

A lightness filled his chest. "And . . . you wished to see me alone?"

She nodded. "I've been thinking about you."

He stilled.

She'd been thinking about him? What thoughts had she been having, exactly?

"Oh? And just what thoughts were you carrying about me, Ellie-girl?"

"I'd like you to court me."

Chapter 18

My dearest Wesley,

You worry about me giving my heart to another when you are gone. How can you still not know, my heart belongs to you, and only you?

Lovingly Yours

Since she'd made her statement, Wesley had simply stared at her, with an adorable bafflement, for the better part of a minute.

"I . . ." Wesley shook his head, as the remainder of his words failed him.

Since she'd made her Come Out, all Ellie had dreamed of was dancing with Wesley.

In her mind, they'd have done so away from the prying eyes of Polite Society. She would have closed her eyes and simply surrendered to the feel of his arms about her.

In the end, she'd had her dance—not alone. Not even

just in a crowded room . . . but there with his Miss Sparrow watching on.

And undoubtedly, he'd only danced with her because of his Miss Sparrow.

Ellie sighed. "I've gone and made a blunder of all this."

"All of . . . what?"

"My idea."

"Your idea that I court you?" he asked haltingly.

"Yes—"

Wesley's eyebrows flared.

"No! Sort of."

"Can a gentleman *sort of* court a lady?"

"In this case, he can. That is, *you* can."

"Ellie," he began, his tone so hopelessly befuddled, and Ellie smiled.

She took mercy on him. "You see, Wesley—"

"Actually, at this given moment, I don't see anything."

She carried on over his interruption. "It came to me, tonight. While we were dancing . . ."

"It?"

"That you and I, we are *very* similar, but also very different, and because of that, we might help each other."

Wesley continued to stare at her. Exhaling another sigh, Ellie took him by the hands and guided him to the nearby stone bench. "Sit," she ordered, giving the hard wall of his heavily muscled chest a gentle shove.

He complied in what she suspected had far more to do with his need for a seat than any effort on her part of moving his powerful frame.

"As I was saying, during our set, I thought a good deal about our circumstances—my desire never to marry and your greatest wish to wed."

Amusement lit his sky-blue eyes. "My . . . greatest wish is to marry?"

She nodded. "Your Miss Sparrow." That reminder knocked her square in the heart.

The grin froze on his face, and he stared at her with a peculiar expression.

Ellie dropped onto the narrow bench beside him and took his hands in hers. "As we were dancing, it occurred to me that we might help one another. If you court me, and I encourage that courtship, then all my suitors will at last shift their attentions onto some other poor women. And in turn, when your Miss Sparrow sees your affections have shifted, she will be driven to such jealousy and regret having ever spurned you and wish she'd have written you letters in your absence."

The moment she finished, Ellie smiled. "Well?" she urged.

He continued to look at her in that funny way, and the stretch of silence proved so long, and so quiet, that the ticking of his watch fob awkwardly marked the passing seconds.

Ellie's grin slipped. "Surely you have . . . *something* to say."

Only he didn't. For several other agonizingly long moments.

Finally, he spoke. "How does this end, Ellie?" he asked quietly.

She'd not known what she'd expected when she'd blurted out the idea that had popped into her head earlier that evening, when they were dancing. That Wesley would insist he was no longer enamored of his Miss Sparrow, but that he would help Ellie so she could avoid the gentlemen she wished to avoid.

But he didn't. And why should he? A man didn't fall out of love with a woman who looked like that.

"Ellie?" he prodded, and Ellie jumped.

"I am not sure what you are asking. How does this end? As failed courtships do."

"When our relationship goes nowhere, then your suitors will converge once more—"

"By that point, it will be the end of the Season."

"And then, after that?"

"I will deal with that when it comes, Wesley."

"By yourself?"

She nodded. She could not share this with her siblings.

In the glow cast by the moonlight, she studied his opaque

features: The beautiful, harsh planes of his face, which revealed not so much as a hint of what he was thinking. His dark, sooty lashes, lowered as they were, concealed his thoughts, there, too.

He wasn't going to do it. Because he couldn't see Ellie as anything more than the small girl whom he'd taught how to properly handle a sword.

Or mayhap it is merely that he doesn't know how to be around you now that you've revealed your hideous past.

Mortified heat burned up her cheeks.

Suddenly embarrassed by not only having concocted such a scheme, but by having thought he'd ever even entertain the idea, Ellie jumped up. "Forgive me," she said on a rush. "It was a foolish suggestion. If you'll excuse me." With all the grace she could muster, Ellie turned to go.

Wesley stood and caught her gently by the wrist, holding her in place, keeping her there. Just like that, all the embarrassment from before melted away. His strong gloveless fingers on her bare skin sent heat fanning out from that place where he held her.

Ellie's heart hammered—not from fear over a man's touch, but rather a hungering to know even more of it.

"This plan, Ellie," he murmured. "What exactly does it look like?"

What does it look like?

To which *it* did he refer?

Everything was all clumped and jumbled in her mind.

"This pretend courtship," he clarified.

Ellie blinked slowly. Of course. They'd been speaking about the scheme she'd cooked up. Her heart hammered wildly. He was actually entertaining her proposition.

"Well, it would be a courtship," she said. "But *pretend*."

His hard lips twitched at the corners. "Ah, that clarifies things."

"You're teasing."

"Indeed."

And the smile in his voice, and on his lips, met his eyes, and all the tension melted away.

"Given your courtship of Miss Sparrow, you're entirely familiar with what it entails." Her tone sounded arch to her own ears, as the resentment she harbored for that other woman, who'd known Wesley in a way Ellie had all these years longed to, boiled over.

"Our courtship was conducted in secret."

She drew back.

"At the time, I was merely a miner in her father's employ, and she was too fine to wed one of my station." His gaze slid beyond her shoulder, and she knew he'd forgotten Ellie and remembered another.

Her heart seized painfully, and her lungs tightened, too.

"The time we spent together," he said, "was stolen. There was no formal courtship, as that which you propose now."

And Ellie proved both pathetic and small at the possibility of having at least something from this man that his Miss Sparrow never had.

"You've not thought this all through, Ellie," he said, with a hint of finality.

She feigned a breeziness she certainly didn't feel. "I assure you I have. It would entail all the usual parts of a courtship. You might bring me flowers."

"Might?"

"Will."

"We would take a curricle ride through Hyde Park, so everyone can see how deliriously happy and enrapt we are with one another." Ellie warmed to her telling. "Of course, there'd be a visit to Gunter's for frozen ices. You'd snip one of my curls and tuck it close in your jacket so it was close to your heart, always. And . . . and . . . other things," she finished weakly.

Because aside from those mentioned, as a woman who'd foresworn marriage, she'd no other ideas to proffer.

"What are these *other things*?"

Ellie searched her mind. "You must appear to see only me when I enter a room and scowl so darkly at my other suitors that you send them scurrying with nothing more than a look, and you must look at me . . ."

"Yes." He took a step closer, so that she had to tip her head back a fraction to meet his gaze. "How must I look at you, Ellie?"

Her chest rose and fell quickly. "As if I am the only woman in the world," she said, softly. "As though you will perish if you cannot have me."

Heat blazed from within his fathomless blue eyes, scorching all the way to her soul.

"Like this," he murmured huskily.

Ellie managed a nod. Or she thought she did. Wesley's deep, mellifluous baritone washed over her, making her incapable of coherent thought.

Her lashes fluttered. "L-like that."

He lowered his lips close to her ear, and the soft hint of mint and champagne upon his breath proved far headier than those spirits themselves.

"And whisper in your ear so that women envy the secrets I impart, and gentlemen long for that closeness I've stolen," he breathed, and glorious little shivers raced through her being, tickling her, and a breathless giggle slipped from her lips.

"Th-that, too."

"What of stolen touches?"

"S-stolen touches?" she asked, her voice trembling.

This time, he didn't speak. This time, he caught her wrist lightly, tangling his fingers about her in a hold that was as gentle as it was firm. With the pad of his thumb, he pushed the lacy fabric of her glove down and exposed that patch of skin where Ellie's pulse wildly thumped for him and his touch.

"Like this." He rubbed that callused finger, tracing a maddening little circle.

Oh, goodness.

Again, Ellie *tried* to nod. And failed. How could such an innocuous-seeming touch confer such warmth and cause such mayhem in her thoughts and in her breast?

Suddenly, he stopped that mesmerizing caress, and she bit her lower lip hard to keep from crying out with that loss.

But he did not release her. Rather, he continued to hold her, as if he could not let her go.

"How long, Ellie?"

How long? Her heartbeat slowed, and then picked up its wild cadence as she registered what he was asking her. "We're but three weeks from the end of the Season."

"And after that?"

"After that, you will break it off with me, and my heartbreak will be so apparent to all that no one will even bother attempting to court me anymore." After that, they'd go their own ways, and she'd only see him when his family guilted him into giving up his clubs for a proper affair either they or their friends hosted.

Ellie found herself bereft by that eventuality, and she glanced away, past his shoulder to the glass terrace doors.

Wesley brushed his knuckles over her chin and guided her gaze back to his.

"What of an embrace, Ellie?"

"A-an embrace?"

"One powerful and passionate enough so that whenever you see me, it is the kiss you remember and not the ruse."

Oh, God. "That makes c-complete sense. We should, for the g-good of our plan—" Ellie lifted her mouth to his, and then Wesley's was on hers.

There was nothing tender or hesitant about this. He kissed her with all the hungering of a man who wanted her, which was, of course, preposterous. As he'd indicated, this was a kiss only in the name of their scheme.

And yet, her body didn't care for those distinctions. Her body only knew the feel of his hard lips on hers, devouring her, as if he wanted her in truth, as if he wanted her as she yearned for him.

Wesley caught an arm around her waist, drawing her close, and she happily went and melted against him.

Moaning, Ellie parted her lips, and he swept inside to taste of her, and she drank of him in return. They dueled with their tongues, a bold parry and thrust, and she would never again see her rapier without thinking of this glorious, heated sparring.

Wesley slipped a palm under her buttocks, anchoring her close. The hard ridge of his shaft pressed against her belly and the evidence of his desire for her liquefied Ellie inside.

She tangled her tongue with his. A pleased, primitive, masculine growl rumbled in his broad chest, and she felt that tremble all the way through her.

She wanted to climb inside this man and be as close as another person could be to him.

He had been the only man she'd ever wanted and would be the only man she ever did want.

He—

Wesley slowly pulled back, breaking that kiss, ending the magic.

Ellie silently wept at that loss; she'd wanted this moment to last forever. This moment that had been borne of pretend. The reminder of which brought her roaring back to the present and the whole reason Wesley had kissed her in the first place.

Ellie forced her heavy lashes open, and found Wesley's hooded gaze on her.

"Tomorrow," he murmured.

"Tomorrow," Ellie repeated, her voice emerging breathless from his kiss.

And with her legs unsteady beneath her, Ellie turned and took her leave—all the while feeling Wesley's powerful eyes upon her.

Chapter 19

My dearest Wesley,

*You say you regret not having been able to openly court
me while in Staffordshire, and wish to know my dream of
a perfect courtship. I was never much one for flowers.
The ones I do favor are ones that serve a purpose. Ones
that might be a poultice for one in need. I will, however,
confess to loving a fast ride in a curricle. There is
something quite magical in feeling the wind in my hair
and the sun on my face.*

Lovingly Yours

The following morning, during the respectable calling
hour, and also far earlier than he'd been awake for the
better part of the Season, Wesley arrived at his sister's
townhouse to begin his courtship of Ellie Balfour.

Alas, there'd been one small—but very significant—
detail neither of them had given proper thought to . . .

"Wesley!" his sister cried, as with her hands outstretched, she rushed to greet him in the palatial foyer. "It is so very good to see you, and with flow—" Her words trailed off as her gaze landed on the purple-streaked white petals.

"Wood anemones," she blurted.

Wesley's neck went hot. This was going to be deuced awkward to explain.

Misunderstanding the reason for his discomfiture, Cailin quickly found herself.

"They are beautiful," she hurried to assure him, relieving Wesley of the enormous, ribboned bouquet. "They're just a very unexpected flower."

Her eyes twinkled. "As unexpected as your visit, but no less welcomed, of course."

His sister made to hand the arrangement to a nearby servant.

"They are for Ellie," he said, just as she stretched those flowers to a young, blue-clad servant.

Both his sister and the footman froze.

Confusion filled Cailin's eyes. *"Ellie?"*

Taking advantage of her momentarily stunned state, Wesley rescued the offering he'd arrived with from her suspended fingers.

"Yes. *Ellie*," Wesley said.

Cailin just looked at him.

"Graves!"

"Uncle Wesley!"

That jovial greeting from high abovestairs, mingled with the high-pitched calls of children, brought both Wesley's and Cailin's attention skyward.

With a small girl perched atop his shoulders and a young boy at his side, Wesley's brother-in-law made his way carefully downstairs.

Graves. God, how Wesley despised that aptly chosen title.

"Wesley is here," Cailin said as her husband joined them. She reached for the two-year-old girl.

"Mama!" the golden-haired child squealed, hugging her mother tightly around Cailin's neck.

"I see that. How very good it is to see you, Graves," St. James greeted, stretching a hand toward Wesley.

Wesley switched the floral arrangement to his opposite hand and shook the other man's palm in return. "St. James," he said gruffly.

His brother-in-law's gaze landed on the big bouquet. "*And* you've come with flowers. A lovely gesture, that."

"They are for Ellie," Cailin said.

St. James looked dumbly at his wife. "Ellie?" he blurted.

An awkward silence descended between the adults present. All the while, Cailin and St. James's young son, Henry, held his arms out wide at his sides and raced around their legs.

"Imabird," he cried happily. "Imabird!"

Sophia slapped at a still-silent Cailin's cheeks. "Down. I be a bird!"

Cailin instantly complied, lowering her daughter to the marble floor, and a moment later two pretend birds flew all around the adults' legs.

St. James found his voice. *"Ellie?"*

Wesley inclined his head.

"Yes, Ellie," Cailin said. "As in your sister. That is very kind of Wesley. Is it not?"

When the other duke remained silent under that query, Cailin kicked him in the shins.

St. James grunted. "Uh . . . yes? I . . ." He shook his head several times, and then asked the question any wise, protective brother would. *"Why?"*

Cailin glared at her husband.

Alas, given the scheme he'd agreed to take part in, this exchange had been inevitable. Nonetheless, he'd rather subject himself willingly to one of those blackouts that brought him back to war than have this discussion with Ellie's brother.

Wesley cleared his throat. "I . . . thought I might court her?"

Cailin and Courtland continued to stare at him.

Somehow, even the wild children went quiet.

The collection of servants made a show of looking at various parts of the foyer floor.

Feeling much like he had when he'd stolen Arthur Flanders's lunch meal and earned an earful from his eldest brother about that offense, Wesley shifted back and forth on his feet.

Cailin found her voice first. "That is . . . wonderful?"

The slight uptilt that turned her statement into a question proved the most honest part of her response to Wesley's pronouncement.

St. James narrowed his eyes. "*You* wish to court *my* sister."

Nay, Wesley had been wrong. *This* was the most honest response. That brotherly outrage and incredulity. A scarred, bastard-born fellow didn't go courting ladies—certainly not a woman—good and pure and honest as Ellie Balfour.

"I expect this is something of a surprise," Wesley said.

"An unexpectedly lovely one," Cailin swiftly interjected, as only a loyal sister could. "Isn't that right, Courtland?"

St. James remained stonily silent.

"Isn't that right?" Cailin repeated, giving him a second subtle kick.

The duke grunted. "It is unexpected." He allowed his wife only a partial agreement.

"Why don't you bring the children to the nursery, Courtland, and I'll escort Wesley to the drawing room."

St. James looked like he'd prefer to let his wife lead a wild boar through the house than Wesley to his sister.

Which, given the reputation Wesley had earned as a man who indulged too much, made it even more likely the other man would choose the boar.

"St. James," he said awkwardly, bowing his head.

At the duke's answering silence, Cailin cast him a sharp look, looped her arm through Wesley's, and led him onward to Ellie.

"You have questions," he said the moment they were alone.

"I didn't say that."

"You didn't need to."

"Ellie is a lovely young lady who is spirited and clever, and you are my brother. Do you think I'd find you unworthy of her?"

No, Cailin was loyal and loving and saw good in Wesley where there wasn't any. She'd only ever support him—even if in so doing she found herself at odds with her husband.

His sister patted his arm. "Courtland will settle into the idea of it," she said, having followed his silent thoughts.

Settle into the idea of Wesley courting Ellie. A man would sooner fly himself to the moon and capture whatever remnants existed in the celestial heavens to bring back to people below, than St. James would come 'round to the idea of his sister with Wesley.

As they made their way to the drawing room, Wesley eyed the portraits of various Balfours throughout the generations. Those noble lords and ladies all eyed him back with a hearty displeasure to match the current Duke of St. James.

They approached the next hall, and from around the corner, a swell of laughter stretched out into the corridor. That din of amusement grew louder and louder with every step that brought them nearer.

And then Cailin brought him to a stop outside the mahogany double doors drawn open, and those intricately carved panels made a perfect frame about a tableau better suited to a prettily painted porcelain vase.

Surrounded by a sea of suitors, a smiling Ellie sat perched upon the blue-painted canape.

All of the assembled gentlemen vied for her attention, lifting their hands and waving, and raising their voices to be heard.

Only *one* of those gentlemen, however, had been so bold as to claim a place beside her on the carved beechwood frame.

Wesley narrowed his eyes on the golden-haired Duke of Stenton.

The duke lowered his lips near Ellie's ear, whispering something. As he did, the rogue's gaze slipped to the lace fichu that lined the bodice of her soft yellow silk gown.

Wesley's fingers formed a tight fist about the flowers in his hand; those stems strained under his grip. He made himself relax his palm lest he snap the arrangement in half.

"He has been very devoted in his suit. I believe he intends to offer for her any day." Cailin spoke quietly, a warning there.

Perhaps Wesley should care that his sister had detected the source of his ire. And yet, he didn't. Only because it further fed the believability of the ruse he and Ellie sought to perpetuate.

Except why did that feel like no more than a lie he fed himself?

The duke continued speaking in that intimate way to Ellie.

As if she felt his presence, Ellie froze, and she glanced Wesley's way.

And if awards were given for the most skilled of actresses, Ellie would have been the most decorated upon any stage for the adoring way in which she looked at him—as if Wesley were the only person here.

Despite his knowing this was all a farce, and that very look she put his way was a product of the lesson he himself had schooled her on, an odd feeling shifted in his chest.

"Wesley? *Wesley?*"

Wesley started as the moment was broken.

He glanced to his sister, who stared at him with a peculiar expression. She said something to the servant stationed at the entrance of the room.

The young man stepped forward a bit, and then called out loudly, "His Grace, the Duke of Graves."

A dozen sets of eyes shifted from Ellie to Wesley—with one exception.

Stenton's gaze lingered on Ellie a moment more before moving on to Wesley.

They took one another in. Each man sizing up the other. And from the narrowing of Stenton's eyes, he'd recognized Wesley as the threat he was.

"Your Grace!" Ellie popped to her feet, leaving Stenton in the lurch as she rushed to meet Wesley.

They met in the middle of the pretty pink Aubusson carpet.

"Lady Ellie," Wesley murmured. He extended the bouquet he'd fetched a short while ago, and she hesitated, as if shocked that he'd arrived with that small token.

"Wood anemones," he said quietly, his words only for her. "The first time we met, you danced upon those flowers."

Ellie lifted her gaze from those flowers to Wesley. Her mouth trembled, and then her lips parted. "Oh," she whispered.

From over the top of her head, he caught the hostility in Stenton's eyes.

Dismissing him outright, Wesley returned his focus to Ellie. "I thought I might escort you on a curricle ride through Hyde Park."

Ellie continued to stare at the bouquet as if it were the first time in the whole of her existence she'd seen a flower.

Wesley placed his lips near her ear. "That is, unless you'd rather remain here with—"

"A curricle ride would be lovely," she exclaimed, cutting off that remainder of his teasing.

And a short while later, with a collection of groans from Ellie's disappointed suitors, Wesley escorted her from the room and made for their first public outing.

Ellie sat beside Wesley on the curricle bench. The narrow seat was made all the smaller by Wesley's taller, heavily muscled frame. Her leg kissed his powerful thigh and despite the layers of garments between them, heat radiated from where those limbs touched.

Pushing back her bonnet, Ellie closed her eyes and

tipped her face up to the sun. She basked in those warm rays as they bathed her cheeks in heat, and welcomed the comforting *clip-clop* of the team's hooves as Wesley guided them along a less busy trail in Hyde Park.

He'd come with . . . flowers.

Though she knew all of this was merely a game of pretend he'd agreed to take part in, her heart struggled to sort through the difference.

For he could have brought just any bouquet, and yet, he'd not. Instead, he'd somehow hunted down those wildflowers that grew on his father's forest floor, because he recalled that day—a day which had meant so very much to Ellie. She remembered everything from the peaceful twittering of the goldfinch and the mellow song of the blackbird to the crunch of the dried earth under her and Wesley's steps as he'd taught her the proper way to engage in battle.

Before him, she'd not believed anyone other than her brothers was capable of kindness toward children. But Wesley hadn't treated her as a bothersome, underfoot girl. Rather, he'd teased her and talked with her as if she were an equal, and Ellie, who'd previously expected she'd hate all men, had fallen more than a little in love with Wesley that long-ago morn.

She'd never deceived herself into believing he'd seen their exchange as anything more than the innocuous chance meeting it'd been. After all, she'd been a small girl, and he? Well, he'd been a man hopelessly and helplessly and completely in love with another woman.

Even with all that, Wesley, not unlike Ellie, *had* remembered details from that day. He'd remembered the daisy-like flowers upon the earthen floor.

"You do know, people might remark upon the fact we've not exchanged so much as a word since we began our journey, my lady," he drawled.

A smile played at her lips. "Ah, or they will take me as completely tongue-tied and besotted."

Which she was. Which could also only ever be bad and

dangerous, for this was only ending one way—with their eventual breakup. Her smile faded. When this false courtship ended—when Ellie ended it—could they truly return to being friends? There'd at the very least be a requisite separation. It'd be expected there'd be a wounded party, and wounded parties didn't h—

"What is it?" Wesley's quiet voice brought her eyes flowing open, and her flying thoughts to an abrupt cessation.

Her heart thumped harder. He knew her so very well as to know when her thoughts were elsewhere.

"You brought flowers," she said softly.

"Should I not have? Isn't that offering part of a courtship?" There was a gently teasing quality to his voice, and a light glimmer in his eyes.

"A *real* courtship, perhaps."

Theirs, however, was not. Theirs was a game. A ruse meant to deceive. But also one that was already wreaking havoc upon her.

Wesley guided the curricle to a stop from the main path so that other conveyances could freely and safely pass.

Removing his gloves, he set them down on the bench and stared patiently at her.

Ellie tugged at the fabric of her skirts before registering that distracting motion, and she made herself stop.

"It is just . . . when this ends, I fear we will not be the same, and there will at least be a period where either one of us or both of us is expected to be the spurned party, which means we will not be able to talk and see one another . . . and I will miss having you in my life."

She'd missed him when he'd been away fighting, and she'd somehow missed him even more when he'd been sharing the same London sky and yet had stopped seeing her.

Ellie turned her palms up. "I fear I didn't properly think this through." In so many ways.

As was the case so many times with her. Impulsivity. It was her most fatal of flaws—the one that had led her to ruin Cailin and write Wesley and—

Wesley laid a gloved hand upon hers, and she stared down at his larger, stronger fingers. "Ellie," he murmured. "We will *always* be friends."

"Friends," she echoed softly.

It was the most she could ever expect of or hope for from this man. Suddenly, she possessed an overwhelming urge to cry.

"That will not change," he promised.

No, she knew that. Tears pricked her lashes, and, angling her face so that he couldn't see those crystal drops, Ellie blinked them back.

From the corner of her eye, she caught a glimpse of Wesley reaching inside his jacket.

She tensed.

He'd caught her tears and, gentleman that he was, sought to hand over his kerchief. Was there anything worse than having him see her cry—

Wesley withdrew a tiny pair of silver shears.

"What are you doing?" she whispered.

With his gaze locked with hers, he reached for one of the strands hanging at her shoulder. "May I?" he asked with a solemnity to his request and actions that made words an impossibility for her.

Ellie managed only to nod.

At that acquiescence, he captured one of her tendrils, and then stilled.

His gaze slid from hers, moving to that bit of hair he held, and he gently snipped the end.

With an infinite tenderness, he placed that curl inside his jacket and then patted the front like one who sought to assure himself the treasure he'd found had been secured.

It marked the first time and only time in the whole of her life when the act of cutting her hair didn't conjure the darkest thoughts of her father.

Ellie held her palm out.

Wesley stared at her outstretched fingers, and then turned over the shears.

Reaching up, Ellie snipped a dark lock and placed that

cherished strand inside the pocket sewn into her gown, so that she might keep it. So that as time melted away, and the memory of him in this instant faded along with it, she'd have this tangible piece with which to always remember him.

Chapter 20

My dearest Wesley,

*I do so love to draw. I pretend I do not, however, because
I rather dislike conforming to society's expectations for
women. I'd far rather sketch a person than a petunia, or
any flower, for that matter. Except, perhaps, the iris . . .*

Lovingly Yours

Seated on a blanket in the wooded copse along the Serpentine, Ellie, deep in concentration, narrowed her eyes on Wesley, and then added a line to her page.

It'd been nearly two weeks since she and Wesley had begun their charade. The number of Ellie's devoted suitors had slowly dwindled as their visits had stopped completely—including those of the Duke of Stenton. All the gossips whispered and all the newspapers wrote of the Diamond and the Duke. Bets had been placed in the White's betting books as to when Wesley would propose.

As such, their ruse could be declared a grand success, and they could begin discussing the end of their charade.

And yet, they did not.

Instead, they continued to meet day after day. Somewhere along the way, they'd ceased bothering with being seen at the most fashionable hour, and begun meeting in the earliest part of the morn, when the park was quiet. And it was easy enough to pretend—nay, believe—that something had shifted between them, and he actually wished to be with her. As she wished to be with him.

Ellie paused mid-stroke and stared at the emerging likeness of Wesley upon the sheet.

Which was, of course, ludicrous. He'd given his heart to another long ago.

But given the way he kissed you, he doesn't see you as a small girl anymore, a voice at the back of her mind teased her with that reminder.

Of course, that'd been the second and also the *last* time in which he had kissed her: the first had been an explosive one that had ended with horror and regret parading across his features. The other had been about providing her with a kiss to remember for the intent of their ruse.

Giving her head a clearing shake, she glanced up from her rendering and stole another glance at Wesley, who lounged nearby, and returned to her drawing.

When she'd begun sketching him, he'd discarded his immaculately tailored black jacket and unbuttoned the top two buttons of his single-breasted, gold silk dupioni waistcoat. And she damned herself for the fluttering roused at merely the sight of him in that languidly stretched pose.

Ellie pulled a face. How she abhorred that she had grown into the manner of lady who went all starry-eyed for a man—at that, a man who was thoroughly oblivious to her.

"Unhappy with your work, I take it?" he drawled.

"Unhappy with my model, who moves entirely too much," she lied, and waved her pencil his way. "Now *shh*."

He crossed his legs at the ankle.

Ellie paused again in her sketching and waved her pencil at him. "Be still."

"Like this?"

"'Still' means no speaking, Your Grace."

Wesley grinned.

"There!" Ellie said quickly. "That look. Hold that one!"

"This one?" he asked, and with a groan she lightly tapped his ankle with the bottom of her slipper.

"You *moved*."

"You moved me a good deal more when you pushed me."

"Oh, hush." She softened that scolding with a smile.

Wesley grinned in return, that roguish half grin that never ceased to do wild things to her pulse.

Yes, Ellie and Wesley's ruse had proven a great success. One so successful, even she'd come to believe his interest in her . . . might be real.

At last, Ellie added her final lines to the page, and then turned her sketch pad around. "Finished."

He remained motionless, staring at her likeness of him for a long while before at last saying *something*.

"You—"

Ellie swiftly yanked the sketch pad back. "It's horrible, isn't it?" She assessed the pencil portrait. "I thought I may have added entirely too many lines to your waistcoat, and the distinction between your lawn shirt and cravat is too faint. It . . ."

Wesley pulled himself over with his arms and took up the place beside her shoulder. "It is magnificent," he said, with such a quiet reverence.

His solemn tone lent only sincerity to that praise.

Ellie felt a blush build in her cheeks. Flustered, she glanced down.

"I always enjoyed sketching," she confided. "When my governess, a horrid woman, insisted it was an essential skill for all ladies to become proficient in, I swore to myself I'd never produce so much as a passable piece. And I never did . . . except in the nighttime, when everyone was asleep.

I would sit on the floor by the hearth and sketch and sketch and sketch until the morning sun made an appearance in the sky."

"How did you keep such a talent secret, Ellie?"

Ellie tipped her head up so that she could meet his gaze and smiled. "Why, I burned them, of course."

"You burned them? But . . . *why*?"

"Because if my drawings were going to elevate me in some gentleman's eyes and make it so that some man might want to take me for a bride, then I'd find my joy in creating those works, but happily burn them to be freed from marriage."

Only he didn't flash one of his usual captivating grins, or so much as a half one at her attempt to amuse him.

And she wished she'd not told him that truth. Sadness settled around the hard lines of his mouth, and that sentiment filled his eyes. "Oh, Ellie," he said softly.

Setting her pencil down, she dusted her palms together. "It really is fine, you know. I'm better for it."

He took her hand in his and cradled it so very tenderly, folding his other palm over their joined fingers.

Usually, all thoughts of the abuse she'd endured at her father's and governess's hands ushered in an icy chill. With Wesley, however, that cold did not come. This time, there was only a warmth from how he held her, his touch a lifeline to the present, here with him, and not the past, where memories steeped in darkness dwelled.

"How could any person be better for the hurt you suffered through, Ellie?" he asked with such an aching in his voice, she wanted to run from it.

For even though his pain came from the thought of her past pain, she didn't wish to ever see him hurting.

"What happened to me? What my father and governess did? It made me stronger, Wesley."

"His hurting you, Ellie? It did not make you stronger. You were *always* strong. That strength you possess was always inside you. He taught you fear."

She gritted her teeth. How dare he dismiss the only

sense she'd ever been able to make out of what had been done to her.

Disentangling their hands, Ellie edged her chin up. "It showed me how the world treats women and opened my eyes to the fact that if I were to ever marry, I'd find myself in the exact same position I had as a girl—without rights. Without say. Without anything more than the hope that my husband is magnanimous enough as to not beat me or constantly breed me."

"It isn't always that way, Ellie," he said gently. "You've seen Cailin and your brother. Rafe and Edwina. My father and the duchess."

"It isn't *always* that way, but *sometimes* it is, Wesley." She shook her head. "And that is a wager I'm not willing to make."

No, the only man she could ever entertain the idea of a future with was . . .

Ellie recoiled inside.

Him. It'd always been only him. A man who'd always treated her as an equal and who'd only ever shown her kindness and who listened to her when she talked and kept her confidences. She would love him until her dying day—this man, whose heart belonged to another.

Unable to meet his eyes with hers, Ellie snapped her book shut and made to stand.

Wesley placed two middle fingers at her chin, freezing her flight.

He gently guided her face to his. "You deserved better, Ellie. You deserved so much more."

"I was always getting into trouble." She forced a laugh. "Why, look at how I ruined C-Cailin. A good person d-does not do those things, Wesley."

She sank her teeth briefly into her lower lip to stop its tremble. "And do you know why I did it?"

She didn't allow him to answer.

"I did it because I was selfish. I did it because I didn't want to marry and knew—"

"You knew your brother loved Cailin."

"You give me more credit than I deserve. I knew with my family in dire straits, the expectation would be for me to eventually marry. Yes, I knew he loved her, and he would treat her well. I *also* knew I could not say the same for how any future husband would treat me, Wesley."

Ellie thumped a hand against her breast. "When presented with an option of saving myself by hurting another, I chose myself."

"Oh, Ellie," he said, with such sorrow, she closed her eyes.

"Look at me," he quietly urged.

When she remained stonily silent, he added, "*Please*, look at me."

And it was only because she'd not have this man who was so very proud plead, that she complied.

His solemn gaze met hers.

"It was not your fault, Ellie."

"It w-was." Her voice caught and cracked.

"It was *never* your fault. You deserved to be cherished and loved and protected and your father failed you. Your governess failed you. Your brothers failed you."

"They had their own lives," she said, rushing to defend them. "I was just a child and they were all grown and—"

Wesley pressed a fingertip against her lips. "*So* many people failed you."

Ellie stared at him for a long while, and for an even longer while, neither of them spoke.

All these years, she'd blamed herself. All these years, she'd hated herself for having been born with such a wickedness not even her own father could love her. For the first time, Wesley had helped her see that mayhap it hadn't been Ellie's fault. Rather, it had been her father's soul that was putrid, not *hers*.

Hope filled her.

"It was not my fault," she whispered, that realization washing over her, so very freeing.

Wesley shook his head, and then with a beautiful tenderness that threatened to shatter her, he palmed her cheek in his bare hand. "It was never your fault," he repeated.

It wasn't. She'd spent so long believing she was the problem, it would take time for her to fully accept the truth Wesley had opened her eyes to. In time, she'd heal. Wesley had started her on the path to doing so.

He caressed the pad of his thumb down the curve of her cheek, and up to her lip, and her eyes slid briefly closed under that potent and intoxicating touch. And God forgive her, she wanted to know his touch in every way.

She'd no right to ask anything more of him. He'd already given her so much. Perhaps she was a selfish soul, after all.

"Wesley? May I ask a favor of you?"

"Anything." His answer was instantaneous.

Ellie drew a steadying breath, and before her courage deserted her, blurted it out.

"Will you make love to me?"

*W*ill *you make love to me?*
     Wesley went absolutely motionless, certain he'd heard her wrong, but lustful and wrong enough to pray he hadn't.

His pulse pounded loudly in his chest.

There were a million and one reasons he should say no. Among the greatest ones being, she was St. James's sister. At that, an innocent virgin who deserved marriage, and at the very least, a soft feather mattress under her back the first time she made love. Nay, the list could stretch into eternity.

And there was only one he should not.

Because he wanted her.

He wanted her with a desperate hungering and had for far longer than it had ever been good or proper. Now she offered herself to him, in the most trusting of ways.

And yet, there was a shred of honor in him still.

"Ellie," he said hoarsely. "You don't know what you are asking."

She took one of his hands and placed it upon her right breast.

His fingers curled reflexively upon the soft, supple mound.

She held his gaze with a bold directness. "I know what I'm asking, Wesley. I know what I want. You. I want you to be the only man to make love to me."

He opened his mouth to tell her that someday, there'd be another. That despite her insistence and adamancy to the contrary, some man would come along and she'd be swept away—and Wesley stopped himself.

Because Wesley no more wanted to imagine another man taking her in his arms, and in his bed, than he wanted to walk away from what she was asking of him.

He looked her squarely in the eyes.

"Are you certain, Ellie?"

"More certain than I've ever been about anything," she vowed, and then, leaning over, she kissed him.

And Wesley was lost.

Catching her by the waist, Wesley drew her atop him, so that she straddled his frame. All the while, their lips met again and again in a fiery joining, as he and Ellie at last surrendered themselves completely to the passion that had been simmering between them over these past months.

Never breaking contact with her mouth, Wesley kept one arm anchored about her middle, and worked his hand over her right leg. Perched upon him as she was, her skirts were left rucked about her waist, exposing her lower limbs. He ran his fingers over her toned thigh, sinking his fingers into that satiny-soft flesh.

Ellie moaned, and Wesley slipped his tongue inside to consume her as he'd secretly longed to since the last time he'd held her in his arms. She tasted of honey and cinnamon and lemon drops.

She tangled her fingers in his hair, and then gripped the back of his head so she could better meet each glide of his tongue, in a timeless dance.

Still not breaking contact, Wesley reached behind her and worked at the neat row of buttons down the back of her gown.

"I have never hated buttons more than I do in this moment," he rasped against her mouth, capturing Ellie's breathless laugh on another kiss.

Her laughter quickly dissolved to another little moan.

Wesley continued unfastening her dress, until at last, he'd freed her of the garment.

With her help, he pushed the bodice down, shoving the pale blue silk dress to her middle. Next, he disentangled her arms from the sleeves of her chemise, baring her breasts, and Wesley filled his hands with those satiny-soft swells. Touching them—touching her—as he'd desperately longed to do since the first time he'd found her here, in this wooded sanctuary at the edge of the Serpentine.

He teased and tweaked the swollen pink tips, stroking those sensitive peaks, and then, lowering his head, he took one of them into his mouth, and sucked.

A hiss exploded from Ellie's lips, and her fingers tightened in his hair as she held him close.

Wesley worshiped at one peak, flicking it with his tongue, laving the bud. "So beautiful," he breathed between kisses.

"Wesley," Ellie begged, but he only switched his attention to the previously neglected mound.

Her hips began to move, as she undulated against him, thrusting herself into the hard ridge of his erection.

Never had he wanted another woman more than he wanted this one before him. It was a hungering that bordered on desperation. And yet, somehow, he managed to pull away.

Ellie cried out softly, but he captured the remnants of that regret-filled lamentation with his mouth, swallowing it with his kiss, and then he gentled that exchange, and then stopped altogether.

"Ellie," he whispered against her cheek. "Are you certain this is what you want?"

That *he* was what she wanted.

"Because if you wish to stop,"—if she wished to preserve herself for someone more deserving—"I—"

Ellie kissed the remainder of the words from his lips.

When her mouth left his, he tried again. "If you wish to stop, I—"

Ellie silenced him with another kiss. Then, cradling his cheek in her left palm, she placed her lips near his ear. "If you stop, I shall never forgive you, Wesley Audley."

And Wesley was lost once more, as this time, he surged past the point of no return.

They came together in another fiery explosion, mating with their mouths as they ran their hands all over one another.

Wesley shoved Ellie's dress down over her hips, and she wiggled herself out of that luxuriantly soft satin garment. They followed suit with her chemise, until she sat beautifully bare upon his lap, resplendent in her naked splendor.

He laid his palms upon the small of her back and stroked the narrow expanse.

Ellie instantly recoiled; curling up into herself, she drew away.

"Ellie," he murmured.

Her chest moved hard and fast, as for the first time in all the years he'd known this woman, she faltered. She hugged herself in a sad, solitary little embrace.

"You said yourself," she said, her breath still coming quick. "They are hideous."

"No, I said they are beautiful for they are part of you," he gently corrected.

But he'd not force her, in any way. "May I?" he asked.

Ellie's eyes were a blend of desire and uncertainty. And then she slowly nodded, and, shifting on the blanket, she presented him with her back.

Wesley touched his gaze upon the thin crisscrossing of scars upon her flesh, and his heart and soul ached all over again for what she'd suffered. Then, lowering his mouth, he touched his lips to first one and then the next, and the next, kissing her where she'd known her greatest pain, but also knowing from the marks he carried that nothing ever could. That those scars would live forever, not only upon her once unmarred skin, but within her mind and memories of those darkest days. One could only hope to add joy-filled memories now to drown out the noise of the others. He knew that now. He'd discovered that truth from this woman.

When he'd kissed the last of her scars, Ellie turned in his arms.

Not a word passed between them. Their eyes remained locked as she reached for the lawn shirt and tugged it from the waist of his trousers.

Wesley didn't fight her. He didn't put up any protestations. Rather, he placed his trust in her, as she had him, sharing all, in ways he'd never expected he'd be free to share with another.

Ellie drew the shirt over his head, baring his chest.

Unlike her scars, his were still fresher, and more pink and puckered and raised.

She tenderly traced each one: from the place at his right shoulder where a ball had passed through, to the long gash down his left side, from a saber that had come entirely too close to ending him. Then, lowering her lips, she kissed him, as he'd kissed her.

Her mouth was like a benediction, and he discovered he'd been wrong. From this point forward, whenever he saw those marks upon his skin, he would forever remember Ellie Balfour, and the feel of her kiss and the tenderness of her touch.

When she'd kissed the last of his markings, he caught her in his arms, and she straddled him, pressing herself close, as if she wished to climb inside him.

"You are magnificent, Ellie," he rasped as he trailed his lips over the long, graceful column of her neck. He lightly nipped and suckled that flesh, worshiping that place where her pulse beat.

She moaned, pushing her hips against his.

Guiding her down onto the soft wool blanket beneath them, Wesley straightened, and, never taking his eyes from her, he shoved his trousers off, kicking them to the side so that he too was naked before her.

Ellie, as bold and inquisitive as she'd forever been, ran

her gaze over him, lingering her attention on his massive erection.

She held her arms out to him, and Wesley lowered himself atop her. Bracing himself on his elbows, he lowered his mouth to the tip of her right breast, worshiping it once more.

Ellie moaned and shifted back and forth, undulating against him.

Wesley switched his attention to the other small swell. Reaching between them, he palmed the downy softness of the curls between her legs.

Ellie gasped and parted her thighs and lifted her hips.

"So soft," he praised, sliding a finger inside her sodden channel, and then began to gently stroke her, teasing at her nub, until Ellie keened incoherently in her longing, and the rhythm of her hips grew more frantic, indicating how very close she was to her release.

Wesley removed his hand, and she cried out, scraping her fingers over his back.

"Please, don't stop," she begged.

"Never," he vowed, settling himself between her thighs. "As long as you want me, I—"

"I do. I need you."

As he needed her, as he suspected he needed her in so many ways. A realization which he could contemplate in terror at a time that was not now. Now, there was only him and her, and this moment.

Wesley slipped the tip of his shaft inside her welcoming heat, and a guttural groan built in his chest, and got trapped in his throat.

Had there ever been anything to feel as good as being inside her?

Wesley again worshiped at her breasts, teasing and sucking her nipples until Ellie was incoherent in her want, urging him on with every lift of her undulating hips and disjointed words.

Wesley continued to press himself within her, moving with a slowness and caution that threatened his grasp on sanity, until he filled her tight channel.

He paused and searched his gaze over her heart-shaped face, aglow with a sheen of perspiration.

"Am I hurting you?" he asked hoarsely. Because he'd stop. Because if she said he brought her any pain, he'd end this, even as it would kill him to do so.

Ellie's lashes fluttered open, revealing desire-filled, dazed blue irises. "It feels . . . *you* feel wonderful inside me. As if you were meant to be there," she said softly.

As if he were meant to be there.

With her.

Somehow that didn't feel wrong or impossible for who he'd become, or who she was.

And Wesley began to move; slowly at first, withdrawing, and then filling her once more, over and over.

Ellie arched, tentatively at first, and then with an intuition as old as Eve, she met each downward thrust with a bold, determined rise of her hips. She was pure molten fire, and he was all too happy to be burned up by her.

Burying his lips against her neck, he kissed her, suckling at another little birthmark he'd never noted before this moment, and he wanted to discover every other secret spot upon her. He wanted to know everything there was to know about her.

Ellie's movements grew more frantic, more jerky, and he knew she was close.

Sweat dripped from his brow into his eyes, and he welcomed the sting, for a brief distraction from the need to spend himself within her. It'd been so long since he'd known a woman, and that it was this woman who now gave herself over to him . . .

Wesley gritted his teeth, fighting his own hungering.

Moving his attention back to her breasts, he flicked his tongue back and forth along the peaks of her breasts in the manner he'd quickly learned she favored.

Suddenly, Ellie stiffened. Her entire body tensed in his arms and then she cried out; the sound of her release urged him along to his own surrender, but he fought it, wringing every last drop from Ellie until she went limp, and only then did he withdraw, angling sideways and spending his seed on the edge of the blanket.

With a gasp, Wesley collapsed, catching himself atop his elbows so as to not crush her.

A dreamy smile hovered on her bow-shaped lips. "That was—"

Magic.

"Magical," she whispered.

And yet, as he rolled onto the earthen floor beside her, and drew her against the wall of his chest, he came climbing slowly back to reality. The truth of what he'd done—of what they'd done, together—settled around his mind.

Ellie deserved more than a coupling on a blanket in Hyde Park. She deserved to be revered and honored, and he who'd sworn he'd never fall in love again . . . found himself imagining a future with this woman beside him.

Chapter 21

My dearest Wesley,

You worry about me marrying while you are gone for naught. I've never been an enthusiast of all the Bard's work, but I do believe he was on to something when he wrote: "Who wooed in haste and means to wed at leisure?"

Lovingly Yours

The following evening, seated on the sidelines of Lord and Lady Davenport's ballroom, with her sister engrossed in her book, Ellie searched for just one person.

After Ellie and Wesley had made love in Hyde Park, she'd expected the whole world would know it. How could they not see she'd been transformed by that momentous moment in his arms?

And yet, she'd returned home as she'd done every other time during the London Season, without any sideways looks. Without any knowing expressions. The magic of that exchange existed only in the traces of her own memories.

After she'd called for a bath, she'd laid in those warm waters and thought not about the pleasure he'd given her, but that age-old vow she'd made to never marry. At last she understood why ladies pined and yearned and dreamed of gentlemen.

Lord and Lady Davenport's orchestra concluded their latest set, and the guests broke out into a polite applause before taking themselves from the dance floor. As new partners swapped places, they impeded Ellie's view of the now-bare receiving line. She lifted herself slightly from her seat and craned her neck a fraction.

Nothing.

Ellie plopped herself back down.

This would be the first time they saw one another after they'd made love. A blush heated her body as she recalled all over again the ways in which he'd brought her body to life. Only, how did one act around a man who'd broken down her defenses and made her long for . . . more? Not the pretend arrangement they'd entered into, but a real one?

For a man who'd touched her as Wesley had . . . surely might care for Ellie . . . if even just a little?

What if he does not? a voice needled. *What if your affection for him remains as one-sided as it's always been?*

The orchestra struck up a lively country reel at odds with her darkest worrying.

She curled her fingers.

"He is not here yet," her sister remarked, directing that statement to whatever book she read. She flipped the page. "But I've no doubt he will be."

At last, Hattie looked up and held Ellie's gaze. There was a knowing in her elder sister's eyes. "After all, that is part of whatever arrangement you've agreed do," she said quietly. "Is it not?"

Ellie froze. What was her sister saying?

She found her voice. "I don't know what you're—"

Hattie's inelegant snort cut her off. This time, when she spoke, her sister did so in even more hushed tones.

"My sister who called herself a master tactician and wished to train as a soldier since she was a child, and who's now gone out of her way to avoid every single suitor, suddenly finds herself starry-eyed, and free of all the attention she'd previously been receiving."

Ellie just stared at her sister. She knew all that.

Hattie snapped her book shut. "I know all that."

"How?" Ellie blurted.

"Ellie, you may take me as a silly dreamer, with her head either in a book or in the clouds, but I see things." A gentleness filled her sister's pretty blue eyes. "And I certainly see *and know* my own sister."

"I don't take you as a silly dreamer," she said.

Her sister waved a hand. "Everyone does. But why do you think I've always buried myself in books? Why do you think I prefer fictional stories to actual life?"

She stilled. All these years, she'd believed it was just her, that her spirited and contrary nature, which had set her apart from her siblings, also made it so that she was the only one to suffer the late duke's abuse. She'd assumed her siblings—least of all, Hattie—neither knew her, nor really liked her. Oh, she'd known they loved her. But Ellie had come to appreciate one found oneself family by chance, but friends by choice. She'd accepted that sad reality. Only to discover Hattie knew her far more than she'd ever credited.

"I didn't know," she whispered.

"We all dealt with his cruelty in different ways, Ellie." She edged closer, angling her body in a way that shielded them from half the room's occupants. "I . . . knew he abused you emotionally. He did the same to all of us. I just never assumed . . . I didn't know . . ." Hattie drew in an uneven breath. "I didn't know he'd hurt you other ways. We should have spoken of it." Tears filled her eyes. "At the very least, *I* should have talked to you so that you knew it wasn't your fault. The deficit was his."

Hattie covered one of Ellie's hands with her own, and Ellie looked at their white gloves. "Having known what manner of man our father was, and the cruelty he was capable of, I understood what you were doing when you made your debut. I knew you had no interest in making a match. But something . . . changed, did it not?"

Ellie hesitated, and then it was as though she'd finally been set free by her sister's friendship, and all the truths came tumbling out. She told her everything. She told her of the notes she'd written him, signed in the name of another woman. She told her of the time she'd spent helping him recover and the visit to Mrs. Porter. And she told her how desperately and hopelessly she'd come to love him.

When she'd finished, an enormous weight lifted from her shoulders.

Her sister sat with that information in silence for a moment.

"And you haven't told him . . . any of this yet?"

In other words, of her deception and of her feelings for him.

Ellie shook her head. "I lied to him."

"Your intentions were good," Hattie said, with a loyalty Ellie didn't deserve.

"It does not undo the fact that I betrayed him time and time again. And when I stopped writing him . . ." Her voice grew thick. "And when I stopped writing, he was injured."

Her sister frowned and made a sound of protest. "You were not responsible for the injuries he suffered."

"But—"

"Greedy men and their hunger for power were what led the duke into battle."

Only that wasn't altogether true, either. "No, his Miss Sparrow was."

As if on cue, the servant at the front of the receiving line called out her name: "Her Ladyship, the Countess of Trowbridge and her niece, Miss Sparrow."

Together, Ellie and Hattie looked to the front of the room.

The full-figured goddess commanded the room's attention. But then, with midnight-black curls that, under the light cast by the chandelier, shimmered blue on the ends, Miss Sparrow possessed the manner of beauty that men waged wars—and in Wesley's case, fought wars—over.

To her credit, the young woman appeared oblivious to the attention sent her way. Rather, she searched the crowd, as if looking for someone. And Ellie knew precisely who that someone she searched for was, because Ellie searched for the very same man.

Misery swamped Ellie, and she slumped in her chair.

"She's not *that* beautiful," her sister said, helpfully, though unconvincingly.

Ellie gave her sister a look.

"Oh, very well," Hattie muttered. "But her attractiveness does not diminish the fact that you are a beauty in your own right."

"In my own right," she mumbled.

"What? You are stunning. You've glorious blond curls that I would trade my two littlest fingers for. But either way, Ellie? Your beauty? It extends to the manner of woman you are."

A bitter-sounding laugh spilled from her lips. "And what manner of woman is that?"

Her sister's mouth formed a small moue of surprise. "You really don't know?" she said softly, her quietly spoken question a realization.

"Ellie, you are a person of strength and courage. A woman who never allowed Father to crush you as he did me. One who sought to provide a soldier with some solace. Your heart is good, Ellie. It's only you who's failed to see it."

"But what if he rejects me?" she whispered.

"Then at least you know," her sister said, with sage wisdom that Ellie suspected only came with age.

Hattie's eyes twinkled. "You'll *also* know you saved yourself from marrying a fool, because only a man without a brain in his head would fail to fall head over toes in love with you, Ellie."

A shadow fell over them, and they looked up.

Ellie's chest tightened.

Miss Sparrow.

Wesley's Miss Sparrow was even more magnificent up close. Like one of those immaculate statues on display at the museums Ellie occasionally accompanied her brother and Cailin to. She was incapable of doing anything but staring at her—this woman Wesley had pined for and dreamed of.

"May we help you?" Hattie prodded the young woman with a gentleness and kindness only she was capable of.

A pretty blush filled Miss Sparrow's cheeks.

"Forgive me," the young woman murmured. "You are Lady Eleanor."

Even her voice was beautifully low and soft.

Ellie wanted to weep.

Instead, she somehow managed to nod.

"I was wondering if you would be so gracious as to speak with me?" There was a pleading there, in both Miss Sparrow's question and in her magnificent violet-colored eyes.

Ellie felt her sister's stare. One that indicated if Ellie gave the word, she'd dispose of the enchantress requesting an audience in this very public way.

Somehow, Ellie managed a nod. "Of . . . course." She looked at her sister.

Hattie hesitated, and then, coming to her feet, she retreated to a different row of chairs so she was close at hand, but also far enough to grant them privacy.

"I know this is . . . highly impertinent . . . given the circumstances," Miss Sparrow murmured.

Given the circumstances. As in, Wesley had once courted her, and now he courted Ellie. Which only Ellie—and now, Hattie—knew to be a ruse.

"My being a miner's daughter," the young woman murmured, bowing her head, "I don't have a right to be here, and certainly not to approach a lady of your standing."

"I . . . did not think that."

"Everyone else does," Miss Sparrow said with a frankness Ellie didn't want to admire her for, but did. "If it weren't for my great aunt, Lady Willoughby, I'd not be here. Even so, I've come as her companion."

She'd come to work. Knowing that painted Claire Sparrow in a new, never-before-seen light. For materialistic, indulgent women didn't take on work in any capacity. And yet, this one had, and that reality didn't fit with the reality Ellie had already built in her mind about the other woman.

Miss Sparrow flashed a sad smile. "You are even more beautiful than they say," she said wistfully, her words murmured more to herself.

Ellie was more beautiful? Had those words been spoken with anything other than sincere regret, she'd have believed the splendorous woman mocked her.

"How may I help you?" Ellie asked. How was her voice so steady?

"I'm sorry . . . I've been so forward as to approach you without an introduction and then ramble before you. You don't even know who I am." The young woman grimaced. "I'm—"

"I know who you are," Ellie said gently.

"Wesley and I."

Ellie recoiled, that familiarity of Wesley's name on this woman's lips running her through like a dull saber.

Miss Sparrow's eyes grew stricken. "The duke," she whispered, worrying her hands together. "Forgive m-me. His Grace and I . . . we were once . . . friends."

They'd been more than friends. She too had known Wesley's kiss and laugh.

"It was your idea Wesley seek a commission from his father. Was it not?" Ellie issued that reminder for the both of them.

"It was," she said, her voice faint.

Had Wesley not gone to fight, he'd not have suffered so.

The young beauty stared at her hands a moment. "Before he was a duke or a soldier, he was employed in my father's mines. My father would have never countenanced a match between myself and the duke. Not then, anyway."

Now, with a dukedom, wealth, and lands, Wesley possessed everything that had once kept them apart.

"Yes, I did tell him the only way we could be together was if he made more of himself," Miss Sparrow said. "Yes, I urged him to seek out his father, the duke, and obtain a commission. One that would raise his status, and also someday sell. But me? I didn't care that he was only a miner."

Ellie winged an eyebrow up. "Only a miner?"

Wesley's former love—current love?—blushed. "As a lady, you can surely identify with the expectations the world—our fathers—have for us."

"If I'd had the love of a man like Wesley Audley, I'd have wanted nothing more," Ellie said quietly.

"You do."

Ellie stared at her.

"It's just . . . you said: if you'd had the love of a man like Wesley . . . and you do."

Ellie cursed herself for that slight slipup. "Miss Sparrow, perhaps you say whatever it is you wish to say?"

"Yes. Yes, of course. I . . . saw his brother Hunter at the mines. He told me Wesley was terribly injured while fighting. He said he'd been scarred and that he was unable to walk." Miss Sparrow sucked in a wobbly breath. "This is something I can never forgive myself for."

Ellie kept silent.

Pain ravaged the other woman's eyes. "I knew nothing of what happened to him. I wrote His Grace every day. Eventually my father came across our correspondences. From that point forward, every single note I wrote to Wesley was intercepted."

Ellie's chest buckled. *This* was why there'd never been a letter sent. Not because the other woman hadn't cared about Wesley, but because of her father's chicanery.

"The moment I learned he'd returned, and he'd been hurt, I knew the only way I could be close to him was by coming to serve as my aunt's companion here in London. But it was always with the intention of seeing him again so that I might . . . beg his forgiveness." The woman's pain-ravaged eyes met Ellie's. "I didn't know . . . I didn't expect there would be . . ."

Ellie.

But there wasn't really Ellie. Not in the way Miss Sparrow spoke of. What she and Wesley took part in was a ruse to benefit them both.

"But I've seen him, and he looks so very happy when he is with you," Miss Sparrow said wistfully.

Oh, God. Had the other woman been deliberately wielding a knife and slashing away at Ellie's heart, it couldn't hurt any worse than the words now streaming from her lips.

Ellie wanted to blame this woman for Wesley's having gone to fight, and for so long, she had blamed her. Now, she saw it had ultimately been Wesley's decision. And Miss Sparrow clearly carried enough guilt, still—and likely always would. She wasn't grasping. Nor ugly on the inside. She'd simply sought a future with Wesley, in the only way she could.

"You may have urged His Grace to seek out a commission, but the decision to go was ultimately his," Ellie said softly. "You must not blame yourself for that."

As if Ellie had somehow offered the absolution she'd desperately needed, Miss Sparrow's eyes slid shut.

When she opened them, she hesitated a moment more. "I do not deserve that grace, but I am grateful to you for it. We were desperate to be together, and I believed I'd discovered the way. My father? He is not a good man. He is a cruel one."

Miss Sparrow's features twisted, and she glanced away—but not before Ellie caught the glimmer in her beautiful eyes.

Only a person who'd suffered so, someone like Ellie, would note that subtle but noticeable tightening of her delicate face. Ellie desperately wanted to hate her. She wanted to dislike her for so many reasons, and yet, in her, Ellie also found something unexpected—they'd been united in more than their love for Wesley. They were kindred spirits, too, of the worst possible way—cruel sires.

"What are you asking of me?" Ellie softly asked. For there could be no doubting she'd sought Ellie out for a reason.

Miss Sparrow stopped twisting her fingers about. "I merely wish for you to convey my . . . apologies to him. He is happy with you, and that is all I ever want for him. I know you are his love." Now.

That unspoken word—an incorrect assumption, at that—hung upon the end of the other woman's sentence.

Miss Sparrow loved him. It was as clear as the nose on Ellie's face. And she was putting Wesley's happiness before her own. Even if that meant ceding him to another woman, one whom he supposedly loved.

She was superior to Ellie in every way.

Wesley deserved to know the truths Ellie was now in possession of. At which point, he'd discover her deception in writing him, and he'd also learn his Miss Sparrow had been true to him. That she'd never stopped loving him.

Ellie struggled several more moments, attempting to speak through the pain closing at her throat. "I . . . believe it would be important for you and Wesley, were you to say these words to him yourself."

The young woman's plump lips parted, and then trembled. "Y-you would grant me that kindness?"

"I would." It wasn't a kindness. It was what needed to be done.

For Wesley.

Ellie stared out blankly at the waltzing partners.

All these years, she'd believed herself selfish, putting her own wants and worries first. Only to discover in this moment, losing Wesley as she would, she was more honorable than she'd ever credited.

How she wished she were more selfish, after all. For then, she'd have let him continue believing Miss Sparrow had been rapacious and unfaithful. When all along, they'd merely been star-crossed lovers kept apart by a heartless father.

She felt him before she saw him.

While Wesley's first and only love continued speaking, Ellie looked across the ballroom.

Wesley bypassed the servant announcing guests and headed straight down the stairs. All the while, his gaze remained locked . . . on Ellie.

For just a moment.

His focus then shifted to the woman beside her.

Confusion settled in the harshly beautiful planes of his face. His steps slowed, stopped, and then resumed, as he headed toward her.

Nay, not her. Them.

Ellie and his Miss Sparrow.

"The duke's library," Ellie said quietly, not taking her gaze from Wesley's powerful march. "You'll find it down the center hall, and the third room on the right."

"I can never repay you," Miss Sparrow whispered.

"You needn't repay me," Ellie managed.

And then, he was there. His hard eyes not on Ellie—nay, he didn't even bother feigning that she-was-the-only-person-in-the-world look, but rather, the glorious woman beside her.

Oh, God. She would not survive this. She'd suffered all manner of pain at her father's hands, but this? This was a different manner of suffering, but no less agonizing.

Miss Sparrow scrambled to her feet and sank into a slow, elegant curtsy. Ellie made herself follow suit, standing. Her own curtsy felt a good deal more sloppy and speedy.

"Forgive me," Miss Sparrow said softly. "I will leave you both."

And with that, she hurried off.

The moment she'd gone, Wesley snapped his focus back to Ellie. "Are you all right?" he demanded.

"Fine. She was . . . is . . . lovely."

"What did she want?"

Certain the whole room was aware of the tension, Ellie glanced about. Only no one paid them any notice.

"Wesley, you should talk to her," Ellie managed to say. How had those words slipped out so easily?

Wesley drew back, and then collected himself. "There is nothing to say."

Only there was everything to say.

His obstinacy would cost him the truth—if she allowed it. For a mercenary moment, she considered letting him dig in, because then she'd have him in her life still.

Nay, she'd never had him. Not in anything that wasn't pretend.

"Ellie," he murmured, shifting closer. "What is it?"

She shook her head. "Not here," she murmured. "In Lord Davenport's library?"

He nodded. "Of course."

And without another word, Ellie quit his side. The end of her time with Wesley had been inevitable. She'd known that eventually, they'd have to go their own ways, and live their own lives, apart. Only, now that moment was here, she didn't know how she'd go on without him being part of her life in all the ways she desperately wanted him in it.

Chapter 22

My dearest Wesley,

*All I have ever wished for is your happiness. All I want
is for you to survive. Please, know that. Please, believe
that.*

Lovingly Yours

Wesley stood waiting in the baron's vast, high-ceilinged
library.

Gripping the edge of a mahogany shelf stuffed with perfectly lined leather tomes, Wesley stared absently at the
gilded titles, not seeing the books, but rather, in his mind's
eye, seeing another library—and Ellie in it. Ellie who, upon
his return, hadn't shied away from speaking to him or skirted
the room because of his presence there.

Over the years, Wesley had come to know Ellie Balfour
so very well.

He knew by the sparkle in her eyes when she was up to
mischief, and when whatever curious thoughts tumbling

through her head left her pensive. He could tell the degree of her happiness by whether one dimple appeared in her cheek, or both.

It was how, as he'd approached her a short while ago in the baron's ballroom, he'd also known she was upset. Her sadness she wore as effortlessly as she did her joy. From the slight way her beautiful lips creased down at the corners to the paleness of her cheeks, taut with anguish.

There'd been only one thought—getting to her as quickly as he could, so he could discover the source of her sadness, and then slay the one who'd brought her any misery.

It was why he'd not seen the young lady beside her. He'd seen only Ellie. Until he hadn't.

Until he'd noted the lovely figure seated beside her—Miss Claire Sparrow.

He'd expected, given their past, he should have felt . . . some manner of regret for what could have been. Or sadness for what he'd lost. But there hadn't been anything. There'd only been a franticness for him to get to Ellie.

Ellie, whom, somewhere between stepping into his father's library and holding his hand while his bone had been set, he'd fallen completely, madly, and deeply for. Somewhere along the way, the game of pretend they'd entered into had become blurred, so that he now recognized it for what it was—a ruse he'd been all too happy to go along with, because it allowed him that which he'd missed following their separation—time with her.

He wanted her. He wanted her in every way a man could want a woman.

Having returned from war riddled with scars, and his mind affected, too, he'd convinced himself there could be no normal life or future for him. Only Ellie had shown him that even with the scars he carried, happiness was still possible. He was still capable of loving and deserving of being loved.

A lightness filled his chest, a buoyancy that brought with it warmth that seeped throughout his being.

Click.

Wesley turned quickly to greet her. The smile froze on his lips as confusion suspended the thoughts in his head.

"Hullo, Wesley," she said softly.

Claire closed the door quietly behind them.

She'd always been beautiful. Attired in a pretty pink satin that accentuated her curved frame, she was even more so. Perfectly full-figured, violet-eyed, and possessed of the loveliest golden ringlets, she'd always put him in mind of those Greek goddesses written on the pages of the handful of books there'd been in the Audleys' cottage in Cheadle. And she'd been as unattainable as one of those mythical figures, too.

When he'd first spied her, heading to her father's offices, a lace parasol at her shoulder and a pink ribbon wound through hair the color of sunshine and gold, he'd been captivated.

He'd never seen a woman more exquisite.

He acknowledged her winsomeness still, but found it paled against Ellie's transcendent beauty.

He stiffened. Ellie was due to arrive, and he'd intended to tell her everything in his heart. He couldn't do that were she to discover him with this woman. "Claire," he said. "I'm expecting—"

"Lady Ellie." Claire pushed herself away from the door and started forward. Only she stopped with two paces between them. "She . . . was so very good as to . . . arrange this meeting."

Tension whipped through him.

"She is lovely," she murmured. "In every way. I certainly see why you fell in love with her."

That'd been the plan from the start, the idea proposed by Ellie. Deter her suitors and make Claire Sparrow envious. He'd never really cared, however, about the latter. He'd merely gone along with that plan because he'd hated with every fiber of his soul the thought of another man courting her.

"What do you want, Claire?" he asked quietly, without malice, just eager to cut to the reason for her being here.

She stretched a hand out to him. It hovered there, and then she let it fall quaveringly back to her side.

"I wanted you to know, Wesley, how very sorry I am. For ever having suggested you go seek out your father. For urging you to obtain a commission and fight. I never wished to see you hurt."

"There is nothing to forgive, Claire," he said quietly, and her eyes slid shut.

There'd been a time he'd resented both himself and her for the foolhardy plan concocted. Only now? With even just the slightest passage of time, he found himself grateful. For if he'd never gone, and returned injured, there'd never have been . . . Ellie.

Her eyes glittered with tears. "Thank y-you." Her voice caught. "That is the only reason I came to London. To see that you were well and to make my apologies. Now that I kn-know, I can be at peace."

She turned to go.

There was, however, one thing. Something he'd once needed to know.

"Why did you stop writing?" he asked, and it was more curiosity than any real hurt that prompted that question.

Claire turned back. Confusion filled her expressive eyes.

"When I was away fighting," he clarified. "What made you stop exchanging letters the second time?"

"The *second* time?" she asked haltingly. "I . . ." She faltered. "I didn't."

It was funny how it always started in a library—all the biggest moments, the most significant parts of Ellie's existence happened in that same room, just in different households.

First, the Duke of Bentley's country estate, where Ellie had coordinated her brother and Cailin's ruin.

Then, upon Wesley's return, where she'd fallen more and more in love with him.

And now. Now it was Lord Davenport's library.

Seated upon the floor, with her back against the silk

damask–lined wall and her legs stretched out before her, Ellie stole a glance down the hall to the pretty white-paneled door behind which Wesley now spoke with his Miss Sparrow and then peered at the Louis XV bracket clock.

Twenty minutes. They'd been closeted away for twenty agonizingly long moments.

There'd been no shouting or audible sobbing. There'd been nothing but silence that proved somehow worse.

And Ellie tortured herself.

She tortured herself with thoughts of the excruciatingly beautiful young woman weeping copious tears against Wesley's jacketfront. Of Wesley holding her, while all the secrets and truths at last came out, and his anger and resentment melted away, so that they were reunited in their love for one another.

Squeezing her eyes shut, she knocked her head silently against the wall.

She only wanted his happiness. She wanted it for him, more than even her own. But she would never, ever stop loving him or wanting *him*.

The steady beat of frantic footfalls cut across her misery, and Ellie stiffened, looking toward their source.

Her brother Courtland came tearing down the hall, his hair mussed from the pace he'd set, with panic radiating from his eyes.

The moment he caught sight of her, he drew up short, stumbling to a halt.

"Ellie?" he whispered, and her name was more a prayer. "You're here. I thought . . ."

She stared up at him. "Yes?"

His cheeks, already flushed from his exertions, turned several shades redder.

"Hattie said you disappeared. She was worried sick. *I* was worried sick."

"Worried that I was going to ruin some other couple?" She arched a brow up.

"No." Courtland pulled at his cravat. "Yes? I was worried you were going to ruin yourself."

Appreciating that he'd offered that belated truth, she sighed and rested her head back against the wall.

"Well, you needn't. There will be no one ruined this evening."

In fact, the very reason she'd stationed herself as a sentry in this hall had been to ensure no one accidentally discovered Wesley and Miss Sparrow. It was one thing if Wesley decided he wished to have a future with her. It was quite another were he to find himself forced into it because of propriety and society's expectations.

Ellie tried to take a breath so that she might ease the pressure crushing at her chest.

To no avail.

It hurt to breathe. It hurt to think. Every part of her, inside and out, ached.

The floorboards groaned.

A moment later, Courtland dropped down and joined her on the floor. They sat shoulder to shoulder, thigh to thigh, each staring at the opposite wall.

"Do you want to talk about it?"

"Do you mean the fact that I'm in love with Cailin's brother, a man whose heart belongs to another?"

"Ellie," he said gently. "That isn't t—"

"True?" she interrupted him. "I assure you it is. It's been the only thing true between Wesley and me." At least on his part. Her heart, on the other hand, had forever been engaged.

Tears clogged her throat, and she swallowed several times.

"I . . . don't understand." Her brother spoke haltingly. "Are you saying you do not love him?"

"No!" That quiet denial exploded from her lips before Courtland's question had even been fully formed by her brother. "That is, I do love him." She stared sightlessly at the peacock embroidered into the wallpaper on the opposite wall. "I believe I always have."

She always had. She always would. From the moment he'd joined her in that copse, her heart had been forever his. She'd only fallen more and more love with him along the way.

And the pain of losing him would never not hurt.

Courtland covered her hand with his, drawing her gaze to his.

"Wesley clearly loves you. I'd never have supported his suit had he not."

Wesley very clearly loved her? My, they'd excelled at their performance.

A gurgling half sob, half laugh became trapped in her throat.

Courtland shifted the remaining inch closer. "Ellie?" he asked, concern and confusion all tangled up together in his tone.

"It wasn't real, Courtland."

"What wasn't?"

"Any of it. All of it." A quiet sound of frustration escaped her. "At least, not on his end. The whole reason he courted me was to make his Miss Sparrow jealous."

The muscles in her brother's face tightened; the corner of his left eye ticked. "I'll kill—"

"It was not his fault. He did so at my suggestion."

Courtland's brow creased, his confusion driving away the earlier fury emanating from his person. "Why did you suggest that, Ellie?"

"Because I didn't wish to marry. I never want to marry," she whispered furiously, finally releasing that truth, and it felt so very good. So very freeing.

Only . . . Her shoulders sagged. "Or, I never *wanted* to marry. I . . . saw the manner of man Father was, and . . ."

"What did you see, Ellie?" he asked gravely, when she couldn't bring herself to finish. "Ellie?" he pleaded.

"He beat me," she whispered, at last voicing that truth aloud for the first time to either of her brothers.

Courtland went absolutely still. The blood drained from his face. "Oh, God. He beat me and Keir and I just assumed he'd not touch you or Hattie or Lottie because you were girls and—" He scrubbed the back of his hand across his mouth, muffling the moan that slipped out. "Why didn't you tell—"

Ellie turned her palms up. "I wasn't quite certain I didn't deserve his wrath," she said, her voice threadbare.

Courtland scrambled quickly, scooting himself around so that he faced her. He took her hands in his trembling ones.

"Never," he said vehemently. "Never did you deserve any of what he did. He was a monster and you were and are all that is good and light." His eyes slid closed, but not before she caught the sheen of tears there. When he opened his arms, she crawled over and curled into the crook of his shoulder.

"God, I am so sorry I was not there for you." He buried a kiss on the top of her head.

And she found, once more, something cathartic in sharing those darkest memories.

"Now you know why I didn't wish to marry, Courtland. I didn't want to find myself tied to a man who was cruel like our father. I should have told you that before. I . . . just didn't know how."

They sat in silence for a long moment, and then each found their way back to the original station they'd set up against the wall. "So you and Wesley . . . engaged in a game of pretend to deter your suitors?"

She nodded.

"And I gather, along the way . . . you found yourself falling in love with him."

A crystal sheen filled her eyes, blurring her vision. "I found myself falling in love with him long before that." And just as she'd shared with Hattie, she revealed all to her brother, going back to the moment of her first meeting with Wesley, and the guilt that had found her alone with him in those woods.

When she'd finished, her brother's silence proved deafening.

She stole a glance at him.

Courtland looked heart-stricken. The last she'd seen him pale and shocked so had been that moment years ago, when he'd discovered Ellie had coordinated his and Cailin's ruin.

"My God, Ellie," he whispered, when he'd found his voice. "Why didn't you tell me *any* of this? Did you believe I would *force* you? Have I failed so miserably as your brother that I gave you such reason to doubt me?"

"No! It was never that. Ever, Courtland. Please believe that."

"Then what was it?" he begged. "Please, help me understand."

"It's . . . how I lived my life, Courtland. Since I was a girl, I've sought to escape situations by prevarication . . . and by any way I could."

Another pained laugh built in her chest. "I considered myself a *master* tactician, on the battlefield of life, with every move I made being a different maneuver to exact my desired outcome. I did so to protect myself, and finally realized . . ."

Unbidden, her gaze crept back to that door where Wesley still spoke with his Miss Sparrow.

"What is it you've realized, Ellie?" her brother gently asked.

"Each time I did, I've only brought myself—and those I love—more pain. I don't want to live like that anymore."

And this time, she didn't blink back her tears or brush them away. This time, she let them fall, leaving a warm trail upon her cheeks.

Her brother looped an arm around her shoulder and drew her close. "What do you want, Ellie? Tell me whatever it is, and it is yours."

Only he couldn't do that. He couldn't just secure her that which she wanted most—Wesley, and a future with him.

There was one thing, however, that he *could* do—the next best thing.

Ellie lifted her gaze to his. "I want to leave London. I want to return to the country."

He bowed his head. "It is done."

Chapter 23

My dearest Wesley,

*You worry I'm sending you all my ribbons. Well, you
needn't worry. I really quite despise wearing them. They
look far better as a bright bit of color wrapped about my
letters to you than they ever could wound in my hair.*

Lovingly Yours

This night, there'd at last been answers . . . and closure
on Wesley's past.

But there'd been something *more*.

A letter in hand and more than two dozen scattered
around him, Wesley sat at the floor-to-ceiling-length windows overlooking the gardens of the townhouse he'd recently been gifted by the king.

He sat there reading, just as he'd been since his return
from Lord and Lady Davenport's some hours ago.

Through it, his focus remained fixed on the notes about
him. Periodically he swapped one for the next. Even as he

needn't have bothered reading through them. He remembered every line.

The moment Wesley and Claire had parted ways in Davenport's library—she out a different side panel, while he'd remained closeted away, so as to avoid the potential for scandal or ruin—he'd found himself in a strange place—at both sea . . . and oddly, still at peace.

All he'd wanted to do when he left that room was to find Ellie and tell her *everything* in his heart. To thank her for saving his sanity. For writing him dozens upon dozens of letters, when even his own family's notes had come a good deal less frequently.

Only, when he'd left that library, he'd discovered she, Courtland, and Cailin had gone, and so Wesley returned home instead, closeted himself away in a different library, with his letters—his letters from Ellie—and read.

At some point, the half-moon had swapped its place in the sky to the early morning sun, which made its slow rise to daylight. That fiery orb bathed the dew-soaked grounds in a soft glow.

Wesley reached for the last letter he'd ever received on the battle lines.

> *My dearest Wesley, you insist on knowing my favorite*
> *flower, so that you can return and shower me with those*
> *blooms, and yet, how can you not realize, I do not need*
> *gifts or sonnets or the jewels you talk of gifting me. I*
> *wish only for your return. But as you persist, and I do*
> *not want you to believe me coy, I shall share. It is . . .*

"The *iris*," he whispered, his gaze locked on that one word which had flipped his world upside down when he'd returned last evening. This note, and her mention of the iris in it, had been the one. All along, the clue about the real identity of the woman writing him had lived here on the page of this very last letter.

The note still clasped between his fingers, Wesley lifted his head and looked out the windows at the grounds below.

He did a search, and then found them near a watering fountain—those vibrant purple flowers.

In his mind's eye, he saw a different moment in time.

"The iris shall be the one and only flower I favor."

"A very wise choice, little general."

Ellie's face fell. "The iris may help a soldier heal, but they don't prepare a person to fight."

Of course it had been Ellie.

Ellie who'd written to him.

Ellie whose notes had been the sole bright spot in the hell of war.

During that darkest of times, each letter he'd received had been a balm to his soul. Each one had taken him away— if even for just a short while—from the hell of war, and had instead offered Wesley a reminder that there wasn't death and dying everywhere. That in some place, the place where she was, there still existed a life without pain and darkness. And it had given him hope. *She* had given him hope.

Turning, Wesley consulted the clock.

Six o'clock in the morning, an entirely too early time to arrive with his heart in his hand, and admissions of his own folly for having failed to see that it was her all along—and to ask that she, who had every reason to fear men and their intentions, trust him, and trust that he'd never hurt her. That he'd only ever love her.

Gathering up all his notes, Wesley carefully filed them into the stacks he'd kept them organized in. He tied them with the ribbons he'd received from her through the years.

Heading over to the bellpull, Wesley rang for his valet.

The young man appeared in almost an instant through their connecting doors.

A short while later, after a trip to his private gardens, Wesley collected the reins of his mount from a servant and swung himself into the saddle.

When he'd seated himself, the young man held over the small bouquet, wrapped with a purple ribbon. Wesley accepted it, and then, clicking his tongue, he nudged his horse onward to Ellie's family's household.

He rode through streets still calm, but just beginning to bustle. With every moment, he found himself closer to seeing her and telling her everything in his heart, and an eagerness built inside.

A short while later, Wesley arrived outside his brother-in-law's household.

Dismounting, Wesley stood there, staring for a long time at the white stucco townhouse.

Until he'd begun his pretend courtship of Ellie, he'd never been inside—not even once. For so long, he'd just closeted himself away, shutting his family out—his siblings, their spouses, his niece and nephews. He now knew he'd done so because their bucolic lives had served as a constant reminder of what he'd so desperately yearned for, and that which he'd thought himself incapable of having after the war.

Ellie had opened his eyes to the fact that he could have that idyllic life he craved. She'd shown him the scars he now carried were just part of his story, and that all people lived with wounds of their own. They were all broken in ways, only put back together by love and laughter.

"Need some 'elp, guv'nor?"

Startled from his thoughts, Wesley glanced down.

A small, chestnut-haired street waif stared back with big eyes.

Reaching inside his jacket, Wesley pulled out a small purse and handed over the velvet bag.

The little boy peeked inside. His eyes went somehow even bigger.

"Will you watch after my mount until I return . . . ?" Wesley asked, searching for the boy's name.

"The name is Brynmore, and gor, will Oi ever." The painfully slender boy puffed his gaunt chest out. "You won't find a better watcher of your horse than me, sir."

Wesley turned to go . . . and then stopped. He took the child in once more. The lad was slender from lack of food, and his cheeks hollowed out, and Wesley was hit square in the chest with the evidence of his own self-absorption since his return. It was as Ellie had said that day in Hyde Park: with the title and fortune he'd inherited, there were so many people he might help.

The boy's brow dropped. "You . . . having second th-thoughts? Because I really am good with horses. Watch a lot of them, I do—"

"It isn't that at all." Wesley dropped to his haunches. "I suspect you are one of the best at what you did," he said, in deliberately solemn tones. "If you're looking for steady work, however, I am in need of more stable hands."

Brynmore's eyes bulged. *"Truly?"*

Wesley nodded. Reaching inside his jacket once more, he withdrew a card, and provided him directions to his residence and the name of his butler.

Straightening, Wesley took the eight stone steps, two at a time, and knocked on the sapphire-blue door.

Restless, he tugged out his timepiece.

The door was suddenly opened by the graying, kind-eyed servant.

"Wickham," Wesley greeted the butler as he entered.

"Your Grace," Wickham said, eyeing the bouquet in Wesley's hand.

"I'm here to see Lady Ellie."

Wesley did a sweep of the palatial foyer. Excitement mingled with fear in his breast. What if even after declaring his heart, she did not wish to marry him?

"Lady . . . Ellie?" Wickham spoke her name haltingly, as if it were the first time he'd ever heard it spoken.

Something in his tone penetrated Wesley's clamoring thoughts.

Frowning, he looked to the butler. "Is she not here?" Perhaps she'd gone to Hyde Park. Wesley should have recalled she preferred rising at dawn and visiting those grounds when they were quiet.

"I am afraid not, Your Grace."

"Do you know when she will return?" he asked, restlessly.

Wickham looked pained. "You . . . do not know."

Wesley's heart slowed to a painfully slow, sickly thump. "Know what?" he managed, his words thick to his own ears.

"She, along with the duke and duchess, left just this morning."

"Left," he repeated dumbly.

The butler nodded. "They've retired to Leeds for the Season, and ordered the townhouse closed up."

She'd simply . . . left? Without so much as a word, without so much as a note . . . just nothing. As if these past days and weeks, months, and even years hadn't mattered at all? As if in leaving, she didn't know she'd break him in ways not even the war had or could. Pain cleaved at his chest.

Wickham cleared his throat.

Blinking slowly, Wesley stared blankly at the other man.

"I was told to give you this were you to arrive."

Hope flared to life as he eagerly reached for the letter, all but grabbing it from the servant.

Wickham collected the flowers Wesley had arrived with.

Wesley tore the letter open, and frantically scanned the familiar writing.

His heart fell.

Familiar . . . but also not the one he'd sought.

My dear brother,

If you are receiving this, you now know we are headed for Leeds. Ellie asked that we retreat to the country early. She indicated there was no longer anything for her there. It is my hope that isn't true. It is also my hope that you aren't a great, big dunderhead and that you can realize what is as plain as the nose on your face . . .

Your devoted sister,
Cailin

Wesley crushed the edges of the pages in his hands.

He'd been a great, big dunderhead and worse. He'd been a bloody, stupid arse.

He looked up. "When?" he demanded.

"Your Grace?"

"When did they depart?"

"Just over an hour ago, Your Grace."

They were traveling by carriages, and he by horse. He could catch them.

Turning on his heel, Wesley bolted.

Seated in one of two carriages making the trek to the Balfours' Leeds estate, Ellie stared out the window at the passing countryside. The London streets had long since faded, replaced by greener grounds, bluer skies, and softly rolling hills.

Since she'd been a girl, she'd long loved the time spent at any one of her family's country holdings. In London, there'd been fewer places to hide from the late duke. There'd been less pure air to breathe and less lands to explore. Nay, there'd not even truly been any lands. Not ones that weren't manufactured, anyway, to give off the illusion.

She'd always found solace and joy in being on those lands—anywhere, as long as it wasn't London.

That had been the case.

Until now.

She'd had to leave. Staying in London, watching Wesley reunited with his sweetheart, would break her in ways her father had never managed. It would leave her shattered and aching, and unable to put the pieces of herself back together. She'd not, however, anticipated that pain would still be so very acute, even with all the distance she put between them.

Because leaving didn't make his love of Miss Sparrow not true. It didn't erase the thoughts of the time Ellie had spent with him, or the future she'd secretly dreamed of with him.

She briefly squeezed her eyes shut.

Selfish. Selfish was what she'd always been, but in this, she would not let herself be. In so doing, however, she'd only hurt another.

Ellie pulled her focus from the idyllic landscape, and

with grief ravaging her soul, she looked to where her sister sat reading. "I am so sorry," she said quietly.

Hattie picked her head up. Confusion creased her brow.

"For . . . making it so that you had to leave London," Ellie clarified.

Hattie snapped her book shut. Amusement danced in her eyes. "You think I'm *regretful* about leaving London?"

Ellie stared at her. "You're . . . not?"

Hattie laughed. "Ellie, the *last* thing I wish to do is suffer through another Season."

"But . . . but . . ."

Her eldest sister winged an eyebrow up. "You believe I'm sad at still being unwed?"

"You're . . . not?"

"No!"

"It does certainly point to a Balfour deficit in matters of communication," Hattie said dryly. The mirth vanished from her features, and she grew solemn. "I never wanted a London Season."

Ellie fell back in her seat. For that didn't fit at all with everything she knew about her romantic of a sister. "You read *romance* novels and love fairy tales and—"

"*And* that must mean I must surely dream of those things for myself?"

Ellie nodded.

"I did."

Her own misery was forgotten in an instant. "You are perfectly lovely and witty and you shouldn't cease dreaming of them, or believing you might have them, Hattie," she said, willing her eldest sister to see it might be impossible for Ellie to be lucky in love, but it wasn't so for Hattie.

"I didn't just want those things with anyone, Ellie," she said softly.

Ellie started. "You're in love," she whispered. "Who?" What man was foolish enough to not love her clever, kindhearted sister in return?

A pained-looking smile formed on her sister's lips. "It doesn't matter."

"It does."

"Fine, it does. But his identity is not one I wish to reveal."

That was why her sister, stunning though she was, had always buried herself behind books at *ton* events. It was why their middle sister, Lottie, had gone on to wed before her, and why she'd fashioned herself as more a companion to Ellie during her Season.

"Oh, Hattie, I have been so utterly self-absorbed—"

"Stuff and nonsense. I didn't want anyone to see, but it is why I've been able to realize just how very much you love Wesley and how much he loves you."

"You don't—"

"Know that? I do. I know because I would have traded my soul to have the man I love look at me the way Wesley looks at you. You should have told him, Ellie," Hattie insisted.

"Told him what, Hattie?" she asked tiredly. "That I lied with every letter I sent?"

Only she hadn't. In every note sent, she'd shared parts of her heart, soul, and pieces of books she'd read. He'd wanted all of that. He'd just . . . wanted it from another woman.

Tears stung her eyes.

The squabs groaned as Hattie quit her bench and joined Ellie on hers.

"You should have told him *everything*, Ellie," her sister said softly.

"It wouldn't have changed anything." Her voice emerged a faint whisper.

"You don't know that," Hattie said insistently. "If you told him you loved him, it might have mattered. I believe it would have. I *saw* how he looked at you."

"It was only a ruse." At least for him, anyway.

Her sister made a sound of protest. "I don't believe that."

"Have you spoken to the man you love?"

Hattie's cheeks pinkened. "That is different."

Ellie shook her head. "It isn't. It's only different because it's you."

"You're trying to change the subject," her sister muttered.

"Only partly."

They shared a smile.

Hattie opened her mouth to speak, when the carriage suddenly lurched forward slightly, and then slowed, rolling to a graceful halt.

Quiet filled the carriage.

"Why have we stopped?" Ellie asked.

"Perhaps we broke an axle?"

"It would have been a more jarring stop," Ellie pointed out.

"That is true." Hattie's eyes lit, and pushing back the curtain, she peered out the window. "Do you suppose it is a highwayman?"

"Only you would sound positively delighted at the prospect," Ellie drawled.

Hattie's eyes went big. "There is a man here, with a sword."

A man with a—

Her sister sat back, affording Ellie a look through the window.

Ellie went completely still, unable to move, scarcely daring to breathe. "Wesley," she whispered.

And Wesley as her sister had said, with a sword in hand, and all the misery of leaving him and losing him was forgotten, replaced instead with the joy of seeing—

"Ellie Balfour," he called in a booming voice, as he swung down from his mount.

Then Ellie recalled that which had prompted her flight.

Her heart hammering, Ellie suddenly dropped the curtain.

"Ellie," her sister chided, shoving it back wide. "The man has come all the way on horseback to see you; the least you can do is grant him an audience."

Hattie made the decision for her. She reached for the handle and pushed the door open.

Sunlight streamed inside, briefly blinding, and Ellie shielded her eyes from the glare.

"Hello, Your Grace!" Hattie said cheerfully, giving Wesley a wave.

"Lady Hattie."

The pair of them might as well have been meeting in a ballroom, and Ellie slunk in her seat, praying she remained forgotten.

Alas . . .

"Ellie," Wesley called again in that booming voice.

She'd never considered herself a coward, and yet flight seemed preferable to facing him.

Ellie ducked her head out.

"There you are," he said.

She cleared her throat. "Here I am."

Wesley remained a handful of paces away—his gaze inscrutable. The tense lines at the corners of his lips and the tic at the corner of his right eye, however, were all telltale evidence of his rage.

Somehow she managed to climb out of the conveyance and meet him.

"You are angry," she said, the moment her feet touched the ground.

"Furious."

Ellie chewed at the inside of her cheek. "I do not blame you."

He took a step closer. "I'm here for a fight."

Ellie dropped her gaze to the ground. Oh, God. And he deserved it, too. She forced herself to meet his opaque stare. "I . . . understand."

"You never signed your name, Ellie."

She didn't pretend to misunderstand. Even so, he took her silence for such.

"The letters. Your letters. The ones *you* wrote to me."

Her tongue suddenly grew heavy in her mouth. "Oh. Those," she managed to say. As if there'd been any other he'd obviously sought her out to discuss.

"Yes, *those*."

Ellie hugged her arms around her waist. "I trust you've come to tell me precisely what you think about what I did," she said, her voice catching.

A breeze tugged at his already-windswept hair that had escaped his queue. "Indeed, I have."

He took a step closer.

Ellie registered the clatter of churning wheels, and glanced at the approaching carriage, returning from the opposite direction.

Her stomach fell.

Of course Courtland would double back when he did not see her and Hattie's carriage. Of course, there'd now be a bigger audience for her misery.

Digging deep for bravery from she knew not where, Ellie brought her shoulders back. "You may say whatever it is you wish to say, Wesley. I am deserving of your anger." She deserved all of it and more.

He touched his gaze on every corner of her face.

Did she imagine the softening in his eyes?

"Is that what you believe, Ellie? That I've come to berate you?"

"I . . ." She didn't know. She didn't know anything anymore. She only knew that the only man she loved and wanted stood before her, now in possession of the greatest lie she'd perpetuated.

She dampened her lips and tried again. "You haven't?"

"No," he said gently. "That isn't why I've come."

"To thank me for reuniting you and your Miss Sparrow, then?" she somehow managed through a wave of grief.

"Not for that, either. Miss Sparrow and I parted ways amicably."

"Oh, Wesley." Her heart ached for him. "I'm so sorry."

"I'm not."

Why, then, was he here?

"You said you were here for a fight," she entreated, turning her hands up.

"I am. I've come to fight for you."

She stilled. "For me," she whispered, touching a hand to her breast.

"You, Ellie," he said softly.

"What?" she whispered. "But . . . you're supposed to fight for your Miss Sparrow."

"Are you trying to foist me on another?" he asked, a teasing note threaded through his question.

"No!" she exclaimed. "I only ever wanted for you to be happy, Wesley."

"And I am, Ellie. With *you*. What I had with Claire, it was . . . just stolen moments from two people chafing at the lives we'd been born into. In that limited time, neither of us shared any true parts of ourselves. Not as you did. And not as I did with you."

Dropping his sword to the ground, he palmed her cheek, and, closing her eyes, she leaned into that tender touch.

"You were on every line of every page. I know that now," Wesley said, in husky tones. He smiled wistfully. "And I suspect somewhere, in some way, I've *always* known."

Tears pricked Ellie's lashes. These ones far different than all the ones she'd shed before at the loss of him.

"You are not mad, th-then?" Her voice caught.

"My God, Ellie," he begged, cupping her face in both hands, and crouching down so he could meet her eyes. "How could I *ever* be mad? Your letters? They *saved* me. My only regret is that you stopped."

And this time, she didn't bother blinking back the drops that blurred his beloved face. She let them fall freely, and Wesley caught them with his thumbs. He tenderly wiped away each one and the others that followed.

"I did not want to," she said, through her tears. "But I felt I'd already done you greater harm than Miss Sparrow not writing, and when I stopped, you were hurt. I will n-never forgive myself for that."

"Oh, Ellie. That had nothing to do with you or the absence of your letters. My injuries, they were a product of nothing other than the war. I was no different than any other man who fell or suffered that day."

A sob spilled from her lips.

Wesley drew her into his arms, folding her close, and

she wrapped hers about him. She hung on to him for all she was worth, absorbing all the warmth he conferred.

He kissed the top of her head. "I love you."

Those three words, that one glorious phrase, reached deep within her soul and filled her. She'd only ever wanted this man and his love.

Wesley drew back slightly. "Dare I take your lack of response to mean my feelings are not return—"

"They are!" she exclaimed, and from somewhere near, she caught the sound of either Cailin's or Hattie's crying. Mayhap both of them.

"I love you, Wesley Audley," she said, catching his hands in hers and holding them tight. "I have loved you from the moment I met you when you taught me to fight, and I shall love you until I take my last—"

He pressed an index finger against her lips, silencing the remainder of that vow.

"I only want to think about the firsts to come, Ellie."

Wesley reached inside his jacket and withdrew a small bouquet.

Ellie just stared at the handful of slightly crushed purple irises, as she recalled another moment, long ago, when she'd been only a girl, and when she'd first fallen in love with him. Her eyes flew to his.

"They looked a good deal better when I first set out," he said bemusedly.

"They are perfect."

"The iris, you once said, was the only flower you'd ever favor," he murmured.

"You remember that," she whispered.

"I remember all of it. It was you, Ellie," he said quietly. "It was always you. I've just been too blind to see it."

He dropped to a knee, earning audible gasps from their family and servants.

She and Wesley ignored them. She saw only him.

"I am not blind any longer, Ellie," he said solemnly. "I want you in every way. And if you can trust in me, if you can trust that I will live only for your smile, and will fetch you a star if it means I could spare you any hurt, then I'd ask . . . I'd humbly beg you to marry m—"

Crying out, Ellie launched herself into his arms.

Wesley caught her to his chest, but her weight and the suddenness of her movement sent him tumbling back.

He landed with Ellie sprawled atop him.

"Dare I take that as a—?"

"Yes!" she exclaimed through laughter and tears. "A million times, yes."

And as their family cheered around them, Wesley smiled and leaned up to meet her lips in a kiss that promised forever.

Keep reading for an excerpt from the first
book in the All the Duke's Sins series . . .

Along Came a Lady

In the many years she'd been working as an instructor in etiquette, Miss Edwina Dalrymple had advised everyone from the daughters of powerful members of the gentry to the daughters of obscenely wealthy merchants.

She'd taught women who'd not so much as attempted a curtsy in their life the intricate and essential motions they required among the previously unfamiliar Polite Society.

She'd written articles offering advice to young women new to the *ton*.

She'd even written—although not sold so very many copies of—a manual with her instructions and advice meticulously laid out.

In all the time she'd worked in her respective positions, however, she'd never entertained . . . a duke and duchess.

Though, in fairness, there wasn't an overabundance of those highest of peers below a prince.

Even if there had been, however, they'd certainly never sought to enlist her services.

Or they hadn't before now.

At that very moment, the Duke and Duchess of Bentley stared across Edwina's modest chestnut table. Etched upon their faces were matched expressions of austere confidence and regal power. It was a skill they'd likely perfected in their respective nurseries, and one Edwina had schooled countless students on. And the duke and duchess also represented the closest Edwina had ever found herself to the dream she'd long carried of working among their vaunted ranks.

Ten years. It had been ten years, nearly to the date, that she'd secured herself references that would set her on a course to be the most sought-after and, more importantly, most respected governess.

Folding her hands neatly before her, Edwina opted to train her focus on the Duke of Bentley. "You would like me to instruct your child." Because, really, the matter of that out-of-the-blue request required clarification. A duke and duchess seeking her services. Such an outrageous impossibility, one she'd only ever carried in her dreams. She discreetly pinched her thigh.

No, she was most definitely awake.

The duke nodded. "That is correct. However, he is not a . . . child in the traditional . . . sense."

Edwina sat up straighter on the upholstered armchair and waited for him to say more. "Your Grace?" she asked, seeking clarification.

The duchess silenced her husband with a single look, the manner of which Edwina had used sparingly, and only with her most recalcitrant charges, in order to preserve its effectiveness.

And wonder of wonders, it appeared even dukes could be tamed.

The just-graying gentleman adjusted his cravat and sat back in the sofa he occupied alongside his wife.

For the first time since they'd arrived and the duke had stated his intentions to hire Edwina, the duchess took command of the meeting. "We've come to enlist your services, Miss Dalrymple," Her Grace intoned. "And I gather, from your . . . response, you are wondering *why* we've requested you specifically." The gentleness in the duchess's tone kept that question from being an insult.

The duke frowned at his wife. "We do not mean to offend you . . ."

His wife gave him another look, this one a wry smile that proved just as effective in silencing him. "By everything I've read to you about her, the woman is clever enough to know. She knows that we're aware she's never had a patron among the peerage."

"That is correct," Edwina murmured, appreciating that directness and honesty. People of their station did not solicit her help. Unless they had to. "I have never had a client who was born to the peerage." Once that truth had stung. Edwina, however, in time, and with her work, had come to appreciate her lot for what it was—outside the sphere of the ruling elite. Despite the fact she'd been working her way to establish a place among them from the start. "As such, I must confess to . . . some surprise." And elation. Under her hem, Edwina danced her slippered feet about in a quiet, unseen celebration.

"We may not have had much success with previous instructors," the duke volunteered, and by the chastising look shot his way by his wife, too honestly this time.

Ah, he was desperate, then, and the duchess was determined to reveal no vulnerability. It mattered not. This represented her chance to prove to her father that she was completely capable of moving among his equals. And perhaps . . . even then, earn, if not his love, respect.

"She is going to have to know something of it," the duke said.

Edwina's intrigue redoubled.

And the older woman might have whispered something that sounded very much like, "You're the one responsible for your actions, dear heart."

Had they been attempting to rouse her intrigue, they couldn't have done any better than they were with their sotto voce exchange.

The duke slumped in his chair, giving him the look of a naughty charge. "Get on with it, then."

They were a fascinating, if peculiar, pair. One that fit not at all with the image society pedaled of dukes and duchesses, and yet, mayhap it was that elevated rank that allowed them that freedom of expression.

Her Grace looked to Edwina. "Until recently . . . *very* recently, His Grace had something of a . . . reputation."

"Most gentlemen do," Edwina said pragmatically. It didn't make it right, or anything she wished for her charges' future, but it *did* make it accepted by Polite Society.

"Not like this, Miss Dalrymple. Not. Like. This," the Duchess of Bentley said.

"She hardly requires all the details," the duke muttered.

His wife cupped a palm around her mouth, concealing it from her husband. "He was quite the rogue, really."

Again, most men were.

"I hear you, dear," he groused.

His wife, however, wasn't done with him. "In your mind you have likely conjured rogues and rakes and scoundrels, Miss Dalrymple. My husband would have put them all to shame with the depth of his depravity."

Edwina's mouth moved, but no words came out.

"How many other governesses have you come to before approaching me?" she asked, curious.

"Does it matter either way for our discussion?" the duchess returned.

Edwina considered that question a moment. "No," she allowed. "I suppose it does not." Only in the sense that it would provide her an indication of just how difficult an assignment she was taking on. Nor could there be any doubting or disputing that she was taking it regardless. This represented her first, and perhaps only, chance to gain entry into a clientele previously beyond her grasp.

"As I was saying, we've attempted to enlist the services of others. But governess after governess has refused us. First for the reason of my husband's past as a rogue"—and his not-too-distant one, at that—"and then, there is, of course, the matter of his children."

"She doesn't require details, dear heart," the duke mumbled, a blush on his cheeks. He wrestled with his cravat.

His Grace needn't have even bothered wasting his breath. The duchess would not be silenced. "Until our marriage, just six months ago." The stunningly regal woman leaned forward. "I assure you, my dear, had we been married some years earlier, the duke would not find himself in the very predicament he does now." And in a very unduchesslike way, she winked.

And perhaps it was that unexpected realness from the woman that compelled Edwina to ask her next question. "What exactly is the predicament you speak of?"

"His reputation has been so terribly damaged that the governesses most highly recommended by our peers, well—"

"Won't work for me," the duke said, the color deepening on his cheeks. "I'm not nearly as bad as society has made me out to be."

His wife lifted an eyebrow in his direction.

"Anymore," he allowed. "It was my youth. My distant youth," he added. "Alas, the reputation . . . stuck."

At last, all the pieces of the puzzle were in their proper place, and the reason a duke and duchess wished to hire *Edwina* made sense. They'd not sought her out because they wished for her services. They'd sought her out because there was no one else who'd take on the assignment. Either way, her pride wasn't fragile; her determination to work among the peerage was far stronger.

His wife nodded. "Precisely. My husband has been making an attempt at a new beginning. He wants to . . ." She paused, and glanced at the duke. "Tell her."

"I want to make right my past, where I can." He made that avowal as if it was rote, committed to memory, and mayhap with the commanding woman he'd made his duchess, he'd been required to do so.

Edwina puzzled her brow. The Duke and Duchess of Bentley were only recently married. Which meant . . . Edwina went still.

"They are all bastards," the duke said quietly.

"Illegitimate," the duchess admonished. "They are illegitimate."

His Grace frowned. "They mean the same thing."

"Ah," the Duchess of Bentley said, putting up a single finger, "but one is vastly more polite than the other, and therefore, that is the descriptor we shall go with."

Aye, bastard . . . or illegitimate . . . They both meant the same. Edwina's stomach muscles clenched. Bastard-born herself, a secret that would have destroyed all hope of an honorable existence if revealed, she knew all too well society's opinion of people born outside wedlock. It was the very reason she'd crafted a new identity for herself and lived a life and lie of respectability. She'd carved out a respectable life. Yes, whichever polite word one wished to dress it up with, a child born out of wedlock was nothing more than a bastard, always searching for and never finding society's approval.

But if I can groom a young woman, the daughter of a duke, to take her place among Polite Society . . . What that would do for her business. This represented her entry to the *ton*—that sphere that had previously been closed to her. One she'd sought so very hard to infiltrate.

"There is just one more detail I might mention . . ." The duke's pronouncement went unfinished.

"It is my husband's eldest son."

A son?

And just like that, those eager musings were popped. Oh, blast and damn on Tuesday. "I do not have male charges."

"Correction, Miss Dalrymple." The duchess tipped her lips up in a perfectly measured little smile. "You didn't have them. It is our expectation that after today . . . you will."

How very confident they were that Edwina would simply accept the assignment, no matter how unconventional and outrageous it was. But then, to those of the peerage, the word *no* meant nothing. It was why they weren't incorrect in their assumption that she'd not reject the assignment they put to her outright.

"Oh, and there is just one more thing, Miss Dalrymple."

What else could it possibly be? "Yes, Your Grace?"

"My husband's son? He's no interest in the title, or . . . receiving our company. We've sent our man of affairs . . ."

"Solicitors," the duke put in.

"Investigators. All of them have had little success in securing a meeting."

Edwina puzzled her brow. "Are they unable to locate him?" she asked, perplexed. And how was she supposed to find the gentleman if others had not?

Husband and wife exchanged a glance.

"Oh, no. We currently know where he and his siblings reside. We'll need you to convince the eldest of the lot to join you in London and begin instruction," the duke said.

They were mad. "Me?" A small laugh escaped her. "You expect me, a stranger and a woman at that, one who has never met him, to not only convince him but bring him back to London."

The duchess beamed. "You've stated it all quite clearly."

"And just what makes you believe I shall succeed when you have both failed?"

It was a bold, if accidental, challenge to two of London's most influential peers, and by the like frowns marring their mouths, they chafed at it.

"The fact that you and he both stand to benefit, Miss Dalrymple. That is why I expect you to not only accept the undertaking, but convince him that returning to London and claiming his rightful place as a duke's son is an opportunity neither of you can afford to pass up. If you take on this endeavor and succeed? You'll be richly compensated," the duke vowed. "Five hundred pounds if you manage to convince him to return to London." Her heart jolted, and she choked on her swallow. "And another two thousand upon your completion of his . . . transformation."

Edwina choked again, hurriedly covering her mouth with a fist.

It was a veritable fortune for a woman reliant upon her own skills and work in order to survive. And yet, neither was it enough to see her set. Nay, ultimately, her reputation and her skill set were what Edwina relied upon and would continue to rely upon, regardless of what decision she made this day.

"But I can also promise you far more than that, Miss Dalrymple," the duchess murmured.

Edwina straightened and retrained her focus on the elegant woman across from her.

"Once you transform His Grace's son, Polite Society will see there is no charge you cannot transform." The older and very astute peeress had been wise enough, then, to grasp just how much Edwina's business . . . and reputation meant.

As such, they'd offered all they might to bring her 'round to accepting, and yet she'd not succeeded as she had in the world by not analyzing every situation from every possible angle. She eyed them carefully. "Given the importance of the undertaking, why do you not pay a visit to the gentleman yourself?" she asked, removing all inflection.

"My children don't wish to see me."

Was it merely a trick of the room's shadows responsible for the glint of sadness she detected in his eyes?

Pulling off her gloves, the duchess proceeded to slap those fine leather articles together. "And with good reason," the duchess muttered. "We trust you might be more capable of conveying the benefits of his stepping forward into his rightful role."

They'd cracked open a door, allowing her a peek inside a life that, even with her successes as an instructor, she'd been without—entry to Polite Society and their daughters . . . and the respectability that would elevate her business . . . and set her on a path to independence, the likes of which she'd never known. And that had only existed as a fanciful musing she'd stopped allowing herself. "Very well," she said, forcing calm, while inside giddiness threatened to overwhelm that weak facade. "I shall accept your assignment." Edwina silently tapped her toes about, once more in a private celebration.

"Splendid." The duchess took to her feet, and Edwina

quickly followed suit. Her Grace fished a small stack from within her cloak and placed a heavy packet atop Edwina's desk. "The details we've been able to gather about his sons, Miss Dalrymple, are in there."

Edwina picked up the packet and studied it a moment, as her newly acquired employers started for the door. "Staffordshire?" she asked, picking her head up.

The pair paused briefly. "Oh, we might not have mentioned before . . . Rafe . . . ? He is a coalfield miner." With that, the couple let themselves out.

A coalfield . . . miner?

She choked. That was why the most elite instructors had declined the duke and duchess's request: not because of His Grace's wicked past, but because of his son's rough existence.

She'd agreed to the task of teaching a thirty-one-year-old coal miner how to conduct himself among Polite Society. That is, after she convinced him to accompany her back to London so he might claim a place among the *ton*.

"How difficult can it be to convince a miner to accept the wealth and lands awaiting him?" she murmured.

Nay, the greater difficulty lay in transforming a piece of coal into a diamond that sparkled.

Ready to find
your next great read?

Let us help.

Visit prh.com/nextread

Penguin
Random
House